I0614872

Jillie

by

Olive Balla

Jillie

Cover Art by *Abigail Owen*

The Wild Rose Press, Inc.
PO Box 708
Adams Basin, NY 14410-0708
Visit us at www.thewildrosepress.com

Publishing History
First Mainstream Mystery Rose Edition, 2019
Print ISBN 978-1-5092-2556-9
Digital ISBN 978-1-5092-2557-6

Published in the United States of America

Jillie dropped the metal lid as if it were red hot... Her stomach heaved, and something sour shot up her throat. Panic sent her running to the door where she pounded against the unyielding wood until the muscles in her arms cramped. She fell to her knees and clawed at the floor, ignoring the pain radiating up her arms from torn fingernails...

The sound of approaching footsteps made the tiny hairs on the back of her neck move. Jillie snatched up the broken shovel handle and took a position in front of the door. With her legs slightly bent, she balanced on the balls of her feet as she'd seen a martial arts professional do on television. She gripped the pole in both hands as if it were a sword, aimed its broken, pointed end at the door, and waited.

**Praise for Olive Balla and
her first mystery novel,
*AN ARM AND A LEG***

"A fine read!"
"Compelling from the very first chapter."
"…a thrilling story."
"Thanks for the good read."
"Couldn't put it down."

Dedication

For my siblings:
Richard, Virginia, Joseph, and Ernest,
who've been there through it all
and know where the bodies are buried.

Acknowledgements

Christine Munsey, Criminal Investigator
Carol Burns, M.D.
Dennis Burns, M.D. Professor of Pathology
Heath White, Torrance County Sheriff
Michelle Wells, Torrance County Sheriff's
Administrator
Susan Brazil, Torrance County Planning & Zoning
Maggie Pino, Crime Scene Cleanup
Frank Zubia, Director, Crime Victim Reparation
Lee Havard, Ex-Military Medic & Paramedic
Virginia Hutson, Editing & Beta Reader
Alysia Hernandez, Beta Reader
Ally Robertson, Editor, The Wild Rose Press

~*~

Other Titles by Olive Balla
available from The Wild Rose Press, Inc.

An Arm and a Leg

Chapter One

Trying unsuccessfully to ignore raised voices coming from inside the house where she lived with her sister and brother-in-law, eleven-year-old Jillie Ross stooped to retrieve a green plastic toy soldier and two milky white stones—the latest of many gifts left by a growing number of crows in exchange for the bits of bread she scattered on the porch daily. The toy soldier was missing a leg, but the crystalline stones were pretty. She did a happy dance for the benefit of the crow watching from its perch atop the backyard fence, stuffed the toy and stones into her jeans pocket, and headed for the back door.

Her stomach tightened as it always did when her sister Beth and brother-in-law Digger argued. Usually, she'd walk the mile or so to their neighbor Mrs. Potter's house and hang out long enough for the storm to die down, but for some reason, that day she chose to stay close by.

She sighed, repositioned the eyeglasses on her sweat-slick nose, and shot a final glance toward a sumac bush underneath which she'd seen a huge rattlesnake that morning. After making a mental note to warn Beth about the snake, she stepped to the back door.

"Stop your blubbering, and tell me where it is." Digger Elliott's angry voice blasted through the open door. The sound of flesh smacking flesh confirmed that the argument had escalated, as usual.

Hesitantly, Jillie opened the screen.

"You will tell me, you know," Digger said. "It's just a matter of time. I ain't even started on you good yet." He paused and looked thoughtful. "Or maybe I been going about this all wrong. Maybe it's your little sister I should be working over, the white-haired little freak."

Beth sniffled but otherwise remained silent.

"I'm talking to you," Digger yelled.

"Why would I lie?" Beth said. "I'd tell you if there was such a thing." Her voice sounded tired and sad—like she'd said the same thing so many times she'd lost count. "She doesn't know any more than I do."

"Well now, it's a sad fact of life that innocent folks sometimes get hurt."

Beth's quivering voice rose. "Don't you touch Jillie. I swear I'll kill you if you so much as look at her funny."

"Whooooeee, listen at you threatening me. Just who the hell do you think you are?" Digger growled, the sound like something from a wild animal.

Beth wiped her hand across her face and smeared blood over her mouth, chin, and cheeks. Tears streamed from the bright green eyes. The usually smiling lips were swollen and cut.

"I gotta take a leak." Digger lifted his shirt and unbuckled his belt. "You and me'll finish this when I get back." He weaved, bumped into the wall, stumbled for a couple of steps, then disappeared into the bathroom. The sour smell of booze floated on the air behind him. An open, half-empty bottle of yellowish liquid on the kitchen table offered testimony to his condition.

Beth glanced down the hall then back toward her sister. She shook her head once and held her finger to her lips.

Jillie stood still.

"Go to Mrs. Potter's." Beth's voice was barely more than a whisper. "He's pulled the phone out of the wall, so you'll have to call the police from there."

But Jillie couldn't move. She couldn't stop looking at her sister's nose, all sideways on her face, or at the streaming blood that made parentheses around Beth's mouth before dripping onto her white ruffled blouse.

"You got to go get help." A pink bubble appeared under Beth's nostril, dangled for an instant, and then popped. "Hurry, before he gets back."

The sound of a door opening down the hall, followed by heavy footfalls and cursing, spurred Jillie to action. Wishing for the cell phone Digger had steadfastly refused to buy—*I ain't paying good money so the gov'ment or some foreign hacker can listen to me trash talk my buds*—she tore her eyes from her sister's pleading face, turned, and ran through the kitchen and out the back door.

After only a few steps, she slowed. While she was running away, Digger would be hurting Beth. Her gaze frantically darted around the yard for anything big enough to make him stop.

Sun glancing off metal caught her eye. Digger's machete lay where he'd left it, next to a clump of sagebrush he'd gotten tired of whacking at.

Jillie jumped over a discarded metal detector, grabbed up the machete, and ran back to the house. She flung the screen open, screaming at the top of her lungs, "Leave my sister alone!"

Digger's eyes remained fixed on Beth. "Get out of here, Freak," he yelled "Go on back outside, and talk to your birds." He dropped to his knees astraddle Beth. "You know what I hate? I hate the way you find money for her to feed those lousy birds when I have to beg my parents for cigarette money."

"That money pays the bills, and what's left belongs to Jillie."

"Yeah, yeah, a monthly check for the poor little orphan after her mammy and pappy died." Digger snorted. "That money comes from taxpayers like me, and all's I want is some of it back."

"You'd have to pay taxes to be called a taxpayer."

"Bitch." Digger growled. "Where is it? Ever'body knows it's here someplace."

Beth moved her hands in slow motion. Her eyes grew unfocused, a far-away look in them like she saw things no one else could see.

Digger lifted his fist.

"Stop it!" Jillie hefted the machete above her head. "I said leave her alone." Seemingly of its own volition, the heavy weapon dropped. The blade thumped against the side of Digger's head then buried itself in the spot where his neck connected to his shoulder. He hollered a cuss word and made a grab for the blade. Then he grunted, made a funny kind of *eep* sound, swayed back and forth a couple of times, and collapsed onto the floor.

The sisters stared in stunned silence at the dark circle of blood pulsing outward from Digger's neck.

Beth's voice pulled Jillie away from the sight.

"Here." She held out one arm. "Help me up." She kept blinking and shaking her head like she was trying to clear it. "I need to rest a bit."

"I hurt him pretty bad." Jillie's lip quivered. "I just wanted to make him stop." She glanced back at Digger. "He's going to be mad when he wakes up."

"Listen to me." Beth looked into Jillie's eyes. "He was working himself up to kill me for sure, and you stopped him. You got nothing to be sorry for." She stroked Jillie's hair with shaking hands. "We've got to go. The police'll take you away from me after this."

"But what if he gets better and comes after us?" It'd be like Digger to play possum to trick them into feeling safe before jumping up and whaling on Beth again.

Beth looked at her husband lying on the floor next to her. An odd look came over her face, and she sighed. "He won't be coming after us."

With Jillie's help, she stood, staggered to the sink, and poured a glass of water. She took a drink and immediately vomited. She stood there, her head hanging, and eyes closed, then turned the water back on, cupped her hands under the stream, and splashed her face. Spots of red splattered the counter and the wall behind the sink.

"You're sick." Jillie's stomach felt like she'd swallowed a boulder.

"I'll be okay. Go change out of those bloody clothes. Pack the big suitcase and your backpack with as much as you can get into them. And bring your coat."

"What about your stuff?"

"I'll get my things together after I've rested up a

bit. Get the money we've been saving; it's in the pouch in my right riding boot. And don't forget your sunscreen and hair dye."

Trembling so badly she could barely control her body, Jillie ran up the stairs and into her bedroom. She pulled the old yellow suitcase down from the closet shelf and hefted it onto her bed. Unwilling to leave her art supplies behind, she shoved her sketch pad and tin of colored pencils into the suitcase, then filled it with a random pile of clothes and underwear. When the lid wouldn't close, she sat on it and bounced up and down until it clicked in place. Then she stuffed her backpack with odds and ends before hauling everything downstairs.

"All done," Jillie said as she dragged the bulging bags into the kitchen. Careful not to look at Digger, she placed her luggage on the floor and approached her sister who sat on the floor against the refrigerator.

Beth's face was gray, and her legs were splayed out in front of her.

"Don't you need to pack some stuff?" Jillie said. She touched her sister's slumped shoulder. "Are you asleep?"

Her eyes half open, Beth stared at the floor. Her stomach had swelled up like she was three or four months pregnant.

A cold shiver moved through Jillie's insides. "Beth, wake up." She shook her sister's shoulder, softly at first, then a little harder.

When Beth still didn't respond, Jillie ran out of the house and down the road to their nearest neighbor, "Moms" Potter. She was crying so hard the old woman made her repeat herself several times before understanding dawned, and she called an ambulance.

By the time Mrs. Potter hung up the phone, Jillie was sprinting toward the front door.

"You should wait here for the police," the old woman half yelled.

"Beth needs me," Jillie hollered over her shoulder.

"We'll take my pickup," Mrs. Potter yelled back.

Without a word, Jillie changed course. She ran to the white pickup parked in front of Mrs. Potter's house, pulled open the door, and jumped in while Mrs. Potter started the engine.

Once back at the farm, Jillie hurried through the back door and into the kitchen. Neither Digger nor Beth had moved.

Jillie dropped onto the floor next to her sister. "It's okay, Beth. I called the police. They said they'd send an ambulance." She picked up her sister's hand and squeezed. But when there was no return pressure, she busted out bawling. "Don't die, Beth. Please don't die."

The screen door shrieked open, then banged closed as Mrs. Potter came into the kitchen.

Jillie glanced up at the elderly woman she'd known all her life. "Digger hurt her bad this time, Moms. He hurt her real bad."

Mrs. Potter stepped across the room to Digger, bent over his body, and pressed her fingers against the inside of his wrist. After a couple of seconds, she blew a puff of air out of her mouth, stood, and stepped to a chair near the sisters.

"I don't think she's breathing, Moms." Jillie began to cry.

Mrs. Potter put a hand on Jillie's shoulder. "The ambulance will be here soon, Little One. Be strong for your sister."

Wordlessly, Jillie sat and stroked her sister's hand. She was still there twenty minutes later when the Valencia County Sheriff and an ambulance arrived.

Chapter Two

Within the next few hours, Beth was taken to a hospital, and Jillie was taken into custody. While her sister was fighting for her life, Jillie sat in a small room at the police department answering the same questions over and over. A couple of hours later, she was sent to Bernalillo County Youth Services Center in Albuquerque pending a detention hearing. Based on the evidence at the scene, the District Attorney brought Jillie up on charges of murder, and the court assigned her a Public Defender.

Jillie's attorney requested a female police psychologist to interview her. The woman smiled a lot and talked softly as she asked questions. A one-eyed video camera recorded every sound and movement.

"Were you afraid of your brother-in-law, afraid he was going to hurt you?"

Jillie shook her head. "He yelled, but he never actually hit me. He hurt Beth a lot, though."

"By *a lot*, do you mean he hurt her at other times as well?"

"Not as bad as this time, but he'd been getting worse, mostly after he got drunk."

After several more questions, the psychologist left the room, and Jillie's attorney returned.

"You'll have to stay here for a while," her attorney said.

"I want to see Beth."

The attorney shook her head. "I'm sorry, Jillie. There are some things that have to be done first." She promised to check on Beth then left.

Moms Potter was allowed to attend Jillie's pretrial. She sat silently, smiled, and mouthed the word *Courage*.

After several minutes of discussion, the judge dismissed the charges, stating the defense had offered a compelling argument against bringing the case to trial. Then he gave Jillie the option of either going into foster care or staying with Cleg and Margo Elliott, Digger's parents who'd requested custody.

Though Jillie had never really liked Beth's in-laws, she agreed to stay with them rather than return to juvie to await placement with other foster parents. It wouldn't be long—just until Beth came for her. And anything would be better than juvie.

She shivered at the memory of her fifteen-year-old juvie roommate's threat *to dig her purple-ass eyes out with a spoon and put them in a baby food jar if she didn't stop whining and bawling all night.*

As Jillie exited the courtroom with the Elliotts, people with cameras shoved microphones toward her face and shouted questions. Others stared at her, held their hands in front of their mouths and whispered. Although she couldn't understand most of what people were saying because of all the shouting, she overheard one woman call her a murderer, while another said she must be some kind of monster.

Moms Potter made her way through the crowd to Jillie. "Don't pay any attention to these jerks. Some people get their kicks from other people's pain." She patted Jillie's shoulder. "You did the right thing."

A young woman squeezed through the herd and approached Jillie. "I'll be your caseworker." She pointed to a bench where Jillie's suitcase and nylon backpack sat. "I got permission to pick these up for you. You'll want to look it all over, but your stuff ought to be just as you left it."

Jillie nodded her thanks. "Can I go see my sister now?"

With a sad smile, Moms Potter said, "She isn't awake yet."

"I need to be there when she wakes up."

The caseworker put a warm hand on Jillie's forearm. "I'm sure your family will take you once you get settled. You're a smart girl, Jillie, and you're strong. Beth's lucky to have you for a sister."

Having moved to within earshot, Margo Elliott leveled a hard look at the caseworker, and her lips curled like she'd just discovered a maggot in her spaghetti. Cleg's face was set in its usual blank stare.

"I'll see to Beth," Moms Potter said. "And I'll come see you as often as I can." She turned her head away, but not before Jillie saw a tear fall onto her shirt front.

"We should get going," Margo said.

Jillie picked up her suitcase and backpack. She waved goodbye to Mrs. Potter, swallowed hard, and followed the Elliotts to their brown, rusted-out pickup.

As Cleg got into the driver's seat, Margo motioned for Jillie to scoot in next to him. A satisfied look on her face, Margo squeezed in next to Jillie and slammed the pickup door.

"Now then," Margo said. "Isn't this nice?"

Jillie shivered as if someone had run an icicle up her spine.

Please God, make Beth better soon.

Chapter Three

Except for Cleg's wheezing around the plastic tube that ran from his nose to a metal container with the word *oxygen* written on it, the trip to the Elliotts' house was made in silence. But the way Margo stared at Jillie the whole time made her feel all squirmy inside, and the rotten cheese smell coming from old man Elliott made her wish someone would open a window.

On the outskirts of Belen, Cleg turned the pickup down a washboard-dirt road that led to a circular driveway. At the end of the drive, a two-story house sat hunkered like a huge molting bird of prey out of Jillie's biology book.

Gray, weathered wood siding had pretty well managed to rid itself of any paint, but a few stubborn little patches looked like it might have once been white. With a dirt front yard, partially collapsed brick flower bed clogged with dried weeds, and a cracked front window patched with duct tape and cardboard, the place looked like a house out of a horror movie. The skin on Jillie's forearms puckered into goose bumps.

Cleg turned off the engine, and the three exited the pickup.

Merciless afternoon sunlight poured over Margo's body, highlighting every gap and bulge. Her mouth looked like a slit in an old inner tube, with deep creases running from her top lip up toward her nose. Bright pink lipstick seeped up the creases. A small flap of skin at the edge of one nostril fluttered when she snorted—which was often. Stick figure arms dangled from the short sleeves of a clingy dress covered with a weird blue pattern, and skinny fingers fiddled with the white crocheted collar buttoned up tight. Thin, blue-veined legs held her upright.

"We're taking you in because no young girl ought to have to live with total strangers." Margo's lips barely moved over teeth that stayed clamped shut.

"That's right." Cleg's jaws chomped down on each consonant, like he was chewing something gristly. He paused, wheezed, and sucked air in through his nose. "We don't hold Digger's killing against you; you were just trying to protect your sister. Ain't that right, Honey Bumpkin?"

Margo twitched her pointy nose like a hound sniffing at something dead. She shot a look at her husband that made him hold his hands up like he was praying for rain.

Cleg's eyes dropped to the ground. He cleared his throat then muttered something about telling *that boy* a hundred times his temper was going to get him into trouble.

Old man Elliott's body was exactly the opposite of his wife's. The flesh under his eyes was all puffed out, like someone had pulled the skin back and stuffed the inside full of cotton balls. His bloated, blue lips were wet from constant licking, and small gobs of white crusty residue formed crescents in the corners of his mouth. When he walked, his legs looked like they moved only from the knees down, and his stomach arrived at its destination a full heartbeat ahead of the rest of his body. From the nearly hairless head perched on top of thick shoulders, all the way down to his tiny, tennis shoe-shod feet, the man looked like a human ice cream cone.

"We've come up with a few rules," Margo said. She paused to let those words sink in. "First, you'll be allowed two meals a day. You can choose which two."

Two meals? Beth always made sure she had three hot meals and two snacks a day. She'd said a growing girl *needed sustenance.* A frown drew the edges of Jillie's mouth down.

Margo squinted. "One day you'll thank me. Chubby girls don't get on well in the world. Especially if they look like you." Her lip curled. "All that white hair and pale skin…and those eyes…they're just plain unnatural."

Jillie wanted to scream for Margo to bite the wall. Beth had said her baby fat would go away once she started her periods. Beth said she'd been chubby too, but slimmed down when her hormones kicked in. And once, when she found Jillie crying because a kid at school made fun of her, Beth had promised the mild albinism that gave her porcelain-like skin, thick snow-white hair and nearly purple eyes was going to make her a stunning beauty when she grew up. And Beth was real smart.

Margo pushed her lip-slit into a pucker. "Anyway, Americans eat too much." She glanced at Cleg, who was staring off into space and didn't seem to be listening.

"When can I see Beth?" Jillie said.

Margo's head swiveled toward Jillie and her lip curled upward slightly. "We'll see how things go."

"She'll get better, you'll see. She promised to take me to the Balloon Fiesta, and Beth never breaks a promise."

Margo made a funny sound in the back of her throat and pulled the corners of her mouth up. "The Fiesta's still a couple months away." She bent over so her eyes were even with Jillie's. "A lot can happen in two months."

As if someone had plugged in his power cord, Cleg suddenly came to life. "Maybe I'll take you to the Balloon Fiesta. Would you like that?" He smiled, like a kid who'd just found a chocolate in his pocket.

Margo frowned at her husband then jabbed an elbow in his ribs. "I said we'll see."

As they entered the darkened house, an odor thick as pudding poured over them—like the school's locker room, only a lot worse. Neither of the Elliotts seemed to notice, but Jillie had to swallow hard to keep from throwing up.

She followed the Elliotts into a large room with several windows, each covered with tightly closed venetian blinds. No happy sunlight, no fresh air would be allowed into *that* house.

Margo turned on a lamp atop a table next to a sofa and picked up a piece of grimy paper. She jabbed it toward Jillie. "Your chores."

Though the list was short, the chores looked like something out of the Cinderella story. Every day, Jillie would be expected to prepare all three meals—even the one she wouldn't be allowed to eat—and wash the dishes. She'd do laundry on Saturdays and clean house once a week.

Tapping the paper with a bony forefinger, Margo

said, "It goes without saying that you'll clean your room every morning before breakfast." She turned and headed up the stairs. "Come on. You'll be staying in Digger's old quarters. It's just as it was when he left us to marry your sister."

Jillie gulped. Saliva caught in her throat and set off a coughing spasm. When she could breathe again, she said, "I—I'll be sleeping in his room?"

"Well now," Margo said through those clenched teeth, "He won't be needing it anymore, will he? Besides, all the other rooms are taken."

Digger's old room was a tiny, dark space. One small window overlooked the driveway, its four dirty panes covered by gray curtains. The portion of roof covering the porch lay directly underneath and outside the window. A twin bed sat against one wall, a flattened pillow in a thread-bare pillowcase carelessly tossed on top.

A dust-covered bureau stood against the opposite wall. A large, gray, lidded vase rested on its otherwise bare top.

Margo, a peculiar expression on her face, stood at the door, as if expecting Jillie to either do or say something. "How do you like the room?" If Margo's eyes had been needles, Jillie would have been pinned to the floor like a butterfly on velvet.

"It's—"

"More specifically, how do you like the urn on the bureau?"

"Bureau?"

"Otherwise known as a chest-of-drawers."

Jillie looked at the piece of furniture then back at the woman.

Margo rolled her eyes. "Oh my lord, how have you survived this long being so dense. How do you like the urn?"

"You mean that vase—"

Margo bared her teeth and closed the distance between the two of them, bent at the waist, and brought her face in line with Jillie's. "Not vase, *urn*. This *is*, after all, Digger's room."

Jillie gulped and took a step backward.

Nearly maniacal laughter bubbled up from Margo's chest. "Not to worry, Digger doesn't take up much space, and he doesn't snore anymore." She pointed toward the closet. "Stow your stuff."

Her mouth dry, Jillie put her backpack and suitcase on the floor as far away from the chest of drawers as she could.

Margo pointed to a closed door across the hall. "You'll share the bathroom with Mort. He's not here much, so that shouldn't present any problems." She smirked. "After all, we must treat you like a welcome guest."

Just then, the bathroom door opened, and Digger's younger brother Mort stepped out, zipping his pants. Somewhere in his twenties, Mort was tall like Margo. His head was covered with thick dark hair, as were the parts of his arms uncovered by his short-sleeved T-shirt. He squinted at Jillie and the lips he'd inherited from his father curled into a kind of smirky smile. But, like a line Jillie had read in a mystery novel, *his smile never reached his eyes.*

"Well, well," Mort said, "Never thought we'd have us a murderer living under the same roof. Hope you left your machete at home."

"There'll be no more of that kind of talk." Margo glared at her son. "At least I'm doing something to bring in some money." A funny look flashed across her face as she realized she'd said that out loud. "Of course, we'd take the child in, even if there was no money to cover her keep. The judge said if we didn't, she'd become a ward of the state." She patted the top of Jillie's head as if she were a puppy, only harder.

Mort bent at the waist and looked into Jillie's eyes. "Watch your back, kid." He muttered something then went downstairs.

Margo's eyes hardened into concrete as she stared at her son's retreating back. "Just like his father," she said under her breath. "Useless." Her eyes shifted to Jillie. "Since this is your first night here, you'll eat with the family. But after that, you'll eat in the kitchen. Put your things away and come downstairs." She raked her fingers through Jillie's hair, painfully tugging at tangles. "And do something with that mop. Comb it, or something. You look like you've been pulled through a woodpile backwards."

Margo headed downstairs, her hard-soled shoes clip-clopping on the wooden steps.

Jillie glanced at the urn. With a shiver, she shoved her unopened suitcase against the closet's back wall. Taking care not to look at the bureau again, she leaned her backpack against the suitcase.

She'd not unpack. The thought of putting her clothes in the same drawers that had held Digger's made her feel like hurling her lunch.

Besides, she wouldn't be here that long. Beth would come for her as soon as she got better, and they'd go back home, back to the only home Jillie had ever known.

She spread her thick, down-filled coat on the closet floor in front of her luggage and pulled her teddy bear Mickey out of her backpack. "Your tummy'll be a whole lot better pillow than that smelly old thing on the bed."

Jillie stepped across the hall and into the bathroom where she washed her hands then ran damp fingers through her thick hair. Although she tried her best to smush it down, a glance in the mirror showed her seven cowlicks springing into action, returning her hair to its usual style—what Beth had called her *hedgehog mode*.

At the thought of her sister, Jillie teared up. She swiped the tears away then washed her face. One thing for sure, she'd not let the Elliotts see her cry.

She took a deep breath and went downstairs.

Three sets of eyes followed her progress. The expressions on Mort and Cleg's faces were bland, but the expression on Margo's face made Jillie want to go back upstairs.

"Mort brought pizza," Margo said. "Enjoy it, because after tonight, you'll be making dinner." Her upper lip curled as she dished a piece of pizza onto a paper plate and handed it to Jillie. "One piece for you then it's off to bed. You have an early morning."

Chapter Four

Over the next week, life in the Elliott household settled into routine. Jillie did as she was told and took care of her chores. The rest of the time was spent either outside exploring the surrounding area or in her room reading and drawing.

Beth had always loved Jillie's drawings. Once, when Jillie drew a picture of her favorite teacher, Beth had said it was so realistic it looked like a photo.

Other than ordering Jillie around like a slave, Margo rarely spoke to her. And she never once called her by name. It was *Come here, girl*, or *Do that, girl*.

Cooking the meals for the Elliotts turned out not to be so bad. But doing the laundry was puke-making.

Unwilling to touch any of the Elliotts' underwear, she sneaked a pair of long-handled tongs from the kitchen. Almost giddy with relief at how well they worked, she hid them behind the washer.

Cleg and Margo hardly ever left the house, but Mort came and went at all hours. Once in a while, Mort's cousin Toby Dinkins was mentioned, but he never made an appearance at the house.

Dinner times were always charged and tense. Margo complained about her life at the hands of her spouse, about the state of their finances, and about Mort's lack of ambition. Cleg mostly kept his head down, eyes focused on his plate, and unless someone asked Mort a direct question, he seldom said a word.

Jillie had always been pretty good at reading people's moods, but not Margo's. Things would be calm for a day or two, then some little thing would set her off and she'd yell, throw stuff, and kick the furniture. A couple of times, while Jillie was washing the dishes, she recognized the familiar sounds of flesh smacking flesh followed by Cleg's muffled whimper.

After a couple of days, Jillie's stomach began to ache when Margo went into one of her rages. Then she started chewing her nails—sometimes, so bad they bled.

When the social services caseworker telephoned to set up the first appointment for a home visit, Margo's voice was warm enough to melt butter. "We'll look forward to seeing you tomorrow at two." But as soon as she hung up, she whirled on Jillie. "You say one negative word, just one, and Mort will pay a visit to your sister in the hospital." Her eyelids lowered into slits. "He may not be good for much, but even he could unplug a life support machine. He'd sneak in and out of the hospital before anyone even knew he was there." She pinched the flesh on the upper back of Jillie's arm hard enough to leave a mark. "You hear me?"

Jillie winced and nodded her head.

The same warning was repeated before each of Jillie's court-ordered appointments with a therapist. The kindly psychologist tried to get her to talk about Digger's death and her life with the Elliotts, but she refused to speak.

During the times Mort ate dinner at home, Margo would hammer at him about getting a job. "You think food just magically appears on the table?" She'd shoot dart-looks between her son and spouse. "You're a lazy bum, just like your father."

Since Jillie had chosen breakfast and lunch as her two meals, her evenings were spent trying to ignore a growling stomach. She comforted herself with the thought that once school started, she'd get a free lunch. When that happened, she'd opt to eat breakfast and dinner at the Elliotts'. The thought of eating three meals a day again set her stomach growling.

One night, she sneaked down to the kitchen after everyone had gone to bed. But not only had Margo put a lock on the pantry door, she'd used a black permanent marker to mark the level of milk in the clear plastic carton.

And once, when Jillie's stomach hurt so bad she couldn't concentrate on her homework, she'd tip-toed down to the kitchen and taken a couple of slurps from a bottle of salad dressing. But it had just made her hungrier than ever, so she'd crept to the garage and drank two bottles of water from the cases stored there. That helped, but not for long.

She'd tried to sneak crackers from the unlocked cupboard while doing the dinner dishes. But Margo must have heard the paper rattling, because she came roaring into the kitchen and yanked the box out of her hands.

"I hope you got your fill, because that was tomorrow's breakfast." Margo replaced the box in the cupboard and locked it. A satisfied look on her face, she glanced sideways at Jillie. "I'll know if you cheat."

Although Cleg's plate always looked like he'd licked it clean, sometimes one of the others would leave a bite of pork chop, or a spoonful of beans. Careful to put bones or other inedible scraps on top of the trash where Margo would see them when she did her nightly garbage check, Jillie would snarf down a few bites then quickly wash the dishes.

Nighttime was the roughest. Jillie would lie on her coat on the closet floor with Mickey under her head, stare up into the darkness, and cry.

She sometimes saw Digger in her dreams, standing over her, yelling and cussing, the veins in his neck standing out like ropes. During those dreams, Jillie could neither speak nor move. She'd wake up sweating, her coat wrapped around her so tightly she could hardly breathe.

During the first couple of weeks of Jillie's life at the Elliotts', she'd been allowed to visit Beth only once. The pain of seeing her comatose sister covered with a white sheet, and tubes coming out of everywhere, was nearly more than she could stand. The whole time she was there, she'd held Beth's hand and poured out her soul to her.

"The nurse says you can hear me. I'm doing okay, so you shouldn't worry. Just get well." She'd pleaded with her sister not to leave her and apologized for not keeping Digger from hurting her so bad. "I'll be back as often as I can."

But another week passed, and although Jillie begged to go to the hospital, Margo refused. Her eyes blazing, she'd yelled, "Stop ding-donging at me; it's enough to drive a wooden man crazy. I hate hospitals." She stooped over to bring her eyes level with Jillie's. A funny little smile twisted her lips. "Besides, your sweet sister isn't going to last much longer. She's just a meat sack waiting to die."

"She is not," Jillie yelled. "She's going to get well. She promised never to leave me, and Beth always keeps her promises." Jillie ran out the front door as Margo laughed behind her.

When Jillie's dad died a year earlier, the county wanted to put her into foster care right then and there. But twenty-year-old Beth had promised they'd never be separated. She'd made good on that promise by marrying the first man to ask her, even though he had a reputation for being mean and a womanizer. She said she didn't care about any of that, as long as Digger was good to Jillie. And he had been, for the first couple of weeks.

But life with Digger quickly turned into a nightmare. He didn't try to find a job, refused to do anything around the house, and drank. Obsessed with the rumor that the girls' dad had stashed money somewhere, he'd lived up to his name by digging holes all over the place.

Nearly every weekend he'd get drunk and work on Beth to tell him where their Pop's money was hidden. At first, he'd just pushed her around. But Beth said she'd read that once that kind of thing started, it always got worse.

So, Beth began keeping back a little money from the monthly checks the government sent after their Pops died. She promised once they'd saved enough, they'd get on a bus and not stop until they were good and ready. Some of the best hours of Jillie's life had been spent looking over a tattered old atlas with Beth, giggling, and talking about the future.

But they hadn't planned on Jillie chopping Digger with a machete, or on Beth winding up in what a nurse called the *critical care ward.*

Within the first couple of weeks, Jillie had explored all the Elliotts' dilapidated farm. She didn't do it so much out of curiosity, although there was plenty of that. She did it to get out of that horrid house and because Pops had said it was important to pay attention to her surroundings.

He'd once told her about a hiker who got lost and was never seen again, most likely because he hadn't noticed things. So, during her walks, Jillie often stopped and turned completely around to learn the view from every direction. Those walks were the only times she felt free.

To the side of and some distance from the main house sat a small shed surrounded by tall weeds. Glass shards resembling stalactites and stalagmites rimmed a small window in the door—a gaping hole loosely boarded up from the inside. With warped wood sides and a corrugated tin roof, the little building looked like a place out of one of those scary movies where teenage actors try unsuccessfully to hide from a chainsaw-wielding fiend. Jillie steered clear of the little building.

Often, when Jillie returned from a walk, her eyes were drawn to Cleg's pickup. Sometimes, the temptation was nearly overpowering to grab his keys off the kitchen counter where he regularly tossed them and drive to the hospital to see Beth.

But other than the family tractor, she'd never driven a car or truck. She'd probably end up in a ditch. Or she might get stopped by a policeman and get thrown back in juvie.

But mainly, it was Margo's threat that kept her from doing anything of the kind. She shivered at the image of Mort going to the hospital to finish what Digger started.

As day after day dragged by, Jillie fantasized about ways to get out of the house, to the hospital, and back again without the Elliotts knowing she'd gone. Idea after idea sprung up, blossomed, then died. But a couple of possibilities stuck in her mind and turned into the beginnings of a plan.

She'd have to be sneaky...sneaky and smart. And she couldn't let her guard down even for a second because Beth's life depended on her.

Chapter Five

One evening after dinner, Jillie pulled Beth's brown leather money pouch from a side pocket in her backpack. With Mickey looking on, she untied the knot and poured the contents onto her coat. Paper rattled and coins clinked together as for the hundredth time she counted the fifty-two dollars and sixteen cents Beth had managed to save.

She separated a five-dollar bill and four ones from the stack and replaced the rubber band around the other bills. Four dollars would cover the cost of a day pass on the Railrunner, a commuter train that ran north all the way from Belen to Albuquerque.

Five dollars should buy her lunch in the hospital cafeteria, then she'd take the train back to the Elliotts'. Since the train station was only a couple of miles away from the house, a half hour of fast walking should get her back before the afternoon school bus made the drop-off at her stop. That'd leave several hours to visit Beth.

Humming a happy tune, Jillie stuffed all the money into the pouch and replaced it in her backpack. She laid down on her coat, hugged Mickey, put him under her head, and tried to calm her racing mind. Eventually, she drifted off to sleep.

****

Jillie awoke earlier than usual the next morning.

She jumped up from her coat-bed, dressed, double-checked her money, and hurried downstairs to make breakfast. Her body sizzling with anticipation, she willed herself to act normal as the sleepy Elliotts made their appearance.

Her eyes lowered to prevent Margo from seeing her excitement, she filled their plates before returning to the kitchen to eat. After doing the dishes, she went upstairs to wash her face and comb her hair.

Cleg's voice floated up the stairs. "I hear the bus, girl. Better hustle."

Jillie grabbed her backpack and ran downstairs. She got to the bus just as the driver was closing the door.

"I have a ride today," she said through the partially opened door.

The driver nodded her head, pulled the door closed, shoved the bus in gear, and drove off.

Jillie glanced back toward the house, relieved to see it wasn't visible from where she stood. She sucked in a huge breath and let it out slowly.

Her body felt light, like she could fly if she just flapped her arms hard enough. For the first time in weeks, she felt like she was in control of her life.

She sang under her breath and marched in time to the tune. The whole day was hers.

When the train station came into view, she smiled to herself. She'd sing and tell stories to Beth, just like her sister had done for her every night before bed. She'd tell her how much she loved her and pretend that everything was okay.

But just as Jillie reached the station entrance, someone grabbed her arm from behind.

"Sorry, kid," Mort said. "Life just isn't that easy."

Jillie pulled free from the grip. "Let me go, I'm going to see my sister."

"Not today, you aren't."

"I want to see Beth."

Mort shook his head, a look of what seemed to be sadness on his face. "Not happening. The school called the old woman when you didn't show up."

"Please, she needs me."

"None of that's going to work on me. Haven't you learned anything yet?"

The two walked to the pickup in silence, and in silence they drove home.

Her shoulders slumped, Jillie stepped from the pickup and trudged toward the house.

Margo stood just outside the front door, her arms cocked and fists on her hips. Jillie had witnessed the woman's temper tantrums, but she'd never seen anything like what happened next.

With fists balled so tight the knuckles looked white, Margo screamed words people probably used in R-rated movies. Flecks of saliva flew from her mouth; tiny gobs of spit dangled from her chin, and her nose flap whipped back and forth with every snort and growl.

The flap's gymnastics drew Jillie's focus, and her mind wandered as Margo's screeching voice droned on. Why had the woman never had the thing removed? Maybe she was proud of it. Or maybe she couldn't afford to go to the doctor. Or maybe the thing had been cut away several times, but always grew back. Maybe it was filled with puss, like a zit, so if someone squeezed it, the insides would come out and leave a little sac, kind of like a tiny deflated balloon.

In spite of herself, Jillie felt the beginnings of a smile tug at the corners of her mouth.

As if she'd been slapped, Margo's head jerked up, and her eyes narrowed to slits. "Did I say something funny?"

"No...I..."

"You think you're so smart," Margo said. "But you're stupid, just like your sister. From now on, Cleg will walk you to the bus stop." She jabbed her index finger toward Jillie's nose. "And in case you're thinking of trying anything like this again, just remember what I said could happen to your precious sister. And it'll be your fault."

"I want to see Beth. You can't keep me from seeing her.

"You'll see her when I say." Margo's eyelids came down again until they nearly closed over the glittering pinpoint eyes. "I'll be watching you."

Jillie should have remembered about the school's policy to call a parent or guardian when a student didn't show up. Margo might be right, maybe she *was* stupid.

"By the way, in case you're thinking you could walk to the hospital from the school," Margo said, "It'd take you days to get there." A thoughtful look came over her face, and she cocked her head. "Or maybe you think you could hitch a ride. Ooooh, that's a really bad idea. I heard on the news about a girl your age who was hitching and got picked up by a mass murderer. They found pieces of her wrapped in newspaper in three different dumpsters."

Jillie gulped.

"Now go get started on lunch while I think of a

suitable punishment." Margo whirled and stomped back into the house.

"I told you to watch your back," Mort whispered out one side of his mouth.

That night, during dinner, Margo made her announcement. "You'll be docked one meal per day for the next week. If you do as you're told, after that you'll be allowed the usual two." She used a fingernail to dig something out of her teeth before adding, "You mess up again, and I'll make you wish you'd never been born. You *and* your sister."

Chapter Six

Over the next couple of days, the only contact Jillie had with the Elliotts was when she served them their meals. The rest of the time she fled to her room to read or draw.

One afternoon Jillie got home from school early. When she walked into the living room, Margo's head jerked up as if she'd been caught stealing Moms Potter's strawberries.

"Thank you so much," Margo said into the cell phone no one else was allowed to use. "I'll call you back once we've had a chance to talk to her." She snapped the phone closed, slipped it back into a pouch dangling from a sling around her neck, and turned to Jillie. "What're you doing home so early?" Her voice was unusually high and squeaky, and she had a weird look on her face.

"Today was early release because of Labor Day," Jillie said. "I brought a letter home from the principal a couple of days ago."

Margo walked to the sofa, sat down, and patted a spot next to her. "Come sit down, there's something I need to tell you."

But Jillie stood still. She'd probably pay for that bit of defiance, but right then she didn't care. A feeling of dread clawed its way up her throat.

Margo sneered. "Okay, Miss Smarty-Pants, don't

sit." She harrumphed then smiled slightly. "We just got a call from the hospital."

"Is it about Beth?"

"I'm afraid it's bad news. Beth never regained consciousness; she died late last night." The corners of Margo's mouth twitched before resuming the usual straight line. "Sorry."

"You're lying," Jillie shouted. "You're just saying that to be mean." Tears blurred her sight and poured down her cheeks.

"It's hard to lose someone you love, isn't it?" Margo cocked her head sideways. "Why don't you go to your room for a few minutes before making dinner."

Jillie started toward the stairs, but Margo's screeching voice stopped her mid-stride, "Cleg and I'll be your legal guardians now." She held her hands out palms down, fingers splayed, and inspected her new manicure. "We are, after all, your only living relatives."

Something in Jillie's chest hardened. "Not to mention the eight hundred dollars a month you get from the county for keeping me as your personal slave."

Margo snorted out the nose-flap. She took a deep breath, smiled, and peered up at Jillie. "You'll stay here until you're eighteen, then you'll get that house and all that land."

The house Jillie grew up in. The house Mommy, Pops, Beth, and she had lived in, laughed in, played games in. The land with the huge old cottonwood tree made sacred by her parents' ashes scattered around its base.

"Are you listening?"

Jillie jerked her eyes back toward the hard face.

"Don't you worry about anything, we'll look after

you." Margo ran her tongue over her lips. "Just like we looked after your house while you were in jail."

"It wasn't jail, it was—"

Margo's voice grew louder and harsher. "While you were in jail with all the other juvenile delinquents. Did you know we had to have crime scene cleaners clean your house?" Her eyes drew down into slits. "Do you have any idea how much that cost? They had to pull up the linoleum and replace part of the wall because there was so much blood."

Hideous images swam through Jillie's mind, and she swallowed hard. It hadn't occurred to her...she hadn't realized—

"Oh, did baby-kins not concern herself with someone having to clean up her mess?" Margo's voice grew sing-song. "Not just anyone can do that, you know. There are laws." A thoughtful look crept across her face. "We should take you back to the house this weekend. I can't think why we've waited this long. Who knows, we might even find some things that need to be put someplace for safe keeping."

"I don't—"

"Oh, and you needn't worry, I'll take care of funeral arrangements for your dear sister," Margo said. "The county will do an autopsy to find out exactly what she died of." She stared hard into Jillie's eyes, a wicked light in her own. "They'll cut her to pieces, you know. Like they did with our Digger. Then I think we'll have her cremated; that's the cheapest." She puckered and un-puckered her lips a couple of times, and added, "You know what cremation is?"

Jillie tried to blot out the hateful voice. She visualized sunshine on the waxy sumac leaves, tried to remember the smell of clean, rain-washed air, tried to put herself somewhere else—anywhere else but in the Elliott house listening to Margo's words.

"Well? Do you know what happens to a person's body when it's cremated?" Margo paused to let her words sink in and studied her fingernails again. "Of course, if there was any money, we could see to it that your sister had a proper burial, with a nice headstone and all."

"I don't...there isn't..." The image of a headstone under the cottonwood with all three names on it popped into Jillie's head, and her thoughts flew to the money Beth had saved. "How much would that cost?"

As if she'd been struck by lightning, Margo's head jerked up, a look on her face like she'd just won the lottery. "Oh, at least ten thousand dollars." Her eyelids dropped again to half-mast, and she hammered on. "So, your daddy *did* tell you where he hid the money he brought back from his trips."

"What is it with you people? There isn't any treasure." Jillie tapped an index finger against her temple. "Think about it. Did we live like we had piles of money?"

For as long as Jillie could remember, Pops had left for a few weeks about twice a year. Beth said he worked out of town doing something that paid well, but all Jillie knew was that he always came back with money enough for new shoes and clothes. Once he even brought back enough to get a new car.

For a second, Margo looked as if her head were about to explode. Then she shrugged and said, "I guess you didn't really love your sister after all."

"Stop it," Jillie shouted. Her eyes pricked, and even

though she tried her hardest to keep from crying, tears poured down her face.

"By the way, just in case you decide to call that stupid caseworker and complain, I'll be keeping Beth's ashes here." Margo lowered her eyelids. "You even whisper anything against us and those ashes get flushed down the toilet." She leaned forward, her index finger jabbing the air toward Jillie's face. "You heard me, down the toilet. She'll spend eternity in the sewer with the rest of the—"

"Why are you so mean?" Jillie ran upstairs to her room. She slammed the door behind her, collapsed onto the closet floor, lifted Mickey from her coat-bed, and buried her face in his fur to muffle the sounds of her crying.

After a while, something Pops had said floated into Jillie's memory: People are more than the skin-house other people see. The real person is the invisible spirit that lives inside. He said the Creator made people so that even when the body turns back into stardust, the spirit lives on. He said the spirit's made of pure energy and although energy can be altered, it can't be destroyed. Ever. That meant Beth was still Beth, even if her body got burned up.

She sifted through her memory for the things Beth had to take care of during the days following their pop's death. But Beth had left Jillie home and gone to the funeral home on her own, so details were sketchy. She'd probably wanted to protect Jillie from knowing what was going on, but that meant Jillie would have to figure everything out for herself.

You're still the best big sister in the whole world.

Jillie ran her palms along her cheeks to wipe away

the tears she couldn't seem to stop. How long would an autopsy take? Would the cremation happen at the hospital, or would they send her someplace else for that?

But Margo had said Beth had to have an autopsy first. If she wasn't cremated yet, maybe there was still time for Jillie to see her one last time. She stood at the window and considered her options.

She'd have liked to just pack up and walk out the front door in the middle of the night, but the stairs squeaked so loudly, anyone in the house would know what she was up to. The only other way out of the house was through Digger's window, though its small size might make for a tight squeeze. Then there was the steeply slanted tin roof Jillie knew from experience would be slippery.

But once she'd got past those problems, the plentiful thick branches of the huge dead cottonwood just outside the window would be easy to maneuver. Like climbing down a ladder.

With the memory of her sister's smiling face, Jillie went downstairs to cook dinner...dinner that night, breakfast, and dinner the next day—twenty-four hours to set her new plan in motion... Hopefully, that would be long enough.

Chapter Seven

That evening, Jillie pooled bits of food from the dinner plates. Pieces of napkin-wrapped dinner roll formed an inviting lump in the nylon fabric of her backpack. For whatever reason, Margo slacked off a bit on her surveillance, and Jillie sneaked a banana and an orange into her cache.

The next morning, she prepared eggs, sausage and frozen biscuits. But this time she made four extra patties of sausage, two extra hardboiled eggs, and three extra biscuits.

"You know by now how much food to cook." Margo bent over to bring her face inches from Jillie's. "You think I don't know what you're up to?"

Jillie gulped loud enough for anyone within earshot to hear.

"You think I'll let you have the extra food rather than let it go to waste?" Droplets of spit peppered Jillie's face, jettisoned from Margo's mouth with every "s" and "t" in her rant.

Jillie wiped the slobber away with the back of her hand then hung her head in what Beth had called her *contrite act*. "Sorry. It won't happen again."

"You got that right. Just because breakfast is one of your meals here doesn't mean you can eat twice as much as the rest of us." She pointed at the now-cold sausage and biscuits. "That'll be your dinner."

Smiling inwardly, Jillie hung her head.

"Honey Buns?" Cleg called from the living room. "It's time for our show."

Margo narrowed her eyes. "Now clean up this mess. Tomorrow morning we'll go to your farm."

"The show's starting," Cleg's whine floated into the kitchen.

"I'll be there in a minute," Margo shouted back. "Lord, why is it I'm the only one in this house with the sense to take care of things." She glowered at Jillie then left the kitchen.

In spite of her growling stomach, Jillie folded the food scraps up in a paper towel instead of snarfing it down. She finished the dishes then stuffed the package of food under her baggy T-shirt.

"I gotta go to the bathroom," she hollered toward the living room.

Margo yelled back, "If you miss the bus, I'm not taking you."

Music from re-runs of a once-popular crime show meant the Elliotts would be stuck like zombies in front of the tube for the next hour or so.

Glad that Margo hadn't followed through with her threat that Cleg would walk her to the bus stop, Jillie ran upstairs and stuffed the latest wad of food into her backpack. Then she pulled the sheets from her bed, along with two more she'd washed and stashed in her closet. As quickly as she could, she tore the faded, threadbare things into strips, which she stuffed under the mattress. She ran out the door just in time to catch the bus.

Supper was spaghetti. The cooking smells made Jillie's empty stomach growl, and when Margo left the kitchen for a couple of minutes, she slurped down a spoonful of the tangy sauce and sucked up several strands of half-cooked pasta. The food burnt her tongue and put a blister on the roof of her mouth, but she didn't care. She kept her mind busy by going over the details of her plan.

That night, she waited until the household was silent, except for Cleg's foundation-rattling snore. She retrieved the strips of bed sheet and braided them the way she'd learned in Girl Scouts. Hopefully, the makeshift rope would be strong enough for what she needed. She didn't let herself think about what would happen if it weren't.

After pulling one end of the rope through the handle of her suitcase, she circled it around the handle and tied a square knot then threaded it through the straps of her backpack. She hefted the load a couple of times then congratulated herself when the rope held fast.

Jillie heaved the suitcase and backpack onto the bed. Ancient, rusty springs squealed, and she froze, holding her breath. When no feet pounded on the wooden floor toward her room and no voice questioned what she was doing, she planted her hands against the wrought iron bed frame and pushed the whole thing toward the window.

But the bed's iron legs scraped so loudly against the warped wood floor, Jillie had to bite her lip to keep from panicking. If the Elliotts discovered her trying to escape, they'd probably put bars on the window. Or they might even move her someplace where they could lock her in. She'd die without ever finding her sister.

She shivered. *Help me, Beth.*

For the next several minutes, she moved the bed a few inches at a time, stopped to listen, and moved it a few more inches until it rested just beneath the window sill.

Careful to put her feet on the iron bedframe under the mattress, she grabbed the wrought-iron headboard and pulled herself up onto the bed. To prevent the rusty springs from squealing again, she slowly moved her feet along the metal frame until she stood under the window.

After wrapping one end of the braided rope around her waist to keep it from being yanked out of her grasp by the weight of the luggage, she pushed the suitcase and backpack through the window. Once the luggage bumped against the tin roof outside the room, she unwound the rope from her waist.

Relieved when the cadence of Cleg's snore continued unbroken, Jillie carefully played out the braided rope. As she'd hoped, the luggage slid down the roof as if the corrugated tin were a water slide.

But Jillie's sweat-slick hands lost their grip, and the rope burned her palms as it shot through her fingers. Instinctively, she opened her scalded hands and flapped them as the suitcase and backpack thumped onto the packed dirt beside the house.

Once the pain subsided, she held her palms in the moonlight spilling through the open window. No blood, only the redness and soreness caused by rope-burn.

Cautiously, she squeezed through the window—arms first, as if she were diving into a swimming pool. When her fingers came into contact with the roof, she carefully pulled her legs and feet the rest of the way through the window and then righted herself. Clutching the window sill, she stood still long enough to catch her breath.

Her tennies offered little traction on the steeply slanted, corrugated tin, and she nearly slipped several times before managing to inch her way to the roof's edge. Fear of being caught made a boulder in her throat as she began to shinny down the old tree.

But when she reached the lowest tree limb, she realized it was still a long way to the ground—a lot further than it had seemed during her earlier reconnaissance. She'd have to hang from the limb by her arms and hope she didn't hurt herself in the drop.

After slowly lowering her body off one side of the limb, she dangled for several heart-stopping seconds, then took a breath and let go. She landed with a *plop* onto the hard dirt next to her luggage, pain like an electrical shock shooting up the leg that'd taken the brunt of the fall. She sat on the ground and rubbed her ankle until the pain lessened, then stood and stepped to her luggage.

She untied the sheet-rope from her bags, wound it up, and hid it in the gap between the tree and house. Then she slipped the straps of her backpack over her shoulders, lifted the suitcase, and made her way down the driveway's outside edge toward the road.

Cool night air washed over her, and she inhaled as deeply as her lungs would allow. The light breeze smelled like dirt, trees, animals, weeds and dried flowers.

It smelled like freedom.

But instead of singing and dancing for joy as was her impulse, Jillie moved quietly. As soon as the Elliotts discovered her missing, they'd be out looking for her.

And she didn't want to think about what they'd do if they got her back into that house again.

Chapter Eight

Avoiding the roads, Jillie headed cross-country. The suitcase and backpack grew heavier with each step, and she often had to stop and straighten her aching back.

Maybe she should ditch the suitcase. She'd only packed it because Beth told her to.

At the very least, maybe she could unload the Nancy Drew book, or one of the bottles of water. But the book had been Beth's, and she'd need the water. Although less to haul would have been a relief, like Hansel and Gretel's breadcrumbs, anything she left behind would lead searchers right to her. She took a deep breath and tightened her grip on the suitcase handle.

Cool night air teased its fingers upward under her jacket, and her teeth chattered. She busied her mind with memories of past trips on the train with Beth before Pops died. They'd take sandwiches for lunch and stop off along the route to visit museums and parks, window-shop, and people-watch. By the time they got home, they'd be too tired to do anything but take a bath and go to bed.

Sudden anger bubbled up from Jillie's insides. Mommy, Pops, and Beth—all gone.

Life's not fair, Chili Bean. We just do the best we can. Beth's words brought tears to Jillie's eyes. "I miss you," she breathed into the silence.

If all went well, she'd get to the train station before the Elliotts discovered her missing. She'd get off in Albuquerque then board the city bus that stopped in front of the hospital. She'd hunt up the kind-faced nurse who'd patted her shoulder and told her they were doing everything they could for her sister.

Two problems popped into her mind. One was the question of what to do with her luggage. A kid carrying that much stuff would catch people's attention. Second, the Belen station didn't open until five thirty in the morning. And according to her wristwatch, that was still a couple of hours away.

The luggage problem could be resolved by renting one of the station's lockers Beth had pointed out during one of their day trips. Depending on the cost, she might be able to rent one for several days. But the only way to deal with the second problem was to wait for the station to open.

Within a few minutes, the train station came into view. Except for lights dotting the parking lot, the place was dark and empty.

Jillie dropped her suitcase into the roadside ditch. She sat on the ground in front of it, leaned back against the hard plastic, and glanced at her watch.

Two hours before the station came to life. She could rest her eyes, just for a few...

The sun's warmth on Jillie's face jolted her awake. Panic-stricken, she looked at her watch.

Nearly eight o'clock. The Elliotts would be up and ready for breakfast.

When they found her gone, they'd probably call the police or social services. In no time, every train and bus station in the state would be crawling with police. Her picture would probably be plastered all over television.

Her eyes scanning in what Pops had called surveillance mode, she hoisted her luggage and hurried toward the station while searching the parking lot for signs of unusual activity. None of the vehicles looked familiar and she didn't recognize any of the people who bustled in and out of the automatic double doors. No police were in sight.

She jammed her baseball cap down to cover as much of her hair as possible and stepped onto the asphalt at one end of the parking lot.

Just then, Mort's pickup chugged into the lot opposite to where Jillie stood. Alone in the vehicle, his head swiveled from side to side as he slowly drove up and down the lanes.

Panic sluicing through her stomach, Jillie hauled her suitcase back up the hill, dropped it behind a large sage brush and fell to her knees beside it. She watched through gaps in the bush while Mort parked and went inside the station.

Her heart pounding and ears alert to every sound, Jillie grabbed up her bag and again headed cross country. If she didn't stop to rest, she should be able to cover the ten miles to the Los Lunas station by nightfall. She'd stash her suitcase in one of the lockers there and catch the evening train to Albuquerque.

With renewed determination, Jillie tramped across fields and down turn rows. Ignoring the constant pain in her shoulders and stitch in her side, she adjusted her direction based on the position of the sun.

Pops, Mommy, Beth, if you can hear me, please help me be strong.

Exhausted beyond anything she'd ever experienced before, Jillie marched on.

Chapter Nine

Over the next couple of hours, Jillie's elation slowly eroded into the realization that she'd miscalculated how long it would take her to get to the Los Lunas train station. With daylight fading and exhaustion making her breath come in gasps, she had to find a place to hole up for the night.

The sight of a barn on the horizon brought relief pouring through her. No house nearby meant the place was either abandoned or used only for storage.

When her careful search for signs of life came up null, she hurried toward the barn. With its wood door standing slightly ajar, the place felt forgotten.

Jillie pulled her belongings into the darkness. Her ears pricking at every creak and groan the old timbers made in the heightening winds, she hollowed out a nest in a pile of dry, dusty hay, ate a few bites from her food stores, and considered her plan of action.

If she'd been a typical kid with typical looks, mixing in with a crowd wouldn't have been all that hard. But everywhere she went, people stared.

Then she remembered the hair color Beth had insisted she pack.

After retrieving the box from her suitcase, she read the instructions, put the vile smelling stuff on her head and left it for the fifteen minutes the directions demanded.

Sacrificing one bottle of her precious water, she washed her hair as best she could. She then tore the hair color box into tiny pieces and stuffed it along with the empty water bottle into her backpack for later disposal.

Her hair still wet, she nestled into the hay, pulled Mickey up to her chest, and fell asleep.

****

The wail and whistle of high winds through the gaps between the barn's walls brought Jillie awake. Temporarily disoriented, she moved her legs, rustling the hay upon which she lay. The not-unpleasant smell of old, dried alfalfa filled her nostrils.

A glance toward the barn door showed the sun was preparing to come up. Still tired, she yearned to roll over and go back to sleep in her warm nest. But she sat up, pulled on her Broncos baseball cap and quickly packed her things.

The barn had seemed safe the night before. But from the moment she woke, an ominous feeling in her stomach had been growing in intensity, and she'd learned never to ignore it.

She grabbed up her stuff and carried it toward the ditch beside the road. No sooner had she jumped into the gully than her ears pricked at the sound of an approaching vehicle. She lifted her head over the berm as headlights approached the barn.

Dust and pebbles shot out behind the tires as Cleg drove up the overgrown path to the barn. From her perch on the passenger's side, Margo swiveled her head like a barn owl in search of a mouse.

As soon as Cleg turned off the engine, Margo threw open her door, jumped out, slammed the door behind her, and headed for the barn. After a short pause, the second pickup door slammed and Cleg ambled after his wife.

The skin along Jillie's arms and neck crawled like thousands of fleas were invading her body. Barely breathing, she hunkered down and waited.

Voices floated on the breeze to her straining ears.

"I told you she'd hide out here," Margo said. "Look at that hay. She made herself comfortable while you and Mort chased your asses."

Cleg mumbled something.

"You thought?" Margo shrieked. "That's the problem, you didn't think, as per usual. She'll most likely find another hidey-hole...maybe at the Posey's old place."

"It's breakfast time, Sweet Lumps. Can't we grab a bite before heading over there?"

"No, we can't grab a bite before heading over there," Margo mimicked Cleg's whine. "You could live over a month off the blubber you've got stored up. Come on."

Doors slammed, the pickup engine roared to life, and a cloud of dust testified to the Elliotts' departure.

Long after the engine noise receded into the distance, Jillie sat deep in thought.

She'd have to avoid the roads—especially highway forty-seven that ran north from Belen to Los Lunas. No doubt the Elliotts as well as the police would be patrolling that route.

The day was turning out to be overcast—an unusual occurrence in the high desert. The good news was that clouds never hung around long, and she'd soon be able to use the sun for direction. The bad news was, other than the roads she'd memorized, she was completely unfamiliar with the area.

Eyes and ears alert, she walked along the arroyo until it intersected the raised sides of an irrigation ditch. Leaving her luggage in the arroyo, she climbed out, stood atop the berm, and scanned the area—only fields and pasture land as far as she could see.

For the next several hours, Jillie hauled her luggage over barbed wire fences and slogged her way across soggy, irrigated fields in the direction she hoped was north. The day wore on, but low, darkening clouds refused to give her even a glimpse of the sun. Then the little daylight sifting through the clouds dimmed.

Panic drove away the hunger grinding in Jillie's stomach as her eyes scoured the area. No houses, not even a dirt road. Nothing looked familiar.

She was lost, and a storm was brewing. She'd always loved New Mexico rain storms, but just then, the idea terrified her. A storm meant lightning, and lightning could put an end to anyone who got caught out in it. Jillie had to find shelter, and she had to find it fast.

Chapter Ten

Muddy, exhausted, and so hungry she could hardly think straight, Jillie plodded on in the direction she hoped lay Los Lunas. With every step, the suitcase bumped against her legs. Blisters raised on her hands, the stitch in her side had developed into a full-blown, stabbing pain, and her breaths came in gasps. Sweat plastered her hair against her forehead, dripped down her face, and ran stinging into her eyes. Her T-shirt was sweat-soaked while her mouth was dry, and the blisters on her heels had popped, making every step hurt so badly she sobbed.

At some point, the clouds evaporated, and a full moon lit up the terrain. Jillie could hardly believe her eyes at the sight of a sign announcing she was nearing the village limits of Los Lunas.

Giddiness made her lightheaded. She'd find a place to rest, then get to the station early the next morning. Hopefully, Beth would still be at the hospital waiting to be autopsied.

With renewed energy, she stashed her bags beside the road and covered them with dead tree limbs and leaves. Watchful of traffic but unwilling to stray very far from the road, she walked toward the village.

Just outside of town, she spotted a small trailer house, not much bigger than the playhouse Pops had built for her in their back yard. Tall weeds grew undisturbed around the trailer's base. No light or sound came from inside.

If abandoned as it seemed, the trailer might be the perfect place to stash her suitcase. Not only would it allow her to save the money she'd have had to use for a locker, but she'd be able to move much faster. She could come back for it after she got Beth's ashes.

Unable to see through the windows made opaque by dirt, she climbed the two creaky wooden steps and went in. Wadded paper and plastic bags, newspapers, and empty cans littered the floor. The scurrying of tiny clawed feet as well as the smell told her no one had lived here for a long time.

What appeared to be a small rug lay just inside the door, but the rest of the floor was cracked, dark linoleum. Tattered floral fabric oozed cotton batting from a sofa attached to the wall at one end of the trailer.

Jillie returned to her luggage and carried it up the small hill. Once inside the trailer, she heaved the backpack and suitcase onto the sofa. Dust flew from the ragged fabric, and she coughed.

With garbage crunching under her feet, she stepped into a short, dark hallway leading to a built-in wooden platform that must have once served as a bed. The mattress was nowhere to be seen, but at least the platform would keep her off the floor.

She'd taken a couple of steps into the gloomy hallway, when a sudden gust of air wafted upward, ruffling her hair and cooling her face. She looked closer at a dark oval in the center of the hallway and goose bumps broke out on her arms.

Just a few inches further, and she'd have stepped into a gaping hole in the floor. While the fall probably wouldn't have killed her, she could have wound up with a broken arm or leg. Because the trailer was so isolated, most likely no one would have heard her screams for help. By the time she could get free, the Elliotts could have got hold of Beth's ashes.

Jillie swallowed hard and looked around the trailer's interior as her eyes grew accustomed to the darkness. She picked up a small, empty cardboard box on the floor next to the sofa, tore off a side panel and placed it over the hole. It wouldn't be strong enough to hold her weight, but at least it would be a reminder of where not to step.

She wouldn't be here long. A few hours' sleep was all she needed.

But gusts of wind kept lifting the cardboard over the hole and then dropping it. There was no way she'd be able to sleep with all that *whoosh-plop* stuff going on. And a hole that size would allow critters to come and go as they pleased. Though she loved animals, Jillie shivered at the thought of a raccoon or family of rats somehow finding their way up that hole with the intention on nestling next to her while she slept.

She returned to the small rug she'd seen by the front door, picked it up, and spread the threadbare thing on top of the cardboard. Once satisfied that the added weight would hold steady against further wind gusts, she threw her backpack past the rug onto the platform. Too heavy to heave over the hole, the suitcase would stay on the sofa.

Taking what running jump the tiny confines allowed, Jillie leaped over the rug. She sat on the platform edge and pulled her backpack toward her. Only two biscuits, an orange, and a squashed banana left. She should have made more sausage for the trip, no matter how much Margo yelled.

After giving thanks for her food, she ate every bite then allowed herself a few sips from her second bottle of water. The remaining bottle would have to be rationed until she could find someplace to refill it.

At the urgent tugging of her bladder, Jillie stepped outside and walked toward a large bush. She squatted, her eyes drawn down the hill.

Headlights from cars carrying people home from work meandered down streets polka dotted by streetlights. Lighted homes sparkled like jewels across the valley below.

Families were eating supper in those houses. Moms and pops were hugging their kids goodnight, and brothers and sisters scrapped with each other before going to bed. There would be food in those houses, clean clothes, warm baths and beds. There would be people who loved each other.

Jillie swiped at the tears welling up in her eyes, pulled up her britches, and returned to the trailer. After spreading her coat on the wooden platform, she lay down and rested her head on Mickey's tummy.

"God," she whispered, "I don't know if Beth can hear me from Heaven, but would you please give her a message? Tell her I love her and that I'm going to find her no matter what. Amen."

Jillie tried to make herself go to sleep. But her eyes kept popping open, drawn upward to an oblong window in the wall above the platform.

About a foot wide, the dirt-encrusted pane ran nearly the width of the trailer. And though its metal clasp seemed tightly locked, she couldn't make herself stop imagining a hideous, distorted face staring at her like the ones she'd seen in horror movies.

Standing on the platform, she twisted the locked clasp and pushed the window open, wincing at the resulting squeal. Good thing the trailer was so isolated, otherwise she might as well have sent a telegraph to the world that she was there.

She pulled the window closed, twisted the clasp, then shoved against the mechanism to test the lock's strength. But even after it became obvious no one could open the window from the outside, she couldn't calm down.

Her ears perked up at every sound and her imagination played tricks on her while hunger shoved bitter-tasting acid into her throat. Outside, the wind moaned, making the little trailer creak and shudder. Finally, exhaustion won, and Jillie fell asleep.

Chapter Eleven

Early morning light fighting its way through the window above her brought Jillie's eyes open. Relieved to see even a bit of sunshine, she glanced at her watch. Nearly six o'clock.

She sat up, picked up her backpack, and retrieved her money pouch. Time to take stock of her finances.

Less the train fare to Albuquerque, she had forty-eight dollars and change. That sounded like a lot of money, but she'd have to be careful. Especially now that her food was gone.

By that time of the morning, Beth would have been cooking their breakfast. Jillie's mouth watered at the remembered smells of bacon and biscuits, the sizzle and pop of eggs frying in bacon drippings, even the glorious aroma of her sister's fresh coffee. Beth had said it probably wasn't the healthiest breakfast, but it was what Grandma Ross ate every morning of her life, and she lived to be ninety-five.

Jillie did some mental math. If she watched what she spent, and ate only two meals a day, her money should last long enough to get Beth's ashes and take them home on the train.

She refused to think about what she'd do after that. One day at a time, that's what Pops always said. And right then, she had to get something to eat.

Using her fingers as a comb, she poked at her hair

a few times, gave up the brief fight with a rat's nest of tangles, and pulled on her baseball cap.

She jumped over the hole in the floor, opened her suitcase, and took out a small wooden box. A gift from Pops on her ninth birthday, the box was a rectangle of about five inches wide, eight inches long, and three inches high. She ran her fingers over the tiny roses carved into the hinged lid of what she called her treasure chest.

She opened the lid and smiled at the brightly colored beads, crystalline stones, bits of colored plastic and glass, and one of the most recent gifts left by the crows—a crusty nickel. Useless stuff really, but she couldn't bear to leave it behind. She closed the box and stuffed it into her backpack.

Beth had made her memorize the street names of all the train stations in case they got separated during one of their days out. Sometimes, after Digger had fallen asleep, the two of them would pour over a road map of New Mexico. Beth's spirit would radiate equal parts happy anticipation and sadness as they made plans to leave the only home they'd ever known.

Jillie said a quick prayer for help remembering the directions, kissed the top of Mickey's head, and stuffed him into her backpack. With any luck, people would think she was just another kid going to school.

About half an hour later, as she neared the station, she spotted a neon sign atop a twenty-four-hour fast food café. Saliva filled her mouth at the smells of bacon, sausage, eggs, and pancakes that poured through the door as a couple of people exited. She adjusted her backpack and made a beeline for the café.

A woman stood behind the counter. The name tag

pinned to her shirt identified her as the manager. Someone standing at the grill laughed and said something to a young man wearing a hairnet and carrying a box out of a huge refrigerator built into the wall. Jillie was relieved to see there were no other customers.

The woman behind the counter smiled. "How can I help you?"

"How much for a plain biscuit?"

The woman eyed Jillie. "This must be your lucky day. We have a special on our sampler breakfast platter. It comes with a little of everything."

"How much can I get for a dollar?"

"Enough for two people. You want orange or apple juice?"

"Apple." Jillie pulled one wadded-up dollar out of her pocket and put it on the counter. Something about the way the woman looked at her tugged at her insides, but she was too hungry to deal with it. "May I use your restroom?"

"Left at the end of the counter."

Jillie was startled to see her image in the mirror above the bathroom sink. Though pleased that the hair coloring completely changed her appearance, she was shocked at how dirty and bedraggled she looked. The good news was she didn't think even her sister would have recognized her.

She washed her hands and arms up to her elbows, tidied her hair as best she could, and replaced her baseball cap. When she returned to the dining room, the manager smiled and motioned toward a red plastic tray upon which sat a white Styrofoam platter piled high with scrambled eggs, two sausages, two pieces of crisp bacon, and three pancakes. Two little square containers of syrup, a packet of butter, and a box of apple juice sat next to the food.

"If you'd like more juice," the woman said, "Just let me know."

"Thank you." Uncomfortable with the woman's scrutiny, Jillie kept her head bowed. But something about the way the woman's eyes kept shifting back and forth between her and the door set her adrenaline pumping.

She carried her tray to a booth and slid into its built-in seat. After gobbling most of the food, she nonchalantly wrapped the sausages in a napkin, stuffed them into her backpack then headed for the front door.

But just as she was about to step outside, a police car pulled around the corner. Its driver looking intently toward the café, the car slowed then pulled over to the curb.

Had her description already been put on the radio? Had someone in the café recognized her and called the police?

She glanced at the manager who was edging around the counter while pretending to be interested in something else.

"Actually," Jillie said, "if you're sure it's okay, I would like another box of juice."

The woman smiled, a relieved look on her face. "Good," she said. "Another apple juice coming up."

As soon as the manager disappeared behind the counter, Jillie hurried toward the rear door beneath a red-lighted Exit sign. Another sign taped to the door said it was for emergency use only and an alarm would sound if it was opened.

With all the strength she could muster, she pushed the bar on the door down and shoved. True to the sign's promise, the alarm whooped loud enough to shatter the eardrums of anyone in the vicinity.

But instead of running through the exit, Jillie stepped back into the café and ran toward an attached indoor playground. She climbed a ladder to the top of a huge tube-slide and hunkered down inside a red, solid plastic square cube barely large enough for her and her backpack.

Her stomach flip-flopped as voices floated up to her.

"She used the emergency exit," the manager said. "I tried to keep her here, but she must have seen you coming."

"Where does the exit lead?" a man's voice said.

"To the alley. But by now, she'll be long gone."

"What makes you think she was a runaway?"

"I have three daughters," the counter woman said. "That poor kid was half starved. And she looked like she hadn't washed or changed clothes in a month."

"Can you describe her?"

"About four and a half feet tall, maybe seventy pounds. She was wearing a baseball cap, Broncos, I think. She looked about eleven or so. At first, I wasn't even sure she was a girl because of the way she was dressed and the short hair."

"Hair color?"

"Brown, from what I could see under her cap. "

"Was there anyone with her, maybe someone she seemed to be afraid of?"

"No, she was alone." Pause. "At least I think she was." Pause. "You think someone could have been waiting outside for her, someone who made her come in for food?"

"It's possible—"

"Oh," the woman interrupted, "she had really pale skin, almost white, and pretty eyes. Violet, I think you'd call them. It's the first thing I noticed about her."

"Violet eyes?"

"Yeah, nearly purple."

There was a pause, as if the officer was writing down the description. "We'll check missing persons. If she comes back—"

"I'll call," the manager said. "It's sad, you know. People don't watch their kids anymore, too busy or just don't care. I don't leave mine by themselves, not with the way things are these days."

After a couple more questions, the policeman thanked the manager for the call and left.

When sounds in the café returned to normal, Jillie scooted a few feet down the tube attached to the cube and peeked through a round hole. Customers came and went. Groups laughed and joked with each other, taking time with their food, while single folks sat alone, ate quickly and left.

A bus load of kids piled through the door and into the playground. Screaming, pushing, and shoving, they converged onto the slide.

By this time, someone other than the manager stood behind the counter. A different cook slapped raw burger patties onto the grill.

Taking advantage of the sudden mob of kids, Jillie took a turn down the slide then walked toward the front door. No one called to her, and no police were in sight.

After making sure the coast was clear, she stepped

onto the sidewalk and walked as fast as she could toward a park she'd passed on her way into town. She'd refill her water bottle at the drinking fountain there and wash up as best she could. Then she'd eat the sausage and head back to the trailer for a clean outfit from her suitcase.

She'd have to be more careful.

Chapter Twelve

A worried look carefully pasted on his face, Mort spoke to the woman behind the counter at the fast food joint. "We're her only family. My mother's worried sick; she hasn't been able to eat or sleep since our Jillie ran away."

The woman whose badge proclaimed her the assistant manager looked thoughtful. "Our manager said she saw a kid this morning. Her hair wasn't white, though, it was brown."

Mort studied the woman's face. "Brown?" How could he have forgotten about the dye he'd found in Jillie's bags when he'd searched them? He forced himself to nod in understanding. He'd thought Jillie was just a dumb kid, but this whole time she'd been doing some serious planning. "Yeah, that was, um, from my mom's box of hair color." He forced a chuckle.

"Our manager said the poor little thing would have cleaned out the walk-in fridge if she'd had the chance." The assistant manager cocked her head, the look on her face suddenly suspicious.

Mort could almost hear the gears grinding as the woman mentally ran through a dawning litany of reasons why a kid would run away from what appeared to be such a loving home and family.

He forced his mouth into a smile. "Thank you so

much for your kindness to our little Jillie." He pulled out his wallet. "Let me pay you for the food she ate."

The look on the woman's face softened, and she shook her head. "No, sir. The manager said she paid what was asked." She pulled a pad of paper and pen from a pocket in her apron, placed them on the counter, and pushed them toward Mort. "If you'll leave your name and number, I'll call if your niece comes back. Another call won't hurt."

"Another call?"

The woman raised her eyebrows and nodded. "Janey, that's our manager, called the police nearly as soon as the little girl came in. She said she figured somewhere a mother was tying herself in knots with worry. But the kid bolted out the back just as the police drove up."

Mort bowed his head to hide the expression on his face. The police would notify social services, who'd check up on the Elliotts. He could almost feel his dreams of a new life slipping through his fingers.

With what he hoped to be a sincere look of gratitude on his face, Mort raised his head. He looked earnestly into the woman's eyes, allowed a tear to form in his own, and reached for the tablet and pen.

No sooner had he written a fake name and phone number than he realized his mistake. Too easy for the police to figure out who he was once the old bag behind the counter described him. And by trying to hide his identity he'd essentially made himself a person of interest.

Resisting the urge to jerk the tablet back out of the woman's hand, he mentally shook himself and smiled. "Thank you so much for your help."

The woman smiled back, a look of sympathy on her face. "*Jillie*, now that's a lovely name. We'll all be on the lookout for her."

Mort turned to go, his teeth grinding. Mistakes were beginning to pile up.

And while he'd been wasting time hanging around the train station in Belen per Margo's command, the kid had been eating breakfast in Los Lunas. He shook his head at the memory of his mother's rampage when he suggested the kid might have left the state.

Red-faced, veins popping out on her forehead, she'd shrieked at him, "If you had half a brain, you'd know she'd try to get to the hospital. And how would she do that?" Pause. "I asked you a question."

"She'd have to take the train."

"Exactly. But it would never occur to you that she'd be obsessed with seeing her sister's body, would it? The whole love-of-family thing never took root in the mass of jelly that passes for your brain. She's still a kid; she doesn't understand the concept of death."

"Seems she understood it enough to do Digger—"

Margo interrupted, a look on her face that could have turned a pile of rocks into lava. "And once she learns her sister's still alive, all our plans are down the toilet." She'd sneered. "Why can't you be more like your cousin Toby?"

"Wait, wait, is this the same Toby who wet the bed until he was a teenager? The same guy who killed our cat and spray-painted Lucia Alton's car after she broke up with him because he was *creepy*?"

Margo sniffed. "At least Toby went to college, something you couldn't manage to do. He wants to better himself, even has a library card and all."

"Right. He dropped out of college after the first semester and now he lives in a trailer house at the back of our property."

"*Our* property?" Margo puffed air through her nose, setting her skin flap horizontal. After that, she'd screamed at him until he'd had enough and left the house.

By the time Mort turned ten, he'd stopped calling the woman who'd birthed him *Mommy* and began referring to her as *Maggot*, after the flesh-eating, carcass-cleaning worms that lived off others' putrefaction.

And now that scrawny little kid Jillie was holding the keys to his freedom.

Mort envisioned himself scuba diving off pristine coral reefs around the world, skiing in Austria, and going out with beautiful European women. People would bow and scrape to him.

He complemented himself on what he called his most superior Master Plan of Action. And it all hinged on one word: patience.

He had no need to waste time and gas money looking for the kid, because no one who loved someone like that kid loved her sister was going to stay away for long. She'd eventually turn up, and then the sisters would go home. That's when Mort would make his move.

Always best to keep things simple. *Sooner or later*—three simple little words that summed up his Master Plan.

Something cold and hard settled in his gut. He started his engine and pulled out into traffic.

Chapter Thirteen

From inside his pickup parked along the curb at a city park, Toby Dinkins took a bite of breakfast burrito. He turned on the radio, and his favorite pop music from the eighties poured into the enclosed air. But the music failed to soothe his jangled nerves.

After diving for lost change among his sofa cushions, he'd barely scraped together three dollars for a mini-burrito—the cheapest thing on the fast-food menu. Not the life he'd envisioned for himself.

What he needed was to win the lottery. No, what he *really* needed was to find a treasure. And, based on what his cousin Mort told him, that was within the realm of possibility.

Toby's upper lip curled. How he hated what he had to do to pay his bills. Gigolo was such an ugly word, and the job description was getting harder and harder to take.

If his plans solidified, however, that lifestyle would soon be history.

He watched as kids shouted at one another, laughed and shrieked, happy to be out in the open. Mommies watched and chatted with other mommies—despised creatures Toby referred to as *Breeders.*

Toby had never fit into the mass of human cattle, even as a kid. He could almost feel sorry for the poor beasts. They with their slow wits, their bestial habits, their enmities and hatreds. They coddled their dogs and cats while destroying their children.

The world was a battlefield, and survival required vigilance. But no one paid attention nowadays. No one took the time to walk around and observe, or to just sit and think. Too busy yakking on their phones, staring into tiny screens, texting everyone in the world, chirping out their miserable activities—as if anyone cared. A turnip was more aware than today's average *Homo sapiens*.

But from the moment of his birth, Toby had perfected a level of hyper-vigilance that would make the CIA look like cub scouts. As a result, although he'd never before been to the park where he sat, within three minutes of his arrival he could have closed his eyes and described the milieu in detail.

Six children ranging in ages from toddler through about eight or nine cavorted on, around, under, and through the playground equipment. Their laughter floated on the breeze as they flitted in their element.

A brief and quickly squelched feeling of sadness pulsed through Toby's mid-section. Cute little kids, but really just malleable *Tabulae Rasae* mirroring their parents' behaviors until they actually *became* their parents.

Four Breeder-mothers kept vigil over their offspring. Perched like exotic birds on a couple of benches at the edge of the playground, they chatted and laughed. Their watchful eyes darted back and forth among each other and their fledglings. Occasionally, one jumped up and ran to a fallen little one to kiss a boo-boo. Then the child would run back to play, everything made better by the mommy-smooch.

Something toxic moved in Toby's gut. Some boo-boos couldn't be kissed away—just one of the many life lessons he'd learned at the knee of his own Mommy-Dearest.

And then the images before him morphed into another life lesson.

A middle-aged man leaned against a huge elm tree at the edge of the park, his hooded eyes fixed in an unblinking stare at the scene, his hands stuffed deep in the pockets of his khaki slacks.

Toby clenched his jaws nearly tight enough to crack his tooth enamel. Although he didn't know the guy, he recognized the type: a bottom feeder, preying on those too young and weak to defend themselves.

Of course, there'd be those who'd point a finger in Toby's face and call him a hypocrite. Maybe even call him evil. But *evil* was open to definition, wasn't it? One man's evil is another man's survival strategy.

He chuckled as the words of a television psychologist popped into his head: *Nearly guaranteed recipe to bake a disturbed personality? Continuous, prolonged criticism, neglect, and lack of affection by the caregiver.*

Some might call Toby a disturbed personality, but so what? He'd read enough to know no one could be characterized as completely sane. Every human had glitches, some more than others. It was all just a matter of degree.

Drumming his fingers on the bottom of the steering wheel, Toby looked back and forth between the breeders and the pervert. He'd bet money that if he knuckle-knocked on any given breeder-head, the resulting sound would be like a mallet striking a wooden block.

He jiggled his right leg up and down on the ball of his foot while wondering if the adoring mommies would grab up their offspring and run screaming back to their hidey-holes if the law of psychic osmosis miraculously kicked in and allowed them to divine what the old man by the tree was thinking? What he wanted to do to their little ones?

He studied the women's faces. Not one of them reflected an iota of awareness of the world beyond their personal space. They all chatted and tittered the forced laughter required in social settings, careful not to allow their glances to stay overly long on another's out-of-style hairdo or too-worn footwear. Plastic smiles firmly in place, they assessed each other's status.

A light breeze wafted through the pickup window, carrying snippets of conversation. "We feel it's important for our little Moonlight to meet people outside our usual orbits," one breeder said, "so we come here at least once a week."

The second mother nodded sagely. "Oh yes, a social conscience is so important to balanced development."

As the women continued their vapid conversations, Toby fought down the urge to jump from his vehicle, strip naked, and run toward them just to see what they'd do. He snickered at the mental image of the mommy-mob shrieking and grabbing up their little ones, their mommy-hands covering the wide-eyed little faces.

Then again, maybe they'd pretend not to see him as long as he didn't get too close. Humanoid turnips, that's what they were. Nothing more than dark green-leafed plumage presented to the world, while their bulb-heads stayed safely jammed into the dirt.

They assumed everyone else thought and felt as they did. But, of course, that was the tragic mistake made by those who just wanted to live and let live. They didn't want to hurt anyone, so no one could want to hurt them. No hard reality would be allowed in their cotton candy lives.

The never-happen-here attitude was a phenomenon Toby called the *Normalcy Bias*. And this scene was a prime example.

The *Bias* made people blind and vulnerable to those who'd moved outside the constraints of morality, humanity, or conscience. It made them prey. It made people ignore the instinctive twinges in their gut and told them bad things always happened to someone else.

The *Bias* assured them the hideous stuff people perpetrated on others—the horrors splattered across the front page and heard on the nightly news—could never touch them or theirs. It filled their heads with white noise and told them to look neither to the left nor to the right.

Undoubtedly put in place by Mother Nature to help keep the population in check, the *Bias* was strongest in the minds of those who'd never had to fight to survive, who'd never had to stay home from school until broken bones mended and bruises faded. Or who'd never stared into the darkness of a soulless breeder intent on obliterating their spirit.

Strange sounds in the night? The Bias says it's just the wind. Shadows on the wall? It's only the trees scratching at the windows. Whispers in the darkness? You're imagining things. Sleep well, children, our world is safe.

With a heavy sigh, Toby studied the man whose gaze was riveted on a spot hidden from Toby's view by a tall hedge. With his hands shoved deep inside his pockets, had the guy been a bird dog, he would have been in full point mode—target spotted and locked.

As if sensing he was being watched, the man looked toward Toby. Their eyes met, and the man quickly dropped his gaze to study the grass in front of him.

Toby shot a look toward the breeders to see if they'd finally registered the elevated danger. No surprise that after a perfunctory glance, none of them paid further attention to either the pervert or him.

That's right, don't look. If you don't look, the danger's not there.

Then, like dogs responding to a whistle only they could hear, the mothers gathered their chicks and flocked toward the parking lot. They waved at each other, called out their goodbyes, and promised to return soon.

Of course, some of the oh-so-loving-mommy attention would evaporate once behind closed doors. Then some of the pseudo-doting breeders would turn into flesh-shredding, eviscerating, soul-cauterizing harpies, weaving their webs of enmeshment—

Toby interrupted the flood of thought before it spiraled upward into what he'd dubbed a "Hate-Spate." He ordered himself to breathe slowly.

Left unchecked, a hate-spate could override his caution and catapult him into doing something reckless, something that would make the police take an interest in him. He couldn't have that now, not when a new life was so close, he could nearly smell it.

Toby finished his cold burrito, wadded up the wrapper and started the engine. Before pulling away, he took one last look around the park.

As if the pervert's shoes had suddenly caught fire, he scuttled toward a small compact car at one end of the park. But instead of getting into the vehicle, he reached through the open passenger side window, pulled out a brown paper bag then retraced his steps.

A kid wearing a baseball cap stepped out from behind the bush and hurried away. Too far distant for Toby to ascertain gender, the kid broke into a run and disappeared up an alley. The pervert furtively glanced toward the mommies as if to ensure they hadn't noticed him, then followed the kid.

Evil *is*, as Evil *does*.

Toby sucked air through his teeth. Never taking his eyes off the pervert, he started his engine and followed the follower.

Chapter Fourteen

When Jillie arrived at the park, she found a spot behind a large bush hidden from view of anyone on the street. She laid her backpack on the grass, unzipped it and retrieved the napkin-encased sausage she'd saved from the fast food joint.

A light breeze blew the smells of dry grass against her face, and noonday sun warmed the back of her neck. Through gaps in the bush she watched yelping kids play on the slide and swings as an old man looked on from the park's edge.

Did the children have any idea how lucky they were to have the freedom to play in the sun? Did even one of them know what life would be like if their moms were suddenly no longer there to see to them?

She looked like she hadn't washed or changed clothes in a month. The café manager's words had stung.

Other than her hair color, Jillie hadn't given much thought to her appearance. She'd been too busy trying to avoid getting caught by the Elliotts or the police.

She heaved a sigh. She hadn't planned to return to the trailer for her suitcase until after she had Beth's ashes. But, although the thought of back-tracking made her insides sink, it would be a bitter pill to get caught just because she hadn't taken the time to clean herself up.

Beth was counting on her.

As Jillie hefted her backpack and slipped her arms into the straps, her eyes were drawn to movement just beyond the bush behind which she'd eaten. The old man who'd been standing around suddenly hurried toward a car at the side of the park, glancing over his shoulder in her direction every couple of steps.

The words from one of Pop's survival speeches rang in her head: *If something doesn't feel right, never ignore it. Pay attention to your gut.*

Jillie picked up her pace.

Once back at the trailer, she hauled the suitcase up onto the ragged sofa and removed two outfits from it. She stuffed a clean T-shirt and pair of jeans into her backpack then removed her dirty clothes and slipped into the second clean outfit.

Her eyes rested on the huge yellow suitcase. The stupid thing might as well have been a neon sign that said *Here's Jillie Ross, runaway.* She needed to ditch it.

A sudden loud knock on the door interrupted her thoughts and made her jump. She gulped, and her heartbeat sped up.

Maybe the owner of the trailer had come back. Or maybe the police had spotted her in the park and tracked her down.

"Hello in there." It was a man's voice, kind of gargly sounding. The man coughed, hawked, and spat. "I know you're in there girlie," he said a little louder. "I been watching you. I followed you from the park."

Her only thought to get as far away from the front door as possible, Jillie grabbed her backpack, jumped over the hole in the hallway, and climbed onto the platform. Pulling her knees up tight against her chest, she pressed her back against the wall of the trailer and held her breath.

"I just wanna help. A little girl all alone can get into trouble, especially a cute little thing like you." When Jillie remained silent, the man added, "I brought you a burger. You must be hungry, not having a home and all."

Jillie bit her lip to keep from whimpering.

"I said open up." Something heavy beat against the door. *Bam, bam, bam.*

Sounds of splintering wood echoed through the trailer. The door flew open and ricocheted off the wall behind it.

The bright rectangle of late afternoon sunlight darkened as a figure entered the trailer.

"Now you've gone and made me mad." The man stood just inside the door, facing the toy-sized stove and built-in kitchen cabinet against the opposite side. He turned to the left and looked straight at Jillie. "There you are."

The man stood still for a few seconds, allowing his eyes to grow accustomed to the darkness, then he took a couple of steps forward.

"See? I brought you something to eat." Returning to what he obviously intended to be a calming voice, the man held a grease-soaked paper bag. "The biggest burger they make, and a ton of French fries. It's cooled down, but it'll still taste mighty good." He sounded like he was having trouble breathing. "Now lookit you, all balled up like a scared little mouse. You won't get hurt if you do as you're told."

The man took another step into the hallway, and his right foot landed in the middle of the rug-covered hole. Bewilderment followed by understanding flashed in his eyes as he flailed his arms to regain his balance. The bag of food flew out of his hand and his right leg disappeared down the hole. His left leg bent at an impossible angle at the same instant a loud crack echoed through the trailer.

"What the..." The man struggled to free himself, but the splintered plywood flooring jammed into his leg, holding him like a vise. "Help me. I'm hurt bad, you got to help me."

When Jillie made no move, the man's pleading voice changed to a bellow.

Her insides quaking like they were made of Jell-O, Jillie grabbed Mickey, her coat, and backpack. After several seconds of pushing and wrangling, she managed to shove all of it out through the window above the platform.

She grasped the window ledge and started to pull herself through but stopped when the greasy smell coming from the bag wafted toward her. Her mouth watering, she stepped from the platform and snatched up the bag of food from the floor where it had landed. Holding the bag in her teeth, she pulled herself through the window.

"Hey," the man shouted. "You can't just leave me here. You gotta help." His voice now so loud it seemed the whole village of Los Lunas could hear. "Hey, I'm talking to you." The man began to curse.

Jillie stuffed the bag of food into her backpack then slipped the straps over her shoulders. For several heartbeats, she debated whether or not to leave the suitcase behind. But if she left it, the police would know she'd been there. On the other hand, the thought of schlepping the thing one more minute made her want to cry.

The man inside the trailer had stopped yelling and was making grunting sounds like he was trying to pull himself out of the hole. The thought of his finding her suitcase and touching her stuff made Jillie's mind up. She hurried around the trailer to the front door, leaped up the steps, and ran to the sofa.

"Hey," the man yelled. "You got to help me, there's something stuck in my leg."

Jillie slammed her suitcase closed and hauled it outside. Keeping to the rear of the trailer, she started down the hill. Her heart pumping a million miles an hour and breath coming in gasps, she'd only gone a few feet, when a vehicle door slammed from somewhere nearby.

After dropping her luggage behind a sage bush, Jillie crept back toward the trailer far enough to see what was going on.

A young man stood beside an old, rust-splotched, yellow pickup. He stared at the front of the trailer for a few seconds then walked toward the door.

At the top of the steps, he paused and looked around as if to make sure no one was watching. Tall and slender, he wore blue jeans, a denim jacket and down-at-the-heel boots. His arms were unusually long, his hands unusually small. Although some people might think the man attractive, there was something about the expression on his face that made the skin on Jillie's arms crawl. It was a face she'd not forget.

When the new-comer entered the trailer, the old man's shouts for help were replaced by words of gratitude. After a few seconds, the old man cried out—

most likely from the pain of being pulled back up through the splintered wooden floor—then grew silent.

Jillie would need to let the police know about him staking out the park and looking for kids. Once inside the train, she'd make a sketch of the old guy so the police could recognize him. Then she'd draw the young man who'd helped, just in case they wanted to talk to him. She could write a note explaining everything and leave it with the pictures somewhere the police would be sure to find them.

Feeling like a weight had been lifted from her shoulders, she hurried back to her luggage, loaded up, and headed in the direction of the train station.

Chapter Fifteen

After arriving at the tiny trailer in time to see the pervert kick in its door, Toby had stood at a distance arguing with himself for several minutes. This was not his battle; it had nothing to do with him.

Then the kid he'd seen at the park hurried around the side of the trailer, stepped through the front door, and came back out carrying a huge yellow suitcase. With the pervert's howls floating through the trailer's busted door, the kid scuttled downhill toward Los Lunas as if running from a pack of demons.

Eventually, the yelps for help coming from inside the trailer faded into grunts of effort. The kid had dodged a life-lesson-bullet, but the pervert's next target might not be so lucky. Of course, the pervert would return to the park, an elementary school, or some other likely hunting ground to pursue his compulsions.

Feelings Toby had kept under control for years bubbled up from the soles of his feet. Without consciously deciding to do so, he entered the trailer.

He'd stood just inside the door for a few seconds while the trailer's sole occupant thanked him for coming to his aid and said what a coincidence it was that he'd just seen him at the park.

Held firmly in the grip of the *Bias*, the pervert had hurried to explain his presence. "…out on my usual walk and thought I heard someone yelling for help.

False alarm, but I got myself in a fix."

His face a mask, Toby had first glanced around the trailer's interior, then approached the flailing man.

The pervert grimaced. "Can't thank you enough. Pretty sure my leg's busted, I think one of the floor boards is sticking into it, so when I try to pull it out, the jagged end just goes in deeper. You got some tools or maybe a saw?" Something in Toby's posture must have finally registered with the pervert, because the man's eyes widened. "Of course, I'd be glad to pay you for your help. I have money put aside."

Minutes later, Toby exited the trailer. He stood on the rickety steps and looked around, ready to take care of any witnesses who might have been in the wrong place at the wrong time.

But there was no one. Whoever the kid was, he'd been smart enough to lay a trap then hightail it after it was sprung.

Toby smiled. The kid was a survivor. It would have been a pity to have to kill him.

Chapter Sixteen

Jillie chewed on her thumbnail, the other nails bloody and so sore she could hardly stand to touch them. Why did time speed up during summer vacation, but drag during a visit to someplace like the dentist? Probably some mathematical equation could explain it. But she wished it would slow down—like those advertisements on television where everyone on the street freezes while one person goes on his way. Right then, it felt like time was going at light speed, and she still had lots of thing to do.

When she was still a long way from the train station, high white clouds of the afternoon began to grow dark and heavy. A light breeze fanned her cheek with the moist smell of rain, warning of an approaching storm.

She'd have to find some place dry to ride it out. And it was getting late.

It seemed the whole universe was determined to keep her from getting to the hospital. But a soaked kid with both a backpack *and* a suitcase showing up late at night to catch a train would be an attention magnet. Whereas a clean kid with a backpack in broad daylight would be nothing unusual.

Maybe she'd dump the suitcase in a ditch. She could take out anything that would identify her. Besides, she was good and tired of lugging the thing around.

Jillie dropped the suitcase on its side, opened it and surveyed its contents. She retrieved Beth's Nancy Drew paperback, one pair of jeans, a T-shirt, two pair of clean underwear, and her art supplies then stuffed it into her bulging backpack, praying that the fabric and plastic zipper were tough enough to hold. Nevertheless, she finally managed to close the thing.

For the next several minutes, hands turned to the sides like hatchets to avoid hurting her sore fingers, she dug in the sandy soil. Although the newly plowed dirt was soft, the pain from accidentally raking a torn fingernail against it was nearly enough to make her decide to just walk away and leave the suitcase in the field. But something told her she needed to cover her tracks and she'd already made enough mistakes.

Once satisfied with the hole's depth, she dropped the suitcase in and shoved dirt over it. The stupid thing would be found next time the farmer plowed the field, but hopefully not before Jillie was well away.

She stood and dusted her clothes off as best she could. Pleased to be relieved of the burdensome luggage, she walked in the direction she hoped would take her to the train station.

Weather permitting, and if her calculations were correct, she should be able to get to the hospital by noon the next day. She could finish her sketches on the train, then wait until no one was at the hospital's information desk and leave her drawings there along with the letter addressed to the police.

Grateful for the absence of street lamps on the narrow county road, she walked along the white line at the asphalt's edge. Whenever a car came by, she either dropped into the ditch and lay spread-eagled against the slanted side or hid behind a bush.

The storm held off long enough for her to reach the edge of Los Lunas.

Dogs barked; music and voices floated through open windows; cooking smells wafted on the breeze, and amber light shone through windows. People moved around in those warm homes. Families were eating, talking, hugging.

Smoke poured from the brick chimney of the house nearest her, filling the air with the smell of burning wood. The unfenced front yard was covered with cacti and rocks in the water-saving style her science teacher called *xeric landscaping*.

An ancient cottonwood tree towered in the fenced back yard, its fall-painted leaves so thick they blotted out the moon. A light breeze made the leaves whisper to each other as they rubbed against the twigs to which they were anchored. A happy buzz raced along Jillie's arms at the sight of what appeared to be a tree house snuggled amid the huge limbs.

Since the fence was too high for her to climb over, she approached the gate at the side of the house. She lifted its handle then froze, as if suddenly turned to stone, when the metal clasp squeaked loud enough to raise the dead.

When no dogs or people showed up to investigate, she tried again. Slower. Once the handle was all the way up, she pushed the gate open just enough to get through and stepped into the yard, leaving the gate open behind her so as not to chance another squeal.

As she'd hoped, attached to the tree's trunk was a wooden ladder, the top of which disappeared into the foliage. She took hold of the ladder and stepped onto the bottom rung.

But as she put her full weight down, the rotted wood snapped, slamming her right foot onto the ground. Pain shot up her leg, and she bit her tongue. Tears sprang into her eyes, and she doubled over to rub her ankle.

Once the pain had subsided, she straightened and moved her fingers along each rung as high as she could reach. Another couple of rungs felt splintered, but most of them seemed to be okay.

After tightening the backpack's straps and taking care to put her feet next to the upright posts, she went up the ladder and stepped into the treehouse. As much as was possible in the darkness, she surveyed the enclosure.

The wall boards fit together tightly, leaving only an occasional sliver of opening through which the breeze filtered. A couple of knotholes in the wall offered a view of the back of the house. Dust, dried leaves, and twigs piled into drifts in the corners. The wood floor was a bit warped in places and creaked when she moved toward the middle, but the structure seemed solid enough. The smell of clean dirt and fallen leaves filled her nostrils. With its low roof, the space felt cozy, kind of like a cave.

Jillie leaned her backpack against a wall. Using her fingers as a rake, she piled the leaves and twigs together. The air filled with an herbal fragrance as leaves settled into the perfect mattress.

The storm chose that moment to break. But the claps of thunder, flashes of lightning, and torrents of rain only lasted a few minutes then dissipated.

Pleased that no rain found its way into the tree house, Jillie lay down on the leaves. She pulled her jacket up to her chin, nestled against Mickey's chubby tummy and fell asleep.

Chapter Seventeen

Early the next morning, Jillie was awakened by loud voices. Cold, and briefly disoriented, she clamped her jaws together to stop her teeth from chattering and peered through one of the knot holes.

Two little old ladies in pajamas and robes sat at a small round table in the center of a brick patio. They each had what looked like crocheted afghans draped around their shoulders. Curlicues of steam floated up from mugs on the table in front of them.

"I know what I heard," said one old lady. Short white hair resembling a helmet of cotton balls hung over her unnaturally black eyebrows. Her pajamas were made of some silky-looking fabric in a kaleidoscope of greens, blues, and yellows. Her robe was purple. "That gate screams like a banshee every time it's opened. And I found it ajar this morning."

"You're full of beans," the second old lady said. "You probably just forgot to latch it. Besides, I didn't hear a thing." Her hair was white, too, but it was pulled back into a tight bun. Without any visible eyebrows at all, she wore light blue pajamas with a matching robe that looked like it had been made from a huge bath towel.

"You wouldn't have heard a bomb explode," Cotton Top said. "Once you take your hearing aids out, you're deaf as a stump. You wouldn't even know when you fart, if not for the jar followed by the dead-possum-in-the-woods fragrance."

The Bun chuckled. "Got me there. But if someone's been in the back yard, why isn't anything missing?"

Cotton Top *harrumphed* and said, "Other than my veggies, there's nothing back here worth taking."

"Dix, Dix," The Bun said. She shook her head, like she couldn't believe what she was hearing. "Just listen to yourself. Not only is there nothing missing, but there's absolutely no evidence of anyone's having been in our yard."

"No evidence except what I heard, and the gate's being left open."

"Then what's the problem?"

"You don't get it, Lil. I don't like the idea of someone having to sneak around our house late at night. It might be someone in need of help."

"Spare me." A small oblong box on the table squawked and spit static as the woman named Lil moved a knob on its front.

"Good Lord," Dix said. "Wherever did you find that old thing? Isn't that your transistor radio from high school?"

"Yep, still works, too."

"You know listening to the news is the quickest way to get depressed. You can't change anything; it just messes with your head."

"I want to hear the stock market report." Lil fiddled with the knobs, picked the radio up and shook it, then worked the knobs again.

"Is money all you ever think of?"

"It's called being financially responsible; you

should try it sometime."

The static coming from the radio was suddenly replaced by the clear sound of a masculine voice.

Police report finding the body of an unidentified man appearing to be in his fifties in an abandoned trailer just outside of Los Lunas. The death is being investigated as a homicide. Police reports indicate there are currently no suspects.

Jillie gasped. She'd figured the young guy would help the creepy old man; in fact, she'd thought that was why the old man suddenly stopped yelling. Not only had she listened to someone being murdered, but she'd seen the murderer's face.

Should she immediately go to the police? But that would mean abandoning Beth. Maybe she could make an anonymous call. But where could she find a phone? Jillie tasted blood and realized she'd been chewing her tongue.

On the patio below, Dix reached across the table and turned the radio off. "I told you, that's no way to start the day. Murder and mayhem during breakfast, no thank you."

Lil squinted at Dix. "Were you not paying attention, Pollyanna? I've driven past that little trailer a million times; it's not all that far from here." She leaned across the table. "You said yourself, you think someone came into our back yard in the dead of night. What if you happen to be right? What if someone's wandering around killing people?" She stood and draped the afghan over the back of her chair. "I'm going to get an alarm system."

"You're kidding, you mean you're actually going to pay someone to install—"

"Get real." Lil started toward the door. "I'll do it myself, how hard can it be?"

Dix choked on the sip of liquid she'd just taken, coughed, and laughed.

Lil cocked her head at her sister. "What's so funny?"

"Just the supreme irony of your being willing to buy a security system. You're so tight you squeak when you walk. Always have been."

"And that, oh pauper sister of mine, is why we have a house in which to live rather than a yurt." Lil returned to the table, picked up her plate and cup, and headed for the door. "If you need me, I'll be at the hardware store shopping for a motion detector spotlight."

Dix scooted her chair back from the table and started toward the house. "I'm going to the library."

"A suggestion before you go out in public," Lil said. "You might want to re-do your eyebrows. One of the joys of sitting across the breakfast table from you is tracking their migration. The left one's not only a full inch higher than the right, it's arched way too high. Makes you look like you just saw Elvis in pajamas roller blading down Main Street."

Dix snorted. "At least I'm careful of my appearance, as opposed to your extraterrestrial alien, slab-of-meat-with-eyeballs look."

"I don't pretend I'm not getting older. A woman's hair thins with age, it's the natural order of things. I would have thought you'd *prefer* the natural look."

Dix lifted both hands, cupped and palms up. Her right hand raised as if she were a scale weighing something, she said, "Fake, but somewhat human in appearance?" Lowering her left hand, she said, "Or natural, yet scary enough to frighten children and stampede cattle."

"Says you."

"You don't see your face; everyone else does. Have a little compassion, why don't you."

"Hypocrite." Lil stepped into the house.

"Skin flint," Dix shouted after her.

In a few minutes, two vehicles pulled out of the garage at the side of the house—one small and tan, the other a red convertible. The tan car moved slowly, but the red car's tires squealed as it sped away.

Her backpack slung over her shoulders, Jillie climbed down the ladder and glanced around the yard. Morning sunlight sparkled off green, yellow, and red vegetables growing in the garden she'd spotted the night before. In near-perfect rows, tomatoes, carrots, lettuce, cucumbers, bell peppers, green beans, and other plants she didn't recognize called to her like the Sirens she'd read about in mythology. Her stomach growled.

She pulled up two carrots, plucked a huge tomato from its fragrant vine, and then gathered a fistful of green beans. After washing the vegetables with the garden hose, she ate them, drank her fill from the hose, then washed her face and hands. She pulled her treasure chest from her backpack, selected some things from it and returned to the garden.

When she'd finished her task, she again hurried toward the gate. But she stopped in her tracks at the sound of a car pulling into the driveway.

Holding her breath, she edged backward and plastered herself against the side of the house. Hopefully, whoever it was would find no one home and go away.

The sudden electronic *beep, beep, beep* of someone punching numbers into a cell phone wafted through the open window above Jillie's head. "I forgot the library's closed today; I'm going to work the garden. Lunch will be ready at noon sharp. If you're not here, you either don't eat or you fix it yourself." Dix's voice grew fainter as she moved away from the window.

Without thinking, Jillie scooted back to the tree and up the ladder where she hunkered down against a wall.

Immediately, she reflected on the stupidity of that move. Why had she not run when she had the chance? She could easily have outrun the little old lady. But with only an instant to decide what to do, panic had taken over. If Dix had heard the squealing gate again, she'd most likely have called the police. Then they'd have discovered Jillie, and the nightmare life at the Elliotts would never end.

How long would the hospital keep Beth's body before taking it to wherever they burned people up? Or did the hospital do the burning?

The double glass door slid open and Dix came out, her arms filled with gardening implements. She carried the tools to the garden and dropped them onto the ground. Slowly, she moved up the rows, emitting sounds of surprise.

Dix stood in the center of the garden and looked around the yard. As if sensing Jillie's presence, she stared up at the treehouse, pulled a lanyard from around her neck, took a cell phone from the tiny attached bag and punched the screen. "I don't care what you're doing," she said into the phone, "you have to come home right now." Pause. "No, now!" Dix jabbed her finger on the tiny screen again, slid the phone back into its little bag, and dropped the whole thing down the front of her blouse.

Chapter Eighteen

Jillie held her breath, her cheeks pressed against the wood below a knothole, as cotton-headed Dix walked slowly around the yard. Clutching her rake, she studied the ground and mumbled to herself. In a bit, she dropped the implement and headed back into the house.

Within a few minutes, a car door slammed, and The Bun Lil came out onto the porch.

Dix motioned for her sister to follow and marched toward the garden. "See?" She pointed to the tomato plant.

"All I see is a garden that's costing us more to water than the same stuff would cost at the store."

An offended look on her face, Dix said, "You're not paying attention. Someone's taking our veggies. Our *organic* veggies."

"What? You sounded like it was a matter of life and death. You're losing your chili over missing carrots?"

"If by *losing my chili* you mean I'm upset, then you're right. For such a cynic, you refuse to accept what happened here."

Lil snorted. "That's rich coming from a woman who believes extraterrestrials walk among us."

Dix lifted her head and pointed her chin at her sister. "Anyone who believes we're the only planet out of the billions in the universe that can support life is just plain ignorant."

"Heard it all before."

"Here's something for you to chew on, *Puma Punku*."

"Poo…what?" Lil said.

"Puma Punku."

"What the hell is that, some kind of Hippy bean dip?"

"Ha! Shows how much you know. Puma Punku was built thousands of years ago out of blocks of rock weighing several tons each." Dix jabbed her index finger toward Lil's nose. "Solid rock, squared to within something like a millionth of an inch. And it was built when our ancestors were still chipping flint into spear heads. Now where do you think those folks got that kind of technology, huh?"

"Here it comes, the aliens-walk-among-us speech." Lil shook her head.

"At least I'm open to new ideas. Why can't you accept that there are things that defy explanation?"

"Just because we haven't found an explanation yet doesn't mean there isn't one."

"You always have an answer."

"Pretty much. It's all about mathematics."

Dix mumbled something.

Lil pointed her index finger heavenward. "Wait, wait. Just to be clear, are you suggesting your veggies were taken by a gang of extraterrestrials?"

"Go ahead, make fun."

Lil flapped her arms like a bird. "After they've crossed a galaxy or two to get here, surely you don't begrudge them a few veggies. Maybe they think they've abducted native life forms. Maybe they've lined your tomatoes up on a table to probe…

"Enough already," Dix said. "I'm telling you, someone's been in the garden."

"Ah, has Gumshoe Granny detected footprints?"

"Pretty hard to leave footprints on mulch. But there are at least two carrots and one tomato missing." Dix held up three jewel-colored plastic beads. "And I found these in their places."

Lil peered at the beads. "So what? And how do you know how many carrots are missing, anyway, do you count them? Lord, you need to get a life."

Dix shot back, "I don't care what you say, tonight I'm keeping watch. When our burglar returns, I'll be ready."

"And what will you do if you actually catch someone pulling up a carrot? Hold him at bay with your gardening shears?" Lil stood, adopting a fencing pose, legs splayed and bent at the knee, one arm above her head, and the other holding a make-believe weapon.

"Of course not." Dix lifted her chin, her face reddening. "But I'd confront him. He might be a homeless person down on his luck, but whoever he is, he's hungry."

"You don't have what it takes to *confront* anyone," Lil said. "I don't even think you know the meaning of the word. Now me, I'd pepper his backside with rock salt and teach him a lesson."

"That's so like you. Violence never settled anything."

"Really? Tell that to General George Custer. Violence settled his hash pretty well."

Dix shot a defiant look toward her sister. "I'm going to find something to wear." She headed for the sliding back door.

"Something to wear? You got a hot date? More important, has he asked you for money yet?"

Dix glared at her sister. "You're never going to let me forget that, are you? At least I've loved someone. You've never even really *liked* anyone."

Lil laughed. "Now you're just trying to cheer me up."

Dix cocked her head to one side, a thoughtful look on her face. "I think I'll wear my black turtleneck and leggings. Maybe smear some of that Halloween camouflage makeup on my face so I'll blend in with the darkness."

Lil lifted her hands to her face and opened her mouth wide. "Horrors," she said. "You mean some poor unsuspecting schmuck will be subjected to the retina-searing vision of you jumping out at him in your ass-hugging, black spandex leggings? You're too cruel for words."

"Smart aleck," Dix said.

"Wimp," Lil answered.

Tossing snotty comments at each other along the way, the sisters went into the house.

With all the curtains in the house opened, Jillie didn't dare move from her spot. The morning wore on, during which the sisters moved back and forth from the house to the patio.

She could hardly keep from pulling her hair in frustration. Should she run regardless of the little old ladies? Or should she stay put and wait for the chance to escape?

As far as the knot holes and gaps in the tree house walls would allow, she scrutinized the tall wooden backyard fence. Near a corner, one of the boards stood at an angle to its neighbors, exposing a small gap. A few seconds was all she'd need to shinny down the ladder and squeeze through.

Dix stepped onto the patio. "I said I think I'll hide out in the tree house tonight," she yelled over her shoulder.

Jillie's heart thumped so hard it felt like it would jump out of her chest. She held her breath until gray dots swam in her vision.

"Right, and how long has it been since you've climbed a ladder?" Lil's voice rang out from inside the house. "You'll break your neck. Find someplace else to hide." Pause. "Good Lord, I'm beginning to sound like you."

Dix went back into the house then returned carrying a hoe and rake. For at least a couple of hours, she worked in the garden digging, weeding, and watering.

As if talking to a class of kindergarteners, she spoke to each plant. She promised plenty of water and fertilizer and commanded the garden to *live long and prosper*. She sang songs about the sun and happy people; she even whistled.

Smells of cooking food wafted up to the tree house, taunting Jillie's growling stomach.

"Dinner's ready," Lil shouted through the open kitchen window.

Dix propped her garden tools against the side of the house and went inside. Almost immediately, the women brought plates heaped high with food onto the patio.

They argued about whose turn it was to do dishes, griped about how the changing weather was making their joints ache, and complained about their bowels. They tossed snide jabs at each other and argued about the state of world affairs.

Jillie consoled herself with the knowledge that she still had a couple of hours of daylight left. It might be possible for her to get to the station yet. If the little old ladies would just go inside for the night...

When the women finally finished dinner, picked up their dishes and went into the house, Jillie scooped up her backpack and headed for the ladder. She'd just stepped onto the top rung, when Lil returned with a book and cup of something hot.

Her stomach in her throat, Jillie fought down the urge to tear out her hair. The train station couldn't have been more than two or three miles away, but it might as well have been in China.

She stepped back to the knothole and pressed her face against the wooden wall.

Lil had pulled a crocheted quilt over her legs, propped her book on top of the table and began to read.

Daylight dimmed, and with it Jillie's hopes of getting away. At that rate, the station would be closed before she could get there. Another night gone.

Sometime later, Dix stepped onto the patio and sat in the empty chair across from her sister. "If you're going to stay out here all night, you can stand watch, and *I'll* sleep all cozy and warm inside like nothing's going on right under our noses."

Lil hooted. "Not bloody likely. This is your game." She shook her head and shot a sideways glance at her sister. "What a waste of time. But then, I suppose everyone needs a hobby. What I don't understand is how you can ignore the news report that someone was murdered not three miles from here. Now that's worth worrying about."

"And if whoever came into our yard had murder in his heart, we wouldn't be just *sleeping* like the dead. It's obvious that someone was hungry."

Until the sun went down, the sisters wandered back and forth through the glass double doors, never staying inside long enough for Jillie to get away.

When the moon and stars came out, so did Dix. With her body completely covered in black, the bright moonlight highlighted her hair, making it look like a low-hanging, floating white cloud. She mumbled something about Lil's messed up outlook on life and squatted behind a huge chest from which she'd pulled lawn furniture pads earlier.

Twice during the long night, Jillie assumed Dix was asleep and started down the ladder. But both times the old woman either sat up or shifted her position and muttered something.

Between Jillie's hunger, her body's high-pitched hum to get moving, and random ground-shaking snores, barks, growls, and whoops coming from behind the trunk, she got little sleep.

Chapter Nineteen

The sun was barely up when a loud voice woke Jillie out of a fitful sleep.

"Yo, Mutant Ninja," Lil shouted through the back door, "breakfast's ready."

Dix, huffing and puffing like a bear, got to her feet. She rubbed the small of her back and groaned then headed into the house.

Immediately, Lil came out carrying two plates heaped with food. Dix followed carrying a pair of steaming cups. The smells of coffee, bacon, and toast set Jillie's stomach to howling.

"So, what did you learn last night, Grasshopper?" Lil said.

"Don't start," Dix said. "I didn't get a wink of sleep." She rubbed her eyes with the palms of her hands, smearing black greasepaint upward and into her hair.

Lil chuckled. "Now there's a sight." She took a bite of food. "Have you counted your carrots yet?"

"I watched all night, and no one showed up. Maybe he got cold feet."

"Or maybe he saw you in that fetching outfit, decided this was a house of horrors, and gave up his life of crime. He's probably turning himself in to the police as we speak."

"More likely, he caught a glimpse of you taking a

shower and decided to become a monk. You really should close the bathroom blinds, you know."

Chewing between remarks, the women finished breakfast and headed back into the house.

Within a few minutes Jillie thought she heard both cars leave. She flew down the ladder, ran to the garden hose, turned it on full blast and drank until her stomach felt it would burst. After washing her hands and face, she refilled her water bottle, stuck it in her jacket pocket, and raided the garden again. As before, for every vegetable she took, she left a selected bit of treasure the crows had left for her.

As she turned toward the gate, a huge cucumber nestled under the vine's leaves caught her eye. But just as she reached for it, Lil stepped out the back door.

"Gotcha, you little brat." She sprinted to Jillie and grabbed her arms. "Who are you?"

Dix rushed out the door. "Stop that. You're hurting her."

Lil held Jillie's arm up high, like she'd just won a prize fight. "Here's your thief."

"I said let her go. What harm can a child do? Just look at the little thing."

"You obviously don't know your history. Children have been known to commit the most heinous crimes imaginable. Look it up online." Lil squinted down her nose at Jillie. "Type in *evil children*. You'll find enough stuff there to keep you awake nights."

Dix moved to stand between Jillie and Lil. Her eyes kind, she said, "What's your name, Sweetheart?"

"Jillie."

"Nice to meet you, Miss Jillie. I'm Dixie, but you can call me Dix." She pointed to her sister. "And this is

Lillian."

"Why don't you give her our Social Security numbers while you're at it." Lil frowned at her sister.

Ignoring her sister, Dix continued, "Where did you come from, Miss Jillie?"

"I used to live—"

"Don't let her get away." Lil pulled her cell phone from a scabbard attached to the belt of her blue jeans and began punching in numbers. "We'll let the police deal with her."

"Please don't," Jillie said. She tried to stop her lips and chin from quivering.

Dix knocked the phone from her sister's hands. "Stop that." Tiny pieces of glass and plastic skittered across the brick patio.

Lil's head snapped up, a surprised look on her face. "You broke my phone. You're going to pay for that."

"So, add it to my tab already." Dix pulled the pink crocheted lanyard from between her breasts, snatched her own phone from the pouch and jabbed it toward her sister. "Here. Take mine until you get a new one."

Lil ignored the outstretched phone, turned and took a step toward the house. "I'll use the landline."

"You'll do no such thing." Dix wrapped her arms protectively around Jillie's shoulders. "We'll have a chat; then I'll make a nice lunch." She stooped to bring her eyes level with Jillie's. "How's that sound?" She stood, and turned toward her sister, her smile gone. "You know what'll happen once she gets caught up in the legal system. If you make one move to call the police, I'll pack up and move out tonight."

Lil's mouth fell open. "Whoa, you've never threatened to leave before."

"I mean it. Can't you see she's in trouble? We can't just turn her out."

Lil threw her arms into the air. "Why not just go ahead and save the whole world while you're at it, o-you-who-ignores-reality?" She turned to Jillie. "You got a crew hidden out somewhere waiting for us old softies to lead you to our valuables?"

"I'm not—"

"Stop it, Lil," Dix interrupted. "We're going to feed her and listen to her story." She made a slashing motion with her hand. "Don't cross me on this."

Lil peered at her sister, eyes closed to slits. "Did you grow a pair when I wasn't looking?"

"Lillian Jean Ruiz, such language." Dix sniffed. "No police until after we've heard her out. Understood?" Her eyes bored into her sister's.

Lil turned toward Jillie, a scowl on her face. "I'll give you two hours. After that I'm calling the police, even if I have to sneak out of the house to do it."

Dix rested her hand on Jillie's shoulder. "Come on inside. You must be starved." She shot a meaningful look at Lil. "Show her where she can wash up."

Lunch was spaghetti with meatballs, garlic toast, and salad from the garden. Jillie gratefully accepted Dix's offer of seconds.

During the meal, Lil kept glancing at Jillie out of the corner of her eye. The expression on her face left no doubt she expected Jillie to either stuff the silverware in her pockets or attack the sisters with the bread knife.

After lunch, Dix brought out desert, something she called *Banana Split Bread a la Dixie*. She poured two cups of coffee and a huge glass of milk then sat down. "Tell us why you're here."

Beginning with Digger's death, Jillie poured out all that had taken place over the past few weeks. Her voice caught in her throat, and she fought not to cry when she talked about Beth. The two sisters never took their eyes off her face.

When Jillie fell silent, Dix stood. She took a deep breath and said, "No way are we going to take this child to the police." She looked back at Jillie. "What's your plan?"

"I have to find out what the hospital's done with Beth, so I can spread her ashes around the tree with our parents."

Dix's eyes teared up. "I'm not sure the crematory would give ashes to someone so young without an adult family member. They might even call the police."

Jillie's shoulders drooped. "I hadn't thought of that."

Dix lifted her chin. "We'll talk to our nephew. He's a detective with the Los Lunas Police Department."

"Now you're talking," Lil said. "I'll use the landline to call him. He can be here in a half hour."

Jillie's breath caught in her throat. "Please—"

"Stop it, Lil. Can't you see she's terrified?" Dix smiled and put her hand on Jillie's forearm. "Don't worry. We'll invite our nephew to dinner and ask a few *hypothetical* questions." She turned to Lil. "Least we can do is explore options. When he's gone, we'll make a solid plan."

Lil jumped up from the table. "What? You're going to let her stay for dinner? Have you finally lost the last bit of what passes for your mind? We've only got her word for what happened. Or did that whole I-killed-my-brother-in-law-with-a-machete thing not register?"

All gentleness melted from Dix's face. "Don't start with me Lillian Jean. I'll call Davie while she takes a bath. She'll eat before he gets here then hide in my bedroom." She turned to Jillie. "It's right at the top of the stairs. I'll leave the door ajar, so you can hear every word. Is that okay with you?"

Lil shot a look at Jillie. "Don't touch any of my stuff. I don't care what my bleeding-heart twin says. I don't like kids. I especially don't like *thieving* kids."

"She's not a thief." Dix held her opened hand toward her sister, displaying the colored beads and stones retrieved from the garden. "She left something lovely in place of every single veggie she took."

Lil made a sound something like *humph* and crossed her arms.

Dix held the beads in her open palm. "Thank you for these, but I can't accept them. Consider the veggies a gift."

After a couple of beats, Jillie took the beads and stuffed them into her pocket.

Dix continued, "There's a jar of bath salts by the tub, sprinkle a scoop into the water while it's running. The shower gel is on the little ledge."

"Thank you," Jillie said.

Lil sniffed and wrinkled her nose. "Better make it two scoops." At Dix's horrified look, Lil shrugged. "What?"

Dix put an arm around Jillie's shoulders. "Come on." She pulled a huge, fluffy white towel and matching washcloth from a closet in the hall and motioned toward a door at the top of the stairs. "That's the bathroom. Give me your clothes, and I'll start a load of laundry. There's a robe hanging from a hook behind the door. You can put that on while your clothes wash."

Jillie took the towel and cloth and headed upstairs. She filled the tub, sprinkled in the lilac-fragranced bath salts, stepped in, and lay back. Lack of sleep and exhaustion coupled with the soothing warm water tugged at her eyelids.

Dix's tapping on the bathroom door jerked her awake. "We're all set, Davie's coming to dinner." Dix rattled the doorknob. "Jillie?"

Jillie lifted the lever on the tub that would allow the now-cold water to drain. "Coming."

"I don't like anything about this," Lil shouted from downstairs.

"Noted," Dix hollered back.

Jillie stepped out of the tub, dried off and pulled on the bathrobe. She opened the door to find Dix waiting just outside.

"As soon as your clothes are dry, we'll sit down and make a list of questions for Davie. But for now, how about I show you my toy Slinky collection? Got a whole room full, all sizes, some almost as big as you." She chuckled. "The biggest ones make so much noise going end-over-end down our wooden staircase you can't hear yourself think."

Jillie glanced toward the bottom of the stairs where Lil stood glaring up at her. The expression on the woman's face made her stomach feel queasy.

Beth was right, some people wouldn't like you no matter what you did.

Chapter Twenty

Detective David Ruiz climbed out of the rented bass boat, moored it to the marina, and headed for his rented cabin. He'd always loved coming to Elephant Butte lake, had fallen in love with the place when his aunts brought him as a child. Some of his best memories were of the three of them paddling around on inner tubes, splashing each other, and eating hotdogs they'd roasted over a grill.

He sat on the easy chair he'd pulled onto the porch and stared at the lake for one last time before heading back home. Why was it that looking at water soothed the human soul?

The silence was broken by the chirping of his cell phone. He squelched a sigh, glanced at the screen, then punched the answer-dot. "Hey, Aunt Dix, what's up?"

"Are you back in town yet?"

"No, but I will be this afternoon," David said.

"We were hoping you'd come to dinner tonight." His aunt's gentle-yet-persuasive voice poured across the ether.

"Dinner would be great. What can I bring?"

"Just your appetite," Aunt Dixie said. "We're having your favorite, chicken paprika with brown Basmati rice and pickled cucumber salad. Around seven-ish?"

"Sounds good." David replaced the receiver in its

cradle.

Dinner would not only be a good time to catch up with his aunts, it would relieve some of the guilt he felt for not spending more time with them.

David's father Ben had adored his two sisters. Poor to the point of poverty-stricken after David's grandfather's early death, the burden of taking care of the family had fallen on nine-year-old Ben's shoulders.

While his mother drowned her sorrows in pills and a bottle, Ben sneaked into the county zoo and collected fresh eggs and meat from animal cages to feed his siblings. At the age of twelve, he got a job pulling corn tassels on a farm just up the road from their trailer house, and little by little, things got better.

By the time David's grandmother died of cirrhosis of the liver, successful entrepreneur Ben had put his twin sisters through college. But a life of hard work had taken its toll, and Ben suffered a heart attack at forty-two, leaving behind a young widow and ten-year-old son David.

David was twelve and showing signs of rebellion when his mom remarried. Unable to get along with his stepson, the new husband demanded he be sent away to live with relatives. Teary-eyed and apologetic, his mother had asked her psychologist sister-in-law Dix to take him.

From the day David moved in with his aunt Dix, she treated him as an adult. And although he'd made a few self-destructive choices, she never expressed the slightest regret at opening her house to him. Even through her three disastrous marriages and subsequent divorces, Dix had made time to help him with his homework and meet with his teachers.

When Dix's last husband absconded with her life savings, leaving her with a hefty second mortgage and the clothes on her back, the two of them moved in with Aunt Lil.

Although from the same ovum, the two women could not have been more different. Where free-spirit, aging hippie Dixie was gregarious and sociable, Lillian, a retired accountant, isolated herself from the world.

David not only loved his two aunts with all his heart, but he owed them big time. And while to the outside observer their style of interacting with each other might sometimes seem harsh, to him it was normal. More than normal, it was what had made their house a home.

After hauling the chair back to the cabin, David packed his belongings, loaded his Jeep, returned the cabin keys to the owner, and headed home. His stomach growling in anticipation of dinner that evening, he headed home.

****

At exactly seven David pulled into his aunts' driveway. He retrieved a bouquet of daisies from the passenger seat and headed for the front door.

"Lil," Dix yelled from the door she'd opened before David could press the bell. "Davie's here."

David smiled. He'd just turned thirty, and they still referred to him by the moniker they'd hung on him when he was a toddler.

Aunt Dixie enveloped him in her customary wrestling-championship-competition hug and nearly dragged him into the house, while Aunt Lillian offered her usual pat on his shoulder. The smells coming from the kitchen made David's stomach growl, and he marveled that anyone still used that room for anything other than microwaving cups of soup and coffee. He'd heard that in some large cities, apartments no longer even came with a kitchen.

Conversation around the table started off in the usual vein.

"So, Davie, anyone special in your life nowadays?" Her eyebrows penciled into black arcs of perpetual surprise, Dix chewed a mouthful of savory chicken.

David swallowed a groan and said, "Not yet. When I meet someone, I promise you two will be the first to know."

"You just haven't met the right one," Dix said. She pointed her fork at her nephew and smiled.

Lil snorted. "This from someone who's met at least three right ones."

Beyond the standard verbal jabs at each other, the two acted strangely through the meal. While Aunt Dix repeatedly aimed innocent expressions in his direction, Aunt Lil refused to look him in the eye.

A series of prolonged silences and weird vibes kick-started a sense of dread. Was one of them ill? Had they invited him over to break some horrible news?

Careful not to allow his inquiring gaze to linger overlong on either aunt, David obliquely studied their faces while the muscles in his neck tightened. Something was definitely up.

After dinner, over a cup of strong coffee smelling faintly of cinnamon, it was Lillian who finally got to the point. "Hypothetically speaking, what if a runaway showed up on someone's doorstep looking for help? What could be expected?"

Dix shot a look of what appeared to be censure

toward her sister and quickly added, "Lots of stories in the news lately about runaways. We just wondered."

David studied his aunts' faces while a feeling of unease toyed with his gut. "If the child is under twelve, the adult, or adults, could be charged with kidnapping. That is, unless they called the police immediately." He looked pointedly at first one then the other wrinkled face and caught the victorious look Lil shot at her sister.

Like mercury in a thermometer, the gentle throb at the base of David's neck began to move upward. "The hypothetical adults could be in a whole lot of trouble."

A nearly telepathic conversation passed between the twins, and they immediately changed their facial expressions to ones of light interest.

"Surely that can't be right," Dixie said. "I mean, what if the poor child ran away to escape some terrible situation?"

"It may not seem right to you, but believe me, there are plenty of people out there willing to profit from a child's misery," David said. "The laws are in place to protect the child."

"And if the kid's already twelve?" Lil said.

David shook his head, the action kicking the ache up a notch. "It's not like finding a puppy and deciding to keep it. The police should be notified."

Dixie took a deep breath and let it out slowly. "What would happen to the child?"

"Child Protective Services would pick him up and put him into foster care," David said. "Or they'd return him to his parents."

"But what if the child was already in foster care, and the foster parents were horrible?" Dixie said.

"Then the judge would put him somewhere else."

David looked closely at the women. "Even then, the people who found the child wouldn't be allowed to keep him until they'd gone through the foster care screening process. And that can take a while."

A cold breeze suddenly ruffled the table cloth and set Dix's kitchen chimes tinkling. Tiny metal replicas of pots, pans, and skillets clinked against each other as if a spoiled elf-child was having a tantrum.

"The wind blew the door open again," Lil said. She stood and headed toward the offending house part, yelling at Dix over her shoulder, "I thought you called someone to fix the thing." After slamming the door, she stomped back to the table.

The pain meter in David's head neared the red zone. "What are you two trying to keep from telling me?"

Again, the sisters did that telepathic thing.

"Just hypothetical," Dix repeated.

Her lips compressed, Lil stared into space above David's head.

Suddenly, both women stood, thanked David for coming, offered him plastic containers of leftovers, and almost pushed him out the door.

David sat in his car for several seconds before slipping the key into the ignition. Whatever the hell dinner had really been about, right then he didn't want to know. All he wanted was to go home and hit the sack.

"Welcome back to reality," he murmured.

He started the engine and turned the radio to a station that played classical music.

"That was The Magic Flute by Wolfgang Amadeus Mozart." The soothing voice of the female disc jockey poured over David like warmed honey. "We'll return in sixty seconds with Debussy's *Clair de Lune*."

Again pushing aside the uneasiness that kept forcing its way into his thoughts, he promised himself the next day he'd get to the bottom of whatever had his aunts riled up. With the siren songs of two extra-strength aspirin calling to him from his home medicine cabinet, David backed out the driveway.

Chapter Twenty-One

Jillie's shoulders sagged as she listened to the conversation around the dinner table. Although the sisters didn't come right out and tell David about her, he'd asked a lot of questions and didn't seem completely satisfied with the answers.

Dix had been nice. And even though Lil had fussed about Jillie's being there, she hadn't told the policeman about her. But the old ladies could get into a lot of trouble for trying to help her, maybe even go to jail.

After a few more minutes of listening, Jillie had slipped down the hall and to the guest room where Dix had put her backpack on the bed. She stared at the fluffy, down-filled comforter topped with two thick pillows and almost changed her mind.

She was so tired: tired of running, tired of being alone, tired of dreaming about hollering, bleeding Digger. Mostly, she was tired of being alive when her sister was dead.

But Beth was counting on her.

Jillie straightened her shoulders and picked up her backpack. Careful to put her feet down next to the posts at the side of the stairs to avoid squeaks, she tiptoed downstairs and toward the front door. She'd just reached for the knob when the sound of chairs scraping on the dining room floor warned dinner was nearly over.

Quickly, she pulled the front door open. A fierce gust of wind pushed it toward her so hard she had to put her weight behind it to keep the thing from smashing against the wall.

Cold outside air shoved the warm, food-fragranced indoor air aside. It rattled the dried leaves and colored corn husks of a fall decoration hanging on the entryway wall.

Leaving the door open, Jillie scurried outside where she hunkered down behind a sage bush shrouded in darkness. Barely breathing, she peered through spaces between the leaves toward the back-lit doorway.

"I thought you said you were going to call someone to fix this thing," Lil had shouted over her shoulder as she reached for the doorknob. Muttering, the old lady slammed the door and shot the deadbolt home.

Like a flaming sword, distant lightning blazed its initials across the sky. Jillie counted the seconds between the lightning and thunder. Fifteen seconds meant the storm was about three miles away. Hopefully, she'd make it to the train station before it broke loose.

Based on what Dix had said about someone at the hospital calling the police, Jillie didn't dare go there. Besides, Beth's body might already be at the mortuary waiting to be burned up. In that case, her trip to Albuquerque would be wasted.

Like Dix had suggested, although Margo was perfectly capable of doing something awful with Beth's ashes, it'd be more like her to put the urn on the mantel or in the middle of the kitchen table where she could gloat over it with her morning coffee. As Jillie thought it over, she felt certain that at some point, Beth's ashes were going to show up at the Elliott house.

As suddenly as it had blown up, the storm fizzled. Clouds scooted away, stars twinkled, and the air grew colder. Jillie picked up her pace.

Memories of the Elliott house made her queasy. But after weeks of cleaning it, she knew its every nook and cranny. If Beth was there, she'd find her. If she wasn't there yet, Jillie would wait until they brought her.

Her memory flashed on the little wooden shed that stood several feet from the Elliott house. Margo had said the place hadn't been used for years. And there might be old dried-out bags of mulch or something that would make a nice bed. Unless it got too cold, she'd sleep just fine in her down-filled coat with Mickey for company. She could forage for food from the Elliott's pantry and water from their stash in the garage. Best of all, since the shed faced the house, Jillie could watch the Elliotts' comings and goings.

Jillie pulled her hoodie up, adjusted the straps on her backpack, squared her shoulders, and headed toward the Los Lunas train station.

Chapter Twenty-Two

Lil was finishing up the dinner dishes when Dix stormed into the kitchen.

"She's gone."

"What?" Lil said.

"Jillie's gone, she's run away."

"Are you sure?"

"Of course, I'm sure."

"That's the best news I've had since the pigs ate Jeremy Dane."

"Good God, what an abominable thing to say. That's your trouble, Lil, you have no soul. How could we have come from the same mother?"

Lil snorted. "A question I often ask myself."

Dix held up a piece of paper torn from a sketch book. "The note says she didn't want to cause us trouble, but she has to find Beth's ashes."

"Probably realized the jig was up and snuck out."

"But where will she go? How'll she get by? What if that horrible family finds her?"

Lil threw the dishcloth into the soapy water and spun on her sister. "Not our problem. We don't owe that kid anything."

"Jillie. Her name's Jillie."

Lil held up her hand like she was trying to stop a charging rhino. "Yeah, yeah. Call Davie and let the police take it from here."

Dix shook her head. "I love our nephew, but it'll take time for him to find out things we already know. While he's filling out paperwork, that hideous Margo woman could be hurting Jillie. No, we have to find her, that's all there is to it." She pulled a pencil and tablet of paper from a junk drawer in the kitchen and sat at the table. "What did Jillie want more than anything in the world?"

"She *said* she wanted to get her sister's ashes and scatter them around the tree with those of her parents'."

"And where would she get the ashes?"

"If the Elliotts don't have them yet, they'd still be at the mortuary."

Dix snapped her fingers. "Wait, Jillie said Beth had to be autopsied first."

"So?" Lil shook her head.

"I heard of a case where an autopsied body stayed in the mortuary for over a year waiting for someone to claim it."

"I'm going to take a wild stab in the dark that you read that in one of your waste-of-money tabloids."

Ignoring Lil's comment, Dix snatched her phone from the table where she'd tossed it after breaking her sister's. "I'll call the hospital and see if Beth's body has been taken for cremation yet." She Googled the hospital, got its number then punched it in. While waiting for someone to pick up, she said, "I'll bet you dollars to donuts she's headed to the hospital."

A look of disgust on her face, Lil returned to sponging off dishes.

"Hello," Dix said into the phone. "I'm wondering if you can tell me the status of a patient by the name of Beth Elliott." Pause. "Are you sure? Yes, please check again." Pause. "No, that's okay. Thank you for your help." Dix hung up the phone and turned to her sister. "No one by that name has been in that hospital within the past six months. Maybe it's a different hospital."

But when two more calls came up empty, Dix closed her cell and stared into space.

"Ha!" Lil clapped her hands together. "I told you that kid was no good. I'll bet everything she said was a lie."

Dix frowned. "See what I mean? You're so quick to jump to the worst possible conclusion."

"What other conclusion could there be?" Lil shot a look of triumph at her twin. "What a story she dished up. She probably doesn't even have a sister. And you fell hook, line, and sinker for every word, as per usual."

"No, something about that child rang as desperation. If she were playing us, you'd expect to see hints of wily or sneaky, but not desperate. Did you see those fingernails? They must hurt something awful. Not the product of a safe, loving environment, that's for sure."

Lil shrugged. "Everybody's got a sad story, life doesn't discriminate."

"And her feet…blisters on blisters. I had to put ointment and bandages on them."

"Most street kids are tough." Lil took a deep breath. "But so is your average badger, and it's not real bright to get too close to one of those either."

"She's just a child, for pity's sake. She has no business on the street."

"Maybe she's a pathological liar and believes her own fantasies, you ever think of that?"

Dix jabbed the air with her index finger. "If you

won't help me find her, I'll do it myself."

"And what if I'm right? Have you checked your jewelry?" Then as if she'd been thunderstruck, Lil's head jerked up and she headed for the stairs. "If she's made off with anything of mine, I'll haul her to the tank myself."

Dix shot back, "Jillie left something behind for every veggie she took, which she only took because she was hungry. You think she'd grab your trash at the first opportunity?"

Lil's voice floated in the air behind her. "I'll have you know, it's not trash."

The sound of doors opening and closing and of drawers being pulled open and slammed shut was followed by silence.

"Told you," Dix hollered toward the stairs.

Footfalls announced Lil's return to the kitchen. "Okay, so she didn't have time to find my coin collection, but that doesn't mean I'm wrong about her."

Dix shook her head, shot a look of pity toward Lil, then grew thoughtful. "If I were Jillie, where would I look for my sister's ashes?"

"How much more time and energy are you going to waste on this?" Lil sat down across the table from her sister. "Think about it. Since she apparently doesn't have a sister, she won't be trying to find any non-existent ashes."

Dix again retrieved her phone from the kitchen counter. "Wait. I'll do an online search." Mumbling to herself, she dragged her fingers over the tiny screen, then poked it a few times. "Last name Ross from Belen." She smiled ruefully and looked at her sister. "Interesting."

"Okay, so what's *interesting*?"

"It's an obituary for a man named Ross from Belen who was survived by his daughters Bethany and Jillian Ray Ross."

Lil snorted. "So? Doesn't mean any of the rest of her story's true."

"Just a minute." Dix tapped her screen a few more times. "I'm going to call the hospitals back and ask if they have a patient named Bethany Ross."

"You think she kept her maiden name?"

Dix tilted her head to one side and shrugged. "Worth a try." Again, she punched in the hospital's number. She spoke rapidly, her excitement rising with every response from the other end. Nearly effervescent with glee, she broke the connection. "The hospital not only verifies they have a patient by the name of Bethany Ross, but the operator told me what room she's in."

"Hmm, curious."

"Is that all you have to say, Miss People-Are-No-Good?"

"Better make a note on your calendar, because this is a first. I've always been a better judge of character than you."

"Admit it, Jillie told us the truth."

Lil's lips curled. "At least some of it."

"Know what I think? I think that Elliott woman told Jillie her sister was dead to pry information out of her about the so-called treasure. And if the woman's that unscrupulous, the child could be in real danger." Dix headed for the hall closet, flung the door open, grabbed her coat and retrieved her purse from a hook. "We have to find her."

"What *we*? Leave me out of this." Lil pulled the stopper from the sink and allowed the dish water to gurgle down the drain.

"Oh, of course. What was I thinking?" Dix pulled on her coat. "You have to get back to more important things, like saving a few pennies on hot water while the nine-hundred-dollar dishwasher molders away from disuse."

Lil stomped through the kitchen to the entryway and stood in front of her sister. "And where do you intend to go at this hour?"

"I'll drive up and down the streets; she can't have gotten far."

"It's dark outside. That kid's pretty small, but she struck me as being fairly intelligent." Lil squinted at her sister. "If she doesn't want to be found, you're not going to find her."

Dix pulled a wool scarf from her coat pocket and tied it around her neck. "So, I'm just supposed to pretend she never showed up here hungry, filthy, and terrified? Supposed to enjoy a cup of hot chocolate before climbing into my warm bed while that child struggles to survive? Is that what I'm to do?"

Lil shook her head. "You're going to do what you always do, you're going to interfere in business that has nothing to do with you. And then when that brat breaks your heart, you're going to slink back here, curl up in your room, and cry your eyes out for a month." She rolled her eyes heavenward. "God save me."

"She's not a mass-murderer."

"Right, she only has one murder under her belt at this point."

"Not murder, she killed that man to save her sister

who, by the way, is in a coma because of that beating. Even you should be able to understand that."

"That's her story."

"The bottom line is I choose to see the good in people, where you consistently refuse to see anything but the bad." Lil opened her mouth to respond, but Dix held up her hand in a shushing motion. "No, it's more than that. You look for the bad, even if you have to dig for it."

"Oh, please." Lil rolled her eyes again. "Not another lecture."

"Just because you refuse to see that about yourself doesn't mean it's not true. People make mistakes; we're not given a road map at birth. But I believe most people are just trying to survive the best way they know how, just trying to get by."

"And that makes you a sucker. People do whatever brings them the biggest rewards, pure and simple. Your Ph.D. in psychology isn't worth the paper it's written on if you think every monster the world has ever bred was just trying to get by. Your rose-colored view of life ignores the existence of things like greed and hunger for power. Or are those human characteristics not allowed in your fluffy universe?"

"Don't be ridiculous, I'm not a fool. I know there are destructive and hateful people. I know evil exists. But it's a matter of degree. Most people try to do the decent thing."

Lil shook her head. "You just hang on to that thought, why don't you." She snorted. "I agree with one thing you've said, though, people do have to work at being evil, it doesn't just suddenly happen. And they usually start strolling down that path when they're kids." She shoved her index finger to within an inch of Dix's nose. "Mark my words, this'll be just like when you walked in on Darren and his secretary."

"Oh yes, how could I forget that you warned me not to marry him in the first place." Dix faced her sister. "I take it you're not going to help?"

"Help you open yourself up to whatever this situation is going to dump on your head? No thanks. Don't say I didn't warn you."

"You never cease to amaze." Dix moved toward the front door.

"Don't come crying to me when this whole thing blows up in your face."

"Trust me, if I need compassion, I won't look to you." Dix opened the front door. "Don't wait up," she yelled over her shoulder before slamming the door so hard a framed photo on the wall fell from its hook and onto the tile floor. Sounds of shattering frame and glass added finality to Dix's words.

"I'm not cleaning that up," Lil screamed at the top of her lungs. As she stood staring at the front door, a budding sense of dread pushed against her anger. "Gird up your loins and grab your butt, Lil," she muttered, "Here we go again."

Chapter Twenty-Three

Frothy, wind-whipped waves tossed Beth's dream-body toward the rocky shore while moaning winds roiled black clouds overhead. Exhausted, she flailed her arms against the seaweed that threatened to pull her deeper into the darkness.

Like a drowning sailor fighting to reach shore, Beth took what she thought would be her final breath just before the sun peeped through the clouds, and she found herself sunning on a beach.

Warm sand pressed against her back and along her legs. Taught muscles relaxed, and peaceful calm flowed through her body as the hypnotic sound of waves pulsed against the beach.

Again, the scene changed, and she found herself floating above a bed upon which lay a woman's body. Gulliver-like, the form lay immobile, as if a phalanx of maniacal Lilliputians had tethered it with countless plastic tubes and wires. Green and yellow half-healed bruises on the puffy face hinted at recent trauma.

Fearfully, Beth looked closer at the prone figure. Shards of recognition tinged with sadness flashed through the dream-like haze.

Her body.

Instantly, Beth's consciousness moved out of the room. Unfettered by temporal constraints, she floated upward through metal and concrete and into an operating room where a group of white-clad people stood in a circle around a table upon which a sheet-covered body lay.

Machines clicked, whirred, and beeped while blood flowed from a bag hanging on a metal pole and into the body's exposed forearm. Conversation among the medical staff was light-hearted, focused on plans for the weekend.

Then, as if she could see in all four directions at once, Beth floated out onto the hospital rooftop. Seemingly oblivious to her presence, pigeons ascended and descended, warily eyeing a red Converse tennis shoe someone had thrown onto the roof.

Her consciousness suddenly flicked back into her room and, as if the body on the bed housed a powerful vacuum, she was pulled back into it.

The beeping of bedside machines grew louder as pain coursed through various parts of her body. Had she been in an automobile accident? How badly was she hurt?

Had Jillie been hurt, too? *Jillie.*

Beth tried to move her arms and legs. But like a paralyzed dreamer, her limbs refused to obey. At some point, she stopped fighting and floated in and out of consciousness.

Light through her closed eyelids dimmed and intensified with who-knew-how-many dawns and dusks. Then unseen wheels ground to a halt, leaving her wherever it was that Time stood still.

Chapter Twenty-Four

Dix drove in widening circles until she'd searched the whole village of Los Lunas. Her eyes darted down alleyways, along the ditch beside the road and into dark spaces between houses. But other than the occasional passing vehicle and homeless person, she didn't get a glimpse of a child alone and on foot.

If she doesn't want to be found, you won't find her.

Rather than discourage her, Lil's words spurred her on. She drove out of the village limits to wind down country lanes and over bumpy ditch banks. Her fingers grew numb from the cold, but she refused to turn on the car's heater. How could she make herself comfortable while that child wandered around in the frigid weather? According to the temperature readout on her dash, the air outside was only forty-five degrees, low enough to cause life-threatening hypothermia to the weak or unprotected.

Dix pulled her car into an all-night truck stop on Highway Forty-seven, its overhead halogen lights alchemically turning the night's darkness into midday. She paid the young man behind the counter for gasoline, a granola bar, and the largest coffee available. After taking a couple of tentative sips of the scalding swamp-mud-tasting brew, she hurried back to the car where her mind roiled as she filled the tank.

Lil would be worried sick, envisioning all kinds of

horrifying things. Dix had never dealt with her sister's guilt trips very well and yet here she was, dishing up enough fodder to last the next twenty years.

Although she'd been putting it off, it was time to call her sister, if only to let her know she was okay.

Fighting back the sense that she was capitulating to some unreasonable demand, Dix pulled the car away from the pump and parked at the asphalt's edge. Mentally crafting her I'm-okay-but-don't-try-to-stop-me speech, she pulled her cell phone lanyard from inside her blouse.

Her stomach sank at the sight of the empty, useless bag, and she flashed on the image of her phone sitting on the kitchen counter.

She scanned the area around the truck stop for a roadside emergency phone. But sometime during the last couple of decades or so things had changed, and public pay phones were a thing of the past.

Outdated, just like she was. Old school. She'd never even learned how to text…

Yawn.

There used to be a pay phone every…

Yawn.

…few miles…

Dix's eyes suddenly popped open. With blurred vision, she glanced at the clock in the dashboard. Five o'clock. She'd lost an hour.

She stared out the windshield and argued with herself. Should she use the gas station's phone to call Lil? Probably. Then maybe she should call Davie.

But a phone call to Davie would eat up several minutes. Then several more minutes would be spent bringing him up to speed. Added to that was the possibility of some jurisdictional thing-a-ma-jigs to slow the process down even further. There'd probably be hours of paperwork.

Dix shook her head. While all of that was true, she had to admit the real reason she didn't call Davie was out of fear—fear of his anger, fear she'd lose his respect, fear he'd see her as old and useless.

She imagined Davie and Lil commiserating with each other, doing a nod-nod-wink-wink thing and whispering that maybe it was time to put old Dix out to pasture. She envisioned the knowing looks on their faces, the sad shaking of heads, and the aura of pity that would poison the air.

Nope, it'd be best for her to do this on her own. After she'd found Jillie, she'd face the music. And time was ticking.

Based on Maslow's Hierarchy of Needs pyramid, the first things that child would need were food and shelter. But this was an eleven-year-old on a mission. The judgment part of the human brain didn't fully develop until somewhere around the early to mid-twenties. So, the child would be more prone to risk-taking...her decision-making mechanism would be immature...and...

A series of insistent taps on the car window against which her head rested jerked Dix out of a deep sleep. A young man peered through the glass at her, a worried look on his face.

She closed her mouth and worked her air-dried tongue until it was moist enough for speech. Then she powered down her window. "Yes?"

"Are you okay, miss?"

Dix shaped her lips into what she hoped was a

convincing smile. "Everything's fine. Just needed to rest my eyes a few minutes, but I'm good to go now."

"Just so you're all right, you've been sitting here a while." A relieved look on his face, the young man nodded toward the coffee cup. "That'll be cold by now; you want a refresher?"

"Kind of you, but no thanks. I'll be on my way."

The young man headed back to the building. From just inside the door, he stopped and turned back, evidently waiting for her to leave.

Angrily, Dix rolled up her window. She slapped her face, bounced her legs up and down on the balls of her feet, sang, raised and lowered her shoulders, and pinched her forearm hard enough to bring tears. She chugged the cold coffee dregs and considered her next move.

If she were an eleven-year-old searching for her beloved sister's ashes, where would she go? The hospital seemed logical. Jillie had appeared to accept her warning about what might happen if she showed up there, but she was, after all, a child.

Pushing aside the persistent thought that her sleep deprived fuzz-ball brain might not be completely on top of things, Dix sat up straight and squared her shoulders.

She fired up her engine, pulled onto highway Forty-seven and headed back the way she'd come. Twenty minutes of white-knuckle, still-pitch-black-night driving would get her to Interstate Twenty-five. Twenty more minutes would get her to the hospital.

The Universe had called upon her to help Jillie, and she'd not ignore that call.

Chapter Twenty-Five

Beth's eyes fluttered, then opened just enough to make out the fuzzy image of a young man in a nurse's uniform walking around her bed. With the occasional glimpse toward her, he studied monitors and levels of liquid in bags suspended from metal frames then wrote on a clipboard. She tried to call out but only managed to gag around the tube that made her throat feel like it was on fire. The beginnings of fear pulsed in her stomach. She struggled to throw off the bedclothes, but her arms merely twitched where they lay on top of the coverlet.

The nurse's eyes riveted on Beth, and he punched a button. The room suddenly filled with activity. Two nurses rushed in, moved to either side of the bed and held her down while someone injected something into her arm.

Immediately, Beth's muscles relaxed, and a feeling of lethargy pulsed through her body.

"Ah, Miss Ross, you're awake." The young man's voice sounded warm, comforting. "I need you to relax; don't fight the tube. We'll have to do some tests to make sure you can breathe and swallow on your own before we can remove it."

Slowly, in fragments and flashes, images of the beating at Digger's hands bubbled up from Beth's memory—her husband's rage, Jillie's terrified face as she ran to get help, the blood pouring from Digger's neck and his dying spasms.

Jillie?

"Please, Miss Ross, just give us a few more minutes before you try to speak."

After a series of tests, the tube was pulled, and she was asked to swallow several times. One of the nurses drew a tiny hammer-looking instrument down the sole of Beth's right foot and nodded in satisfaction when her toes curled in response.

Finally, everyone but the male nurse and a woman left the room.

Dressed in khaki pants and a button-up blouse, the woman smiled down at her. "I'm Doctor De Bruin." She pulled the chair nearer the bed and sat. "I know you have lots of questions."

After a couple of false starts, Beth managed to whisper. "How long have I been here?"

"Several weeks. You suffered a beating and your brain was swollen. We put you in a medically induced coma until the swelling could go down."

"What happened to my sister? Was she hurt? Do you know where she is? Her name's Jillie, Jillie Ross."

"She's not on this floor." The doctor looked at the nurse. "Do you know anything about her sister?"

The young man shook his head. "This is my first day on this wing, but I haven't come across anyone by that name."

When Beth made a move to pull herself from her bed, the nurse laid a hand on her arm. "Your muscles are going to need some work. A physical therapist will be along shortly to help you with that. Meanwhile, you should rest."

"Someone must know where my little sister is. I'm

the only family she has."

"I'll see what I can find out," the nurse said.

The doctor stood and patted Beth's shoulder. "Welcome back."

Chapter Twenty-Six

Lil paced the floor, watched television, climbed into and out of bed, then paced some more. Roiling anger had long since given way to anxiety, which changed back to anger before finally settling into fear and dread.

Hearing-aids in, she listened for the garage door to open while mentally composing the tongue-lashing she'd give her twin. Her agitation grew as the hour hand on her bedside clock slowly ticked by.

Throughout their lives, the two sisters had often experienced *a twin thing*. By the time they learned to talk, they were finishing each other's sentences. And on more than one occasion, they'd raised the purple-haired, church ladies' eyebrows by bursting into giggles during a prayer or pause in the sermon at something one or the other had thought but didn't need to say.

Then along with the standard hormonal tsunami accompanying their teen years, they simultaneously decided to become non-twins. When Dix chose to wear pink, Lil opted for blue. When Lil decided to get a B.S. in accounting, Dix got a Ph.D. in Clinical Psychology. In an almost frenzied need to touch and be touched, the gregarious Dix had burned through countless relationships and three disastrous marriages while the introverted and supremely a-sexual Lil had been content to remain single.

But though they chose different paths and lifestyles, their near clone-like connection never completely evaporated. And now Lil's gut was twisting and squirming just like it did in junior high school when the creep who lived up the street tried to abduct Dix.

Lil had known her sister was in trouble, even though she'd been roller skating a couple of blocks away. By the time Lil arrived on the scene, the guy had Dix's arms pinned and was trying to haul her into a mud-splattered brown van.

The prick's eyes had grown wide when Lil charged at him. Screaming like something crazed, she'd hurled herself like a bowling ball straight for his kneecaps. He yelped and staggered backward, loosening his hold on Dix to aim a fist at Lil's head.

Then, as the twins later told police, they *went medieval on the jerk's ass*. Two pissed-as-hell twelve-year-old kids kicking, gouging, pulling hair, biting. The guy had seemed almost relieved when a couple of minutes later a squad car pulled up in response to a neighbor's call.

Lil shut down the memory, removed her hearing aids, and again headed for bed.

But when Dix hadn't returned by five the next morning, Lil walked downstairs to the land line in the kitchen and punched in her sister's cell phone number. If Dix thought Lil was going to put up with such behavior, she had another—

Out of the darkness, Dix's 60's rock and roll ring tone erupted from atop the kitchen counter. The phone's tiny green light flashing its location, Lil picked the thing up and jabbed the red disconnect square.

Dix had been out all night. Alone. No way to call

home, even if she'd wanted to.

We should get an in-car emergency phone service, one with satellite connectedness, in case we have car trouble and need to call for help. Dix's words conjured up a truckload of guilt.

"We have cell phones," Lil had said. "We don't need the added expenditure."

"Then we should at least get phone jacks for the car."

But Lil had remained adamant. "Just re-charge the thing every night before you go to bed. Simple. You want that kind of stuff, you pay for it. We don't need it."

Dix had harrumphed and said, "Like the emergency three-day supply of water and food we never managed to set up, we won't need that either." She'd jabbed her index finger in Lil's face in her standard mode of retort. "Until we do. Think Corpus Christi in the sixties, Houston, and east Texas—"

"We live in the desert, in case you haven't noticed. We're high enough not to flood." She'd pitched such a fit about the cost, Dix finally let the matter drop.

And now her directionally challenged sister could be anywhere, stranded, lying in a ditch.

Lil swiped tears away from her cheeks. While she'd been born with an internal combustion that made her uncomfortably warm in temperatures above seventy degrees, Dix was the opposite. Anything below seventy sent her scurrying for a goose down comforter.

And the weather was growing cold.

A grim set to her mouth, Lil prepared a breakfast of eggs, bacon, toast, and coffee then forced herself to eat every bite. Though not the least bit hungry, she had a sinking feeling she was going to need the energy.

She pulled an insulated thermos bottle from the cabinet, filled it with coffee, hurried upstairs to her room, and got dressed. Then she jammed her hearing aids into her ears and put a spare package of tiny round batteries into the breast pocket of her red flannel shirt.

Unsure of what prompted her to do so, she retrieved a can of pepper spray and a fully charged Taser, the scabbard of which she attached to her leather belt. Then she made a beeline downstairs to the kitchen pantry.

Without a wasted movement, she filled a tote bag with the thermos, three oranges, an unopened package of string cheese, and several granola bars. She glanced around the kitchen, her mind furiously ticking off the things she might need if worse came to worst. Then she headed for the garage and retrieved the half-full, red plastic, five-gallon gas container used for the lawn mower.

The sight of Dix's empty parking space sent a wave of renewed fear through Lil's midsection. Trying to convince herself she was probably worried for no reason, that her absent-minded twin was probably enjoying an early breakfast at a Denny's or IHOP, she popped open her trunk, stashed the gas container, and slammed the lid.

She pulled Dix's cell phone from her holster, climbed into the driver's seat, and turned on the dome light. After losing an internal argument over the best way to proceed, she squelched an uncomfortable fluttering of guilt and punched in Davie's number.

"Aunt Dix? What's up? Everything okay?" Her nephew's sleep-fogged voice was tinged with worry.

"It's not Dix, it's Lil. I'm using her phone, long story. Sorry to call you so early, but…"

Broken only by her nephew's occasional question, Lil recounted everything she could remember of what the kid had told her and Dix about Beth, Digger's death, her life with the Elliotts, and her subsequent wanderings.

"You mean the little girl was in the house when—"

"You know Dix has a weakness for strays, always has. The problem is she left last night after dinner to look for the kid and hasn't come home yet."

"Where are you?"

"I'm home." *For the time being.*

"Unless you suspect foul play, Aunt Dix hasn't been gone long enough to do a missing person's report. Do you have any reason to think she's in danger?"

"No, not really. But she can be forgetful when she gets this focused, and she has night-blindness. After several near-misses, I made her stop driving after dark."

"I'll take the day off to look for her." Punctuated with rustling and what sounded like a closet door opening and closing, Davie's words sounded more than a little angry. "Do you have any idea where she was headed?"

"Not for certain, but all that kid could talk about was getting her sister's ashes from the hospital."

"Okay, I'll take it from here."

"I can't just sit—"

"Aunt Lil, I won't be at my best if I have to worry about you as well. You understand? I'll call when I find her." Davie broke the connection.

For the next couple of minutes, Lil sat in the car, her mind a fury of activity. She reached into the console at her elbow, pulled out one of a dozen pair of reading glasses she had stashed in various places, slipped them on, and studied the road map.

She'd often heard that the best lies included a bit of truth. And although some of the kid's story had turned out to be true, Dix had fallen for the whole shebang. Unable to have children of her own, she'd be in raging Valkyrie-Mama mode.

If the kid was to be believed, there were four places she'd be likely to show up: the hospital, the Elliott house, her godmother's house, or her own home.

Since Davie would secure the hospital, that left three other possibilities.

Lil started the engine and backed out into the pre-dawn darkness. She could be in Belen in less than thirty minutes. If Dix were there, she'd bring her home—even if she had to drag her kicking and screaming. And the police could deal with the kid.

Chapter Twenty-Seven

Unable to sleep, Margo Elliott poked her husband's forehead with her index finger until he awakened. "I don't like any of this, things don't feel right. We have to figure out what to do."

When Cleg mumbled something that sounded resentful, Margo smacked his shoulder with her doubled fist. "Get up and make me some coffee." She pulled her tatty old housecoat on over her flannel gown and headed for the stairs. "You've got five minutes."

Margo was pacing the living room floor when Cleg showed up with her steaming cup. "Here it is, just the way you like it."

Between sips, Margo shot lethal glances at her spouse sitting in his easy chair staring at his hands. "You're just plain worthless. I'm trying to do something here, and all you can do is complain about being hungry."

Cleg looked up. "I'm sorry, Sugar Plum." He wrung his hands, his brow furrowed. "I've been trying to figure out where the girl would have gone but can't seem to make heads nor tails of it. You went out of your way to give her a good home and all, even though she killed our boy…"

Margo spun on the balls of her feet, sloshing coffee onto the already-stained carpet. She stomped over to her husband and bent at the waist to bring her eyes level with his. "You don't get it, do you? Not only do we have no clue as to the whereabouts of the treasure, but we lied to the kid about her sister. And now, thanks to that meddling bimbo at the hamburger joint, the police know she's missing. When they find her, everything will come out, and I have a feeling the law won't be too understanding about our good intentions."

"Surely it'd just be her word against ours."

Margo tapped her temple. "Think about it, Marshmallow-Ass, that Social Services girl hated us on sight. Or didn't you notice the way she wrinkled her nose and sniffed when she walked into the living room, or the way she perched on the edge of the sofa like it was coated with manure. Besides, who knows what that kid told the psychologist during her visits." She straightened, crossed one arm over her chest, rested the other elbow on the crossed arm, and tapped her closed fist against her chin. "We have to find her before the police do. Once we have the treasure, we can disappear."

Cleg sat up straighter. "Disappear?"

"Picture us in a place warm year-round with palm trees and a beach. Someplace without extradition." Margo's gaze floated up to the ceiling. "A place where someone young and tanned would wait on me...on us hand and foot. We could live like royalty on very little."

"But what about all our stuff? What would happen to our house?"

Margo jerked her eyes back toward her husband as she moved her hand in an arc. "Is it really all that hard for you to understand why I'd want to leave this place?"

"I know it isn't much, but it's what we can afford on my disability check."

Margo squinted. "If we play our cards right, we won't need your check."

"But—"

Margo made a chopping motion with her right hand. "Shut it. I'm not letting that treasure slip through my hands. Our Digger died trying to find it, and I know he'd want us to have it. I'll think of him while I…while we live the life we deserve."

"But where can the girl go? Seems she'd be pretty easy to spot."

"You're forgetting the box of hair color Mort found in her suitcase. That hamburger-joint woman told him her hair was brown. And eye color's easy enough to hide behind sun shades." Margo took a deep breath, a thoughtful look on her face. "She has no intention of getting caught or she'd have gone to the police by now. That means we still have time to find her."

"She's having to live rough. Either that or someone's already grabbed her." Cleg licked his lips. "A cute little kid like that, she could wind up in some Sultan's harem."

Margo whirled on her husband. "And there it is. You've probably spent hours slobbering all over yourself at the thought of having a harem." She stepped toward Cleg, a look on her face he recognized all too well. "You'd better watch it, Flabbo, or you'll have to start reading your comic books through your fly."

Cleg cringed and a cold sweat popped out along his upper lip. He held his hands up in a pleading motion. "Now, now, Butter Cake, you know you're the only one for me."

As quickly as her temper had flared, Margo's mood changed, and she grew thoughtful. "Mort said no one at either the Belen or Los Lunas train stations said they'd seen her."

Like a lamb unexpectedly reprieved from slaughter, Cleg perked up. "Maybe she caught sight of him looking for her and skedaddled. Or maybe she waited for him to leave then went back."

Ignoring her husband, Margo paced and muttered to herself, "Cross country, that'd be the smart way to go. And she's plenty smart. But once she finds out her dear sister's still alive, all hell's going to break loose." She tapped her cheek with an index finger. "If I were old man Ross, where would I hide a pile of money? Or maybe it's gold bars and jewels. Digger said he Googled it, and there are millions of dollars in lost treasure in various places all over New Mexico."

"How bad can it get…with the police, I mean?"

"You're like a broken record. Stop blathering on about the police."

"But we've not done anything illegal. Not yet, anyways."

Margo glared at her spouse. "Keeping her away from her only surviving family member? Maybe not technically illegal, but some people might frown on that kind of behavior. And who knows what some vote-hungry elected official might decide to call it?"

Cleg gulped, the sound loud enough to be heard across the room.

Suddenly, Margo jerked her head up and smacked her forehead with the palm of her hand. She hurried to the lamp stand by the sofa, picked up her purse and retrieved the pickup keys. "Hustle, Tubby." She tossed the keys at her spouse.

Never a quick study, Cleg blankly watched the

keys' flight as they hit his belly then bounced onto the floor. Wheezing, he bent to retrieve the projectiles. "Where're we going, Peaches?"

"Since the kid still believes her sister's dead, she'll want money for a fancy funeral."

"Aw, that's nice. Don't you think that's nice?"

Margo shot a look of contempt at her spouse. "Focus, Big-Brains. It's been right in front of us all along, she'll have to go back to the farm to get some of the treasure for a funeral and headstone." She strode toward the front door. "Move it or stay here and rot."

Cleg hoisted himself out of his easy chair. Clutching the keys, he grabbed his oxygen tank and hurried after his wife.

Chapter Twenty-Eight

After spending a cold night trying to sleep under a pile of leaves and branches, Jillie dusted herself off as best she could and hurried to the just-opening train station in Los Lunas. Taking care not to look directly at the other passengers, she hunched her shoulders and hurried to the back of the car. Surprised when no one gave her more than a glance, she breathed a deep sigh of relief and tried to review her plans.

But her brain refused to stay focused. After a miserable night, the warm air in the train combined with the rhythmic *clackety-clackety* of its wheels lulled her to sleep. It was pure luck that she'd awakened as they pulled into the Belen station.

She forced herself to walk from the comfortable train into the cold morning air. At first, her teeth chattered. But the walk to the Elliotts' warmed her a bit, and she reached the house at a little before six.

Surprised to see light shining through the downstairs windows so early in the morning, she crouched behind a thick juniper bush just as the front door was thrown open hard enough to knock a hole in the sheet rock behind it. As if chased by wolves, Margo dashed out of the house. With the bottom of her coat flapping, thin legs pumping, and feet pounding the driveway's packed dirt, she headed for the pickup.

Jillie's heartbeat shot sky high. Making herself as

small as she could, she peered through the bush's thick, scale-like fronds.

"Wait up, Jelly Bean." Cleg lumbered out of the house and scrambled after his wife, his face a dark shade of purple.

Screeching threats over her shoulder, Margo hopped into the passenger's seat of their pickup as Cleg struggled to hoist himself into the driver's seat.

Dirt jetted from behind spinning wheels. Dust rose into a cloud, and pebbles *tinked* against metal as the pickup peeled down the drive.

The whole time Jillie lived there, she'd never seen Margo or Cleg move so fast or rise so early. But the good news was their absence meant she could do a thorough search of the house and grounds and re-stock her food stores.

When the sounds of the pickup's engine grew distant, Jillie hurried toward the house's still-open front door. Beginning downstairs, she worked her way through the kitchen, the dining room, the pantry, and the living room. She started upstairs, the familiar feelings of nausea creeping up her throat at the thought of going into her old room—Digger's room, guarded by Digger's ashes.

After one glance at the chest of drawers to ensure a second urn hadn't been added, she hurried across the hall to Cleg and Margo's room. With shaking hands, she pushed their door open.

The air that greeted her made the rest of the house seem like a meadow of blooming wildflowers. Trying not to gag, Jillie stepped into the room, quickly scanned it, then hustled out.

"Yay," she murmured. "I'm glad you're not here

yet, Beth. But don't worry, I won't go anywhere without you."

She re-positioned her backpack and headed toward the well-stocked pantry. Cans of little sausages, crackers, canned cheese, peanut butter crackers and other snacks called to her, and her stomach growled.

Although her empty stomach told her to take everything edible she could get her hands on, it seemed wise not to tip Margo off that she'd been there. She dropped her selected items into her backpack and headed for the basement, where she spent so many miserable hours doing laundry.

While waiting for the laundry to wash and dry, she'd scouted every inch of the place. Even before she ran away, she'd determined the basement would be a handy means of gaining access to the house.

Once down the creaky stairs, she headed straight for one of the two windows that opened out onto the backyard. Until she got Beth's ashes home, she'd most likely be in and out of the house regularly, and an unlocked window in the basement seemed the perfect solution, especially since not once the whole time she'd lived there had Margo or Cleg come downstairs.

She dragged a short step ladder underneath the selected window and climbed high enough to reach the clasp. After several tugs, the corroded mechanism gave way, and she pushed the window open. She clenched her teeth when the hinges squealed loud enough to be heard in the next county then stepped down from the ladder and hurried to a metal shelf against one wall.

Ancient, rusted cans of different sizes, their paper labels splotched with gray and white paint drips, lay scattered among cans of engine oil and half-empty bottles. Relieved to find the WD-40 where she remembered, Jillie grabbed the can of lubricant and returned to the window.

After spraying a thick coating on every moving part, she repeatedly opened and closed the window until it made no sound. Then she returned the can to its spot on the shelf.

With a sense that time was against her, she hurried upstairs to the front door. Cautiously, she poked her head far enough through the door to scan for telltale plumes of approaching dust. Relieved to see the coast was clear, she headed to the shed.

But the nearer she drew to the tiny building, the more her shoulders sagged. With its rotting roof and boarded-up door window, the place would have become home to all sorts of creatures.

The wooden door stood slightly ajar, its green paint peeling like old scabs. An open lock hung from a metal u-bolt attached to the jamb.

Surprised to find how easily and soundlessly the door opened, Jillie stepped inside. She stood still, waiting for her eyes to get used to the darkness.

Odors of rotted wood and who-knew-how-many-generations of mice mingled with the chemical smells of bug spray and fertilizer. Metal implements, most of which were so rusted as to be unusable, had been carelessly thrown on the floor. Several empty burlap bags lay strewn about.

A large metal toolbox had been shoved against one wall, its chrome exterior splotched with rust. Of the kind commonly seen in the backs of pickup trucks across New Mexico, the box stood about two feet high and was long enough to fit snugly behind a pickup's cab.

An oily patch described a semi-circle in the dirt at one end of the box, like something inside had leaked out. Countless footprints in the dust meant someone had been walking around, but no telling when.

Jillie sat on the toolbox and opened her bag of food. Commanding herself to eat exactly one third, she returned the rest to her backpack.

The early morning air grew cooler, it's faintly metallic smell hinting at the possibility of snow. The burlap sacks caught her eye.

She gathered the bags into a pile, coughing at the plume of disturbed dust. Lumpy bags couldn't be called the fanciest mattress, but at least they'd keep her off the floor.

Satisfied with her improvised sleeping arrangement, Jillie sat on the toolbox and pulled her water bottle from her backpack. She had just taken a sip when the crunch of tires on gravel signaled someone's arrival.

Jillie tiptoed to the door and peered through a tiny gap between the door and its frame as Cleg's pickup pulled up the drive. Pickup doors opened then slammed, punctuated by the sound of Margo's angry voice.

"How could you forget to bring a shovel, Butt-breath."

"You didn't tell me—"

"Am I supposed to think of everything? Go on, go get the shovel."

Jillie's stomach flipped and she barely breathed.

"I'm sorry, Sugar Lips," Cleg whined. "The shovel's been busted for years. I've kept meaning to get another one, but I haven't—"

"We'll stop and buy one on the way. That's coming out of your allowance, by the way. And we're going to need the flashlight."

Cleg ambled toward the house while Margo stood by the truck mumbling to herself. When her husband hadn't returned within a few minutes, she let fly a curse word and strode into the house.

Her teeth chattering and toes numb from the cold, Jillie brought her coat up around her chin and hugged Mickey tightly against her chest. Had she made a mistake leaving Dix and Lil's? Maybe Dix would have gotten Beth's ashes for her. But then again, maybe Lil would have called the police on her.

Jillie wasn't sure of what happened to runaways who were found, but she was pretty sure getting caught would keep her from seeing to Beth's ashes.

Reassuring herself she'd made the right decision, she nestled into the burlap bags and closed her eyes. With Mickey's thick fur warming her neck, she fell asleep.

Chapter Twenty-Nine

Having left a message for his boss explaining his need to take a day off, David climbed into his car and headed for the hospital in Albuquerque where Beth Ross was recuperating. He'd considered calling rather than taking the time to make the twenty-minute trip, but he needed to follow up on his aunt Lil's suggestion that Aunt Dix might have driven there hoping to find the little girl.

Beyond that, he needed to question the older sister Beth. It'd been his experience that people often remembered or said things face-to-face they didn't think of on the phone. And if he was lucky, his aunt Dix had figured the same thing.

That Aunt Dix hadn't gone home the night before wasn't as frightening as the fact that she'd not called her sister. To David's knowledge, the two of them had never let more than a day pass without at least touching base. And the highway between Los Lunas and Interstate Twenty-Five was infamous as a dangerous road anytime, let alone at night. Sadly, a T-shirt imprinted with *I survived Highway 47* was gaining in popularity among the locals.

Forcing himself to drive slowly, David scanned both sides of the road for skid marks that would indicate a vehicle out of control.

As the miles crept past, he cursed himself for

ignoring the mental klaxon of his subconscious mind trying to get his attention the night before. He'd known something was wrong during dinner, dammit. He should have pressed his aunts until they came clean, but he'd been too selfish, too focused on his own discomfort.

A detective of six years, he'd gone into law enforcement with lofty ideals and a desire to make a difference in the world. While he'd committed his life to protect those who couldn't protect themselves, he'd had no idea what that commitment would cost him psychologically, emotionally, and even spiritually.

Over time, his proximity to the horrors humans visited on each other had re-shaped the filter through which he saw life, making him jaded and suspicious. He'd been amazed to find that even as perpetrators gave full reign to their selfishness and absolute lack of conscience, they rationalized their behavior, no matter how twisted. The one homicidal maniac he'd helped apprehend had tried to convince a jury he *only killed the ones who asked for it.*

But his twin aunts had always seemed disconnected from the world in which he worked. While their style of dealing with each other messed with his mind, they'd been his safe-haven in a world of chaos. He'd taken them for granted, assumed they'd live forever. Even as he watched them age and the realization dawned that he'd need to be ready to care for them at some point, he'd assumed that day was still far off.

David's breath caught as his headlights picked up black skid marks that ran off the highway toward the elm tree-choked ditch at its side. His mind flashing to scenes of horrific car crashes he'd witnessed, he pulled onto the shoulder. After jamming his gearshift into park, he pulled a flashlight from his glove compartment, jumped from his vehicle, and headed toward the ditch.

Chapter Thirty

When Dix's headlights picked up the Albuquerque city limit sign, it was as if two dangling wires in her brain suddenly connected and fired up a previously unconsidered possibility. Jillie hadn't shown the foggiest understanding of either the length of time or the process involved in having a body autopsied then released to the family for funeral arrangements. In fact, she'd not only been convinced the Elliotts were going to have Beth cremated soon, she was certain that Margo woman would take the ashes to her house.

While it was possible Jillie would make her way back to the Ross farm to hide out and be close to her parents, Dix had never seen anyone more determined to finish a job. She'd not go home without her sister's ashes.

Jillie had said the Elliotts lived south of Belen, just off the road to Mountainair. It'd mean hours of walking for a child, but only an hour or so if she took the train. And Dix could be there within thirty minutes.

She'd find Jillie. Then, by George, she'd take that child to her sister.

Hopefully, none of the Elliott tribe would try to interfere. Although non-violent by nature as well as ideology, Dix had four decades earlier learned a few self-protective moves while an intern at the state mental hospital. And in her subsequent vocation as a marriage and family therapist, she'd had more than one occasion to stare down an abusive client.

Confidence in her ability to deflect an attack while doing no harm to the attacker flooded Dix's sternum. She whipped her car onto the next exit, took the overpass, turned left again, then merged onto Interstate I-25 south.

Senior citizen she may be, but she was a long way from useless.

Chapter Thirty-One

Relief poured over David like a Tahitian waterfall as he inspected the skid marks heading off the road. No wrecked vehicle in the ditch meant the marks could have been made days ago. He unclenched his teeth, and the pain in his jaws subsided.

That Aunt Dix hadn't called him for help in finding the little girl meant his conversation during dinner had frightened her. And he couldn't blame her for not trusting him after the dire warnings he'd given.

It was possible she'd wanted to call but had been unable to find a phone in lieu of the one she left at home. But it was also possible she'd gotten herself into a situation where she was prevented from calling. And David had been in law enforcement too long to off-handedly dismiss the latter.

He took a deep breath through his nose and blew it out through his mouth. For the next several minutes, he reviewed his conversation with his aunt Lil.

If the Ross girl thought her sister was dead and going to be autopsied then cremated, where would she go? Did she have friends who'd pick her up and give her a place to stay? Or were there other relatives she'd call for help? Did the family own any property other than the farm, someplace where she could hide out?

David pounded his hand on the steering wheel and tried to put himself inside his aunt Dix's brain. After several attempts, he finally admitted that he had no clue. In the absence of more information, he could drive around in endless circles, chasing his own tail.

His lips tight, he jammed the gearshift into drive, whipped the car back onto the highway, and sped toward the hospital.

Chapter Thirty-Two

Once inside the hospital, David stopped at the information desk to get Beth's room number, then moved to the elevators. He punched the elevator button then tapped his fingers on his thigh. "Come on, come on, come on."

Losing patience, he'd turned and headed toward the stairwell when the elevator's bell dinged, and its door opened. He jabbed the button for the fourth floor and caught sight of a sign picturing a cell phone with a huge X through it followed by the words *Please do not use cell phones on these floors.*

David turned off his phone and slipped it into his pants pocket as the elevator jerked to a stop. He checked the sticky-note on which the woman at the information desk had written Beth's room number then made his way through the maze of corridors.

Nurses bustled about their duties, offering up the best they could to their patients. Family members wandered the halls, their facial expressions projecting helplessness, anger, and fear in the face of human frailty.

Beth was sitting up in the hospital bed staring at a television set suspended from the ceiling when David poked his head around the open door. The movement caught her eye, and she looked up.

Huge, bright green eyes peered at him from under

thick, black lashes. That, and the long, shiny brown hair, cupid's-bow mouth, pale skin, and cheeks sunken from the extended hospital stay set up an almost physical reaction in David's midsection.

Get a grip, she's only a kid. Way too young for a thirty-year-old. He pasted what he hoped was a professional smile on his face and approached the bed.

"Good morning, Mrs. Elliott. I'm Detective David Ruiz with Los Lunas Police."

"Just Beth, please."

David nodded. "I apologize for the early hour, but I need to ask you some questions about your sister Jillie."

Beth sat up straighter, and her eyes widened. "Have you found her? Oh, please tell me you've found her."

"That's one of the reasons I'm here. Have you heard from her in the last couple of days?"

Beth chewed on her lower lip. "No. I've called the Elliotts every day for the past week, ever since I woke up. But Margo always makes some excuse about why Jillie can't come to the phone. I called Social Services, and they said her caseworker's last visit indicated she was fine and doing well in school. But the nurse said Jillie's only been to see me once, and that's not like her. She'd live in this room if she could." The muscles in her arm trembled from disuse as she pushed the cart bearing a tray of half-eaten food away. "Who would award custody of a kid to the parents of the man she accidentally killed, anyway?"

"It may seem weird, but the judge was pretty well constrained by county policy to put her with family, if at all possible." David pulled a steel-framed, blue vinyl-covered chair closer to the bed and sat down. "And the

Elliotts asked to be allowed to take her."

Her voice quavering, Beth continued, "The Elliotts seem fairly normal on the surface, but they're not. With the possible exception of Cleg, they're vile, truly evil." She struggled to lift a hand to wipe tears from her eyes as a sudden flash of anger brought a flush to her cheeks. "I just know they've done something with Jillie. I know it."

David took a deep breath, let it out slowly, and stared down at the hand he hadn't realized he'd laid on Beth's forearm. He cleared his throat to cover his reaction to the almost electric charge that shot up his arm at the contact and pulled away. For the next several minutes, with his gaze focused slightly above Beth's head to allow him to concentrate, he recounted what he'd been able to find out about Jillie's movements from the day of Digger's death.

Beth shook her head and blew a puff of air through pursed lips. "So, she thinks I'm dead?"

David nodded. "As of last night, she did. Has an elderly woman named Dixie contacted you by any chance?"

Beth's brows came together in a frown. "No. I haven't had any visitors since I woke up. Who's she?"

David explained about his aunts and their involvement with Jillie.

"I'm sorry about your aunt and I hope she's okay, but Jillie's just a kid. She must be terrified. How's she getting food? Where's she sleeping? It can get cold this time of year—"

David held up his hand, palm outward, in a gentle shushing motion. In a voice he hoped sounded more reassuring than he felt, he said, "Your little sister's tough, she's smart, and she's resilient. She's managed on her own for several days now."

"What about sending out an Amber Alert? Has that been done?"

"That only comes into play when the child is taken against her will and considered to be in imminent danger. Since Jillie ran away of her own volition, she's been listed as a runaway and missing person."

"That doesn't seem right. She's only eleven."

"We *have* reported her to the NCIC, um sorry, that's the National Crime Information Center. That means the whole country will be on the lookout for her."

Beth's eyes bored into David's. "You have to find her before the Elliotts do, if they don't already have her. Those people will stop at nothing to get what they want."

David had assumed unselfish love was a figment of artists' and poets' imaginations. Yet here was a woman who'd loved her little sister so much she hooked up with an abusive prick like Digger Elliott to ensure they could stay together. What must it feel like to be wrapped in that kind of love?

Sadness and a sense of loss pulsed through David's midsection. He'd never loved or been loved like that. Not even close.

But that had been his choice. Years ago, he'd decided to allow only veneer relationships—shallow and uncomplicated. Best for all concerned, since over the past several generations the Ruiz men had died young. The term *emotionally unavailable* had been thrown in his face during more than one drama-filled breakup.

He sighed, switched on his electronic tablet, and tapped it open. "Tell me every place your sister might go, any friends she might contact, favorite fast food places, anything you can think of that might help."

Beth looked thoughtful. "She didn't really have many school friends, at least no one she'd want to stay with. Her favorite food?" Beth chuckled. "Anything that doesn't bite back. Then there's Mrs. Potter, Jillie's godmother. She often walked there when things got tense in the house."

"Tell me about Mrs. Potter." David typed furiously as Beth described the woman.

"She's our closest neighbor. She was a good friend of our mom's, kind of looked out for us after mom died."

"I'll check it out. Anything else?"

Beth raised her chin. "If Jillie finds out I'm still alive, she'll find a way to get here. But if, like you said, she thinks Margo's had me cremated, nothing will stop her from finding my ashes and taking them home. It was a pact we made when Pops died. Whichever one of us is next, the other will make sure the family stays together."

"Thanks." David shut off his tablet, stood, and smiled down at Beth. "You've been a great help."

Beth looked up, and her eyes filled with tears. "You have to find Jillie; she's the only family I have left. I don't think I could…"

"I can't imagine what you're going through, and I don't want to minimize the situation. But don't let yourself focus on what might never happen. I promise you this, I won't stop looking until I find your sister." He left the room and headed for the exit.

He'd worked on several missing person's cases over his years on the force. The majority wound up with the missing person showing up and wondering what all the fuss was about. But not always.

A couple of years earlier, he'd helped break up part of a human trafficking ring that dealt exclusively in children. It had been pure coincidence that a passing motorist had seen a child's terrified face staring out a small, round van window the either overly confident or intellectually dim kidnapper had failed to cover. The quick-thinking motorist had snapped a cell phone photo of the van's tags and called the police. Since David's location was nearest the sighting, he'd responded to the call.

After a miles-long, high-speed chase, he managed to stop the van. The driver jumped from the vehicle and ran into the desert, but David brought him down with a flying tackle. He'd handcuffed the smirking bastard then frog-marched him to the police vehicle and locked him in.

The blonde-haired, blue-eyed little boy in the rear of the van had soiled himself while bouncing around inside the van's metal confines. But David held the little guy and told him stories until paramedics arrived and checked them both over.

The female paramedic had eventually pried the little boy out of David's arms. Talking in low, soft tones, she comforted them both, as if sensing the turmoil in David's head—as if she understood his fear that once the child was out of his arms, he might be unable to keep himself from beating the kidnapper into a pile of stinking red meat.

It had taken David the better part of two months to

decide whether or not to quit the force. But the memory of that little boy's face along with the images of what he'd have been enduring made him realize it was more important to help rid the country of that kind of leprosy than to change his career path. Once that decision was made, he'd never looked back.

Back in his Jeep, he clicked open a file on his tablet and studied his notes on Aunt Lil's description of Jillie Ross. With unusual eye and hair coloring, she'd be a high-value target. And at only eleven, she'd be easy to train.

He'd make three stops on his way to Mrs. Potters' place: his aunts' house in Los Lunas to grill his aunt Lil for details, the Elliotts' in Belen in hopes Jillie's foster parents might know something helpful, then to the godmother's in case the little girl had gone to her for help. Hopefully, somewhere along the way, he'd find Aunt Dix.

As he pulled into traffic, David touched his holstered sidearm. He'd learned early on neither to assume anything nor to take chances. Anyone who'd go after a kid wouldn't hesitate to hurt one or two little old ladies who tried to interfere. He had a sick feeling borne of years of experience that someone was going to get hurt.

****

David drove into his aunts' driveway just as the sun was coming up. It didn't seem possible it was only a few hours ago he'd been there for dinner, complaining inwardly at having to listen to his aunts throw verbal spitballs at each other.

Right then, he'd have been overjoyed to hear them going at it again. But, like the timer on a homemade explosive device, the minutes were ticking by. Unable to shake the feeling that he was missing something vital, he rang the bell.

Something someone had said? Something he overheard? Whatever it was, the harder he tried to pull it from the shadows, the further back it slipped.

He rang the bell again and counted to thirty. When no one answered the door, he used the key his aunts had given him and went in.

A quick reconnaissance of the house told him what he suspected—his aunt Lil was out looking for her sister in spite of his request that she stay home.

David couldn't remember ever feeling as angry and afraid as he did right then. Angry at himself for not recognizing the signals he'd sensed from his aunts the night before and fearful of what the next thirty-six hours would bring.

Statistically, the first forty-eight hours were the most critical to finding his aunts and the little girl. After that, a whole new set of data kicked in.

Grim-faced, he left the house, locked the door behind him, and hit the road to Belen.

Chapter Thirty-Three

Cleg frowned at the dull amber light describing a small target against the wall. He hoped there were fresh batteries; he didn't want to think about what would happen if the flashlight burned out while Margo was using it. Of course, it'd be his fault.

Moving as quickly as his trembling fingers would allow, he rummaged in the kitchen's junk drawer. Pushing aside the too-short pencils, rubber bands, and paper clips, he grabbed what he hoped were two good C cells. He tossed the old batteries into the drawer, put in the new ones, clicked the light on and off a couple of times, and then started for the door.

But, like a magnet, the pantry drew his gaze. No telling when he'd have another chance to grab a bite. Margo could go a full day without food, but Cleg's system was more delicate.

He retrieved the key from a pegboard on the wall, unlocked the pantry's padlock and pulled the door open. He eyed the stored food, initially unable to decide what he wanted. Then he grabbed a couple of king-sized candy bars and stuffed them into his right pants pocket and reached for a package of his favorite treat in the world—chocolate-covered marshmallow cookies. He tore open the package, but before he could shove a cookie into his mouth, Margo's voice stabbed through the air, loud enough to pierce his eardrums.

"What do you think you're doing?" She bared her teeth at him like something feral.

In a panic, Cleg stuffed both cookies into his left pants pocket—a move he immediately regretted. Since the girl left, Margo did the laundry. And she'd boil him in oil when she found the remnants of those melted cookies.

"I was just making sure the flashlight works," Cleg said.

Margo grabbed his upper arm and squeezed. "I'm going to take a whiz. By the time I get done, you'd better have the pickup running and the heater on full blast." She threw her coat over the back of a kitchen chair, spun on her heel, and headed for the stairs. Her voice floated on the air behind her, "I hate cold weather. I don't *thrive* in cold weather."

As the sound of Margo's clopping footsteps faded, Cleg took the opportunity to retrieve the cookies from his pocket, gobble them down, then grab another handful of snacks. If he was lucky, he'd have time to eat the candy bars and maybe even some of the caramel popcorn before the woman he'd begun calling *The Shrike* came back.

The nickname he'd first heard in an old Alfred Hitchcock movie couldn't have been more suited to his wife. A tiny, deceptively lovely bird of prey, the shrike impaled its dinner on a thorny bush before leisurely taking time to devour it alive.

Unaware his reveries had eaten up his free time, Cleg jerked his head toward the stairwell at the sound of his wife's flouncing footfalls.

"You still here?" Margo's voice could have shredded beef. She yanked her coat from the chair back, knocking the chair over in the process. "Pick that up." She jerked her head toward the chair and jammed her arms into the sleeves.

Cleg stooped, lost his balance, and nearly toppled over before righting the chair. "I was just—"

Margo stepped to the still-open pantry and peered inside. "I'm telling you, she's been in this house." Something on her blouse caught her eye, and she used a fingernail to peel a speck of food from just above her right breast. She lifted her head and gazed at the wall thoughtfully, "If she still thinks her sister's dead, what will she do next? If I were a kid looking for my sister, what would I do?"

Cleg started to say something, thought better of it, and choked on his own saliva.

Margo whirled on him. "What?" Her eyes narrowed, she took a couple of steps toward him. "Do I hear echoes of a judgmental comment you had sense enough not to say?"

Cleg shook his head. His eyes wide, he stammered, "I was just remembering your own dear sister Chlorine, and how devastated you were when she went missing."

Eyes filled with suspicion, Margo squinted at her husband then resumed pacing. For the next several minutes, she walked back and forth, mumbling to herself.

Suddenly, she whirled, a triumphant look on her face. "The photo."

"What about the photo, Sweet Potato?"

Margo sneered. "You haven't been paying attention. When Mort searched the kid's luggage, he found a photo of her dead mother with a note on the back."

"I don't get—"

"Connect the dots, Jelly-butt. It makes sense that old man Ross would have left a clue for his kids. Now if I could just remember what that note said; it's right on the tip of my tongue."

"But we pulled up most of the floor. And Digger fairly dug up the whole yard. If there'd been anything there, wouldn't someone have found it?"

Margo continued pacing and mumbling. Suddenly, she stood stock still and thrust an index finger upward. "Where your treasure is, there will your heart be also…that's it, that's what old man Ross wrote on the back of that photo."

"Sounds like something from the Bible."

"Makes no difference where it's from, it's got to be the clue we've been missing."

"You think he buried a map with his wife?"

Margo grinned unpleasantly. "That's exactly what I think."

Before he could stop himself, Cleg said, "You mean we're going to dig up that girl's mother?"

Margo made an exasperated noise. "It's just ashes, not a full-on cadaver."

"But surely he wouldn't leave instructions for his girls to dig up…I mean…he wouldn't want his girls digging around…no one would think of—"

"Just listen to you. That's exactly why he *would* bury it there." She strode toward the front door. "Come on, there's work to be done."

Startled by sudden loud knocking on the front door, they swiveled their heads in unison toward the sound.

Cleg looked quizzically at his wife. "Mort forget his key?"

Margo shook her head and motioned for silence.

Another knock, louder. "Mr. and Mrs. Elliott?" The voice sounded young, masculine.

"Who's that at this time of morning?" Cleg whispered.

Margo shook her head. "How do I know? Probably someone looking for a handout." Her upper lip curled into a sneer, and she cracked her knuckles in a way that didn't bode well for the poor sucker at the door. "This won't take long. Go start the pickup."

Cleg took his time moving toward the front door, loathe to miss the coming fireworks, especially since he wasn't the target.

Margo moved to a window, peered out toward the drive then turned her head toward her husband. "Do you know anyone who drives a copper-colored Jeep?"

Cleg shook his head, bewildered.

The young man standing on the porch raised his hand to knock again, but Margo opened the door before he could complete the action. "We don't allow solicitors." She pointed to a dirt-smeared and nearly illegible sign nailed to a cracked wood panel next to the door.

A frown creased the young man's face. He opened his wallet and held it up in front of Margo. "I'm Detective David Ruiz. I'm looking for a young girl and an elderly woman believed to be with her, Jillian Ross? I understand you're her court-appointed temporary guardians."

"Yes?" Margo said.

"May I speak with her, please?"

"What about?"

"Is she here?" The detective's smile grew strained.

"Um, she's not available right now."

"But she *is* here?"

"I, um…"

"We were just going out to look for her," Cleg found himself saying. Margo shot a look at him, and he clapped his mouth shut.

The young man raised his eyebrows, the look on his face just short of a sneer. "I have information that the girl left your house days ago and has not returned. Can you tell me why you didn't report her missing at that time?"

Cleg gulped air in through his nasal cannula and shot a look out of the corner of his eye at The Shrike. He could be wrong, but it seemed the poo was about to hit the fan. And sure as there'd be rain in Seattle, Margo would find a way to pin everything on him. Oh man, his life sucked.

Chapter Thirty-Four

When the detective identified himself, Margo's shoulders dropped. She moved to one side, holding the door open. "You'd better come in."

His nostrils flared, the young man appeared to hesitate an instant then stepped over the threshold. Just inside the door, he stopped and looked around before turning to face Margo and Cleg.

Margo surreptitiously eyed him as his eyes darted around the living room, taking in every detail. Her stomach dropped even further, and her face froze as if suddenly turned to concrete. There had to be some way to spin the mess, some way to keep her in the clear.

She closed the door, moving slowly to allow her frantic mind time to come up with a suitable explanation. How much did this guy know and how much was he just guessing?

Margo led the detective into the living room, Cleg rattling after them. She indicated the sofa. "Please have a seat. Can I get you something to drink? Water? Coffee?"

The detective shook his head. "No thanks." He remained standing. "You say you were just leaving to look for Jillie?"

Cleg's eyes widened and his whining voice climbed up the scale. "We haven't…We didn't actually—"

Margo shot a censorious look at her spouse. Diarrhea of the mouth, that'd always been Cleg's problem. No connection between his brain and his pie-hole.

Her voice cut through his rambling like a scythe through tall grass. "Maybe we made a mistake by not contacting someone earlier." She pasted a contrite look on her face. "But the child has been through so much lately, we just thought she wanted some time to herself."

Detective Ruiz's upper lip curled a bit. "She's only eleven years old."

"Actually, she'll be twelve in a few weeks." At the look that flashed across the detective's face, Margo lifted her hand, palm upward. "But I can see now that we might have been—"

"I'd like to see her room, if I may." When Margo hesitated, he added, "I'm sure you'll want to do anything you can to help find her."

A muscle spasm in Margo's face pulled her mouth into a grimace and set her right eyelid twitching. "Of course. Follow me." She turned and headed up the stairs, the detective close behind.

By the time they got to the top of the stairs, panic had made Margo's breathing so shallow, she was dizzy. If the guy hadn't been so young, she might have tried the life-is-just-so-difficult ploy while batting her eyelashes at him. But something about his demeanor radiated cynicism, like he'd see right through her.

This whole mess was turning sour. And there she was, caught in the headlights with nowhere to run. Margo took a deep breath, steadied herself against the wall and opened the door to Digger's room.

For the next couple of minutes, Detective Ruiz did a thorough search of the room. He looked in the closet, pulled drawers out of the bureau, and pointed to the bed underneath the window where the girl had left it. "Is this the way she got out?"

Margo nodded. "We haven't had a chance to put it back where it belongs, we've just been so worried."

When Ruiz saw the urn on the bureau, he shot a quizzical look at her.

"That's our son Digger's urn. This was his old room."

"And you made that little girl stay here, in the same room with his cremains?"

Margo took a deep breath. "It's the only room that isn't already in use." Even as she said the words, she knew how they sounded. This guy wouldn't buy anything she said after that. And he wouldn't leave a single detail out of his report. She could almost feel the handcuffs snapping around her wrists.

Ruiz made his way through the house and basement then headed back to the living room. He removed a business card from a shirt pocket and placed it on the end table next to the sofa. "If she contacts you, or if an elderly woman comes by looking for her, call me."

As soon as the policeman left, Margo gently closed the door then whirled on her spouse. "Do you think you could have acted more suspicious?"

"What did I do?"

"The only silver lining to all this is that the kid still hasn't turned up." Margo sucked air through her teeth. "Hustle, Tubbo, time's running out and we have work to do."

"But shouldn't we have told the detective what you figured out, Lollipop?"

"What are you blathering on about?" Margo tied her scarf around her neck.

"Shouldn't we have told him you think the girl has been back to get food and stuff? Wouldn't that have made us look less suspicious?"

"What *us*? The only one who looked suspicious was you."

"Maybe we could have told him that we've been leaving food out for her—"

Margo shook her head. "How typically short-sighted of you. If he thought she'd been back, he'd stake out the house. And I don't want him looking over our shoulders."

"Ah." Cleg nodded his head as if he'd suddenly achieved enlightenment.

Margo stepped to the window. She pulled the curtain aside just enough to allow her to watch the detective get into his car, where he sat for several minutes doing who-knew-what.

After Ruiz left, Margo turned toward Cleg. "At first, I thought it might be a good plan to hide out in the kitchen and wait for her to come back. But she's too smart, she'd never just waltz in here without making sure we're gone. And now we're out of time. That cop will report everything he suspects. Next thing we know, the place will be swarming with cops looking for the kid and some old lady. I'm not going to let that treasure slip through my hands, not when I'm so close."

"What do you have in mind, Honey Bits?"

Margo opened the door then turned back toward her spouse. "That kid has managed to completely disappear. Once we find her and get our hands on that treasure, she can stay disappeared. No one'll be the wiser."

"What d'you mean, Lamb Chop?" A series of expressions flowed across Cleg's face, from the despised, empty-headed stare, to thoughtful consideration, and finally open-mouthed shock. "If that kid gets hurt, they'll come after us, sure as the world."

"Not if they never find her."

"If they never…you can't…" As Cleg spoke, his voice raised in pitch, ending in a ten-year-old boy's whine.

"Just listen to you." Margo fought to keep from bashing in the face she'd grown to hate. "At this point we have no choice. Now hustle."

Chapter Thirty-Five

Jillie had watched as the copper-colored vehicle pulled up behind Cleg's pickup, and a man she didn't recognize approached the front door. The man knocked once and was about to knock again when Margo opened the door. He said something then reached into his jacket and held up something for Margo to see.

Although Jillie didn't recognize the newcomer, her stomach twisted into a knot at the sound of his familiar voice. Had Dix and Lil called their policeman nephew after all?

Margo said something then stepped aside and held the door open. Detective Ruiz followed her inside the house. It seemed a long time before he came back out.

As he walked to his car, he swiveled his head and scanned the farm's layout. His gaze landed on the shed, and he turned to Margo who'd followed him onto the porch. "What's the outbuilding used for?"

Jillie's heart skipped a few beats and her mind raced. Frantically, she peered around the shed's small interior for a hiding place.

Her gaze settled on the tool chest. She'd fit, but what about her backpack and Mickey?

"That thing hasn't been used for years," Margo had said. "Cleg used to have a garden, but now it's just rotting away like everything else on this place." She cleared her throat then smiled. "We keep it padlocked.

Of course, we know you'd have to get a warrant to search it, but as you know, we want to help any way we can."

Margo stood in the doorway until David drove away, then spun on her heel, stomped back into the house and closed the door behind her.

Jillie sat on the toolbox. Sooner or later, she'd get caught, that seemed certain. But she had to stay free long enough to take Beth home and put her with Mommy and Pops like she'd promised.

"Beth, please tell me what to do," she whispered.

Her shoulders drooping and head bowed, she swayed back and forth, crying into Mickey's tummy.

Chapter Thirty-Six

David sat in his car mulling over his conversation with the Elliotts. More than the fact that they'd made that little girl sleep in the room with their dead son's ashes, even more than the fact that they hadn't reported her missing, something about the couple had set his antennae vibrating like an off-balance washing machine.

Cleg Elliott hadn't once referred to his wife by her given name, opting for a string of treacly sweet nicknames. But the lovey-dovey mask had slipped once, allowing David a glimpse of undiluted hatred. When the man tried to make a helpful comment, his wife snarled something, effectively shutting him off like a needle valve on a water faucet. A look of fear had flashed across the guy's face, and he'd lapsed into silence, staring into space, his posture near-catatonic.

Margo had managed to squeeze out the requisite tear or two when speaking about *our little Jillie*, but there'd been a glint of pure cold steel in her eyes. And although he'd tried not to stare, David had been mesmerized when the woman's sniffles set a bizarre little flap of skin below one nostril a-jiggling. The look of satisfaction that flashed across her face gave him the distinct impression she'd enjoyed his discomfort.

With all its rotting, scabrous-peeling and odors, the house would have been a grim place for a kid. David had seen worse, but not much.

While he was acquainted with plenty of good folks who'd fallen on rough times, the Elliotts didn't fit into that category. There was a malevolence about Margo. A cruel meanness. Unless David was wrong, a lot worse lay just beneath the surface.

The trouble was, of course, David had been in law enforcement too long. He'd witnessed firsthand the horrors perpetrated by spiteful, control-hungry, greedy people on those unlucky enough to fall into their orbit. As was typical of those law enforcement officers whose days were consumed by dealing with the worst of the worst, he'd grown a thick callus over his finer human emotions. An observer would say those experiences had jaundiced his general view of humanity. And they'd be right.

He often caught himself staring at strangers and wondering if evil lurked behind their benign outer-wrappings, his assessment tinged with adrenaline at the knowledge that just about every adult citizen of New Mexico was armed to the teeth.

After glancing at the house in time to see a face disappear behind a drapery, he pulled his cell from its holder and punched in the number for the dispatch office. "Hey, Betts, it's Ruiz. I'm in Belen, got a missing eleven-year-old girl. I'm going to send you a description and details to post in all the usual places."

Betts said, "That's already been done. Sheriff Sloan from Torrance County called it in earlier."

"When was this?"

"Yesterday, I think. Have you been under a rock?" Betts chuckled. "Or maybe you've been busy with a new girlfriend?"

"So, it wasn't the foster parents who called it in. Has anyone been by to talk to them besides me?"

"Not yet, Sloan's going to see them today. You want his cell?"

"That'd be helpful. Thanks." David clenched his teeth. If he'd checked in, he'd have already known this. That's what he got for taking a couple of days off to go fishing. His only excuses were there'd been no radio at the cabin, and Belen was outside his jurisdiction.

"Are you coming in later?"

"No. My sixty-five-year-old aunt went missing last night. If I don't find her by this evening, I'll contact Missing Persons."

"Is your aunt connected to the missing girl?"

"They met, though I don't have all the details as yet."

"Do we need to send out a Silver Alert?" Betts' voice grew somber.

"No, my aunt's neither handicapped nor mentally disadvantaged. But I'm taking the day to look for her. I'll be in touch."

He broke the connection then punched in his aunt Dix's number. When Aunt Lil didn't pick up, he tried the landline. Again, straight to voicemail.

"Aunt Lil," he said through clenched teeth, "call me when you get this. I'm hoping you're in the shower or haven't put in your hearing aids yet. But if you're thinking of looking for Aunt Dix, please don't. I'll call when I have news."

He jabbed an index finger against the tiny screen, pulled his electronic tablet onto his lap, hurriedly emailed his boss then started his engine and headed toward the old neighbor's house up the road.

If he'd been an eleven-year-old kid, he'd be looking for hot food and a warm bed—just the kind of help a godmother could offer. And if he was lucky, his aunt would have come to the same conclusion.

Chapter Thirty-Seven

After Dix and Lil's nephew drove away, Jillie sat on the toolbox and tried to quiet her racing mind. The policeman had noticed the shed, and that was bad news. It meant she'd have to find someplace else to hide.

She'd been so tempted to holler at him that she'd had to hold her hand over her mouth. Maybe she should have called out to him.

The problem was, she didn't know much about the law. Not only had she run away from the place a judge told her to stay, but she'd been stealing the Elliott's food. Was that enough to get her locked in jail? She shuddered.

Sounds of slamming doors followed by Margo's angry voice pulled Jillie's attention back to the house. She hustled to the shed's door and peered through the crack as Margo stomped out onto the porch.

"She's obviously moving around, so what?" Margo said over her shoulder.

"I still think—" Cleg's voice floated out the door and into the cold air.

"Ye gods and little fishes! What an idiot." Suddenly, Margo whirled on her spouse and punched him in the stomach. "Leave the thinking to me, otherwise you'll strain that pea-sized brain."

Cleg doubled over and coughed a couple of times. By the time he righted himself, Margo had climbed into the pickup's passenger seat, where she stuck her head out the window and shouted, "Get a move on." She honked the horn in several short blasts then held it down until her husband managed to hoist himself into the driver's seat.

Whatever Margo said after that was lost in the roar of the engine. As before, tires spun, and pebbles *tink*ed against metal as if fired from a shotgun. The pickup sped down the dirt drive and onto the road.

Jillie lifted her teddy bear from his resting place on her coat and hugged him to her chest. "I don't know what to do, Mickey. We can't go back to Dix and Lil's, we'd be getting them into trouble. We can't go home without Beth, but we can't stay here."

She gathered her possessions. After struggling to stuff all of it into her backpack, she sat on the tool box, hugged Mickey, and rocked back and forth.

"God, if you would please give Beth a message for me," she whispered into Mickey's tummy. "Please tell her that I'm doing the best I can and that I love her. And please help me find a place to stay. Amen."

Chapter Thirty-Eight

In accordance with Margo's latest command, Cleg ambled into the all-night big-box store and bought the cheapest shovel he could find. By the time he'd paid, hurried across the half block parking lot to the pickup, and put the thing into the back, Margo was nearing the boiling point.

"Where have you been?"

"Sorry, but I had to walk all over the place; then, there was only one checker..." Cleg's voice came in gasps, and he felt light-headed.

"Shut it and drive."

They arrived at the Ross farm a little more than thirty minutes later. Nearly luminescent with excitement, Margo shoved the door open and jumped from the pickup before it had come to a complete stop. "Could you possibly have driven any slower?"

"I did the speed limit, Honey Cakes. I didn't figure we should draw attention—"

"Yeah, yeah." Margo looked at the surrounding area as if expecting to find gold hanging from the trees. "First thing is to make sure the kid isn't around. You check the barn, and I'll search the house. If you spot her, whistle."

"What'll we do if she's here?"

"Why, we'll make her a nice cup of hot tea, what do you think?" Had Margo's voice been a blow torch,

Cleg would have been incinerated. "Time's wasting." She slammed the passenger door and sprinted toward the house.

Cleg compressed his lips, his teeth grinding. How could he have ever been attracted to such a person all those years ago?

Back then, she'd been a tiny, exotic creature with huge eyes—a woman-child. Figuring she'd never give him the time of day, he'd mooned around after her like a starving puppy.

Then when Margo's sister Chlorine announced her own engagement, Margo had thrown herself at Cleg. Unable to believe his luck, he'd fallen instantly and completely in love. In a haze, he couldn't eat, couldn't sleep, and could hardly keep his mind on his work at the hardware store. When she turned up pregnant with Digger, he'd been beside himself with joy. And when Margo proposed marriage, Cleg had said *yes* before she could change her mind.

Margo set their wedding date for two days before her sister's then insisted her own be bigger, better, and costlier. As a result, they started life together heavily in debt.

Like someone said—love is blind, but hate has twenty-twenty vision. Within two months of what he'd expected to be *wedded bliss*, Cleg awakened to the nightmarish reality of life with Margo-The-Shrike.

As time passed, the sisters grew more and more public in their hatred for each other. Their toxic diatribes poisoned the lives of everyone in their vicinity.

When Chlorine's husband had taken all he could stand, he ran off with a local barmaid. After that, although it seemed impossible, Chlorine had become even more vindictive and hateful. By the time Toby was in elementary school, she'd managed to alienate everyone who'd ever known her. No one was exempt. Even the postman hurried past her trailer house.

Of the two sisters, however, Margo had possessed the more hateful disposition. When the slightest bit of frivolity or joy threatened to invade her airspace, she pounced upon the unsuspecting bringer-of-light with an intensity and level of vitriol that often left the victim and any by-standers open-mouthed in disbelief. She could never allow a comment, or its maker, to go unscathed or unchallenged.

No one knew more than she about anything. Ever.

But Chlorine ran a close second in the most-despised category. While she treated the rest of the world badly, she treated her son Toby worse. She all but physically castrated the kid, berating and belittling him endlessly. Cleg had once overheard her threatening to sell him to the first person willing to buy him.

Then Chlorine up and disappeared.

At first, everyone in Belen figured Margo was behind it. But when it was discovered that all her clothes and personal belongings were gone as well, the locals came up with the theory that she must have met someone from out of town, some unsuspecting mook who hadn't been around long enough to know her and had left with him. Some of the locals even placed bets on how long it would take the guy to send her back home. But she didn't come back. And after a few weeks, the whole thing died down.

Cleg had fervently prayed Margo would leave, too. He wasn't surprised, however, when she didn't. She enjoyed making his life miserable too much to move on.

Toby had been a little soldier through the whole ordeal. Although only twelve at the time his mother went missing, he did his grieving in private, maintaining a somber but composed expression in public. Local sympathy ran high for the kid, and donations of clothing and funds for school poured in.

He'd inherited his mother's trailer house and her old, yellow Dodge pickup, complete with a huge, cross-over truck toolbox. Even before he learned to drive, he'd pampered that truck. Sometimes, Cleg would go outside and find the poor kid just sitting on top of the tool chest in the pickup bed, smiling and talking to himself.

Margo had insisted they bring Toby's trailer onto their land for safe keeping. And when Toby turned eighteen, he moved out of the room he shared with Mort and into his trailer.

Of course, when Chlorine disappeared, Margo had acted the part of mourning sister to the hilt. She dressed all in black, adopted a perpetually sad expression, and often lifted a cloth hankie to her nose as if she couldn't stop crying.

But within the walls of their house, Cleg had caught her smiling to herself.

"You done checking the barn?" Margo's flesh-tearing voice suddenly blasted through the open pickup window.

"I was just—"

Margo reached through the window and grabbed a handful of the skimpy hair at the nape of Cleg's neck. "You go ahead and sit there while I do all the work, why don't you?" She pulled and twisted the hair until Cleg whimpered, and his eyes watered. "Good thing for you the kid's not here." She withdrew her hand. "Bring the tools to the tree."

Cleg murmured to himself, "What I don't understand is why Ross left town every so often if he'd buried the stuff somewhere here. That just doesn't—"

The Shrike spun on him, the look on her face striking terror in his stomach. Cleg squeezed his eyes shut and threw his arms up to ward off the blows he knew were coming. But when seconds ticked by and nothing happened, he risked a peek at his spouse.

Margo stood, a pensive look on her face. "Much as I hate to admit it, you might have something there. Although it makes sense he'd want to keep anything of value close by, the only time he had money to spend was after one of his trips." She squinted her eyes and stared into space. "Maybe we shouldn't be looking for a treasure at all; maybe we should be looking for a map."

"Then all that work our Digger did was for nothing?"

"I wouldn't say that. At least we know there's nothing anywhere in the yard or barn. Where's the only place Digger didn't look, the only place he didn't tear into?"

Cleg wracked his brain for the required answer. "Ummm—someplace inside the house?"

"In the walls and under the floor." The Shrike jabbed an index finger against Cleg's forehead. "It'd be someplace easy to get to, someplace no one would think to look, like maybe a floor safe hidden under a rug."

"And a map wouldn't take up much space."

Margo's face broke into a rare smile. "Now we're

getting somewhere. Come on."

During the drive to the Ross farm, Margo shouted instructions, as usual. "You're turning too sharp; you'll hit those bushes. Why are you doing only sixty-five when everyone knows you're allowed five miles over the limit? Pass the truck, Sludge-brain; he's slowing us down."

By the time they turned down the Ross's drive, Cleg's hands and arms ached from gripping the steering wheel. His neck felt like a steel band was tightening around it.

As before, no sooner had Cleg brought the pickup to a stop than Margo jumped from the vehicle, yelling commands over her shoulder.

Cleg climbed out of the pickup. His portable oxygen tank hanging by a strap from his shoulder, he retrieved the shovel and hammer from the pickup bed then turned toward Margo's retreating form.

Suddenly, his stomach shot bitter liquid up his throat. The *slap-slap* of her feet on the ground, unnaturally loud in the still morning air. The claw-like hands dangling at the end of surprisingly strong celery-stalk arms. The head bobbing up and down with every step, as if anchored to her neck by a metal spring. The remembered image of her chewing food—like a camel, her bottom jaw moving in a circular motion instead of up and down like everyone else's. And that hideous flap of skin hanging off her nose he'd repeatedly offered to pay for having removed.

Early morning sunlight glinting off the shovel's blade caught his attention. With its sharp, pointed tip, the thing looked like it could inflict a painful wound. A painful, maybe fatal wound. And the hammer…just one blow from that would do the trick.

Images flooded his mind, fearsome yet seductive in their intensity. He could almost feel the vibration traveling up the shovel handle as the blade connected with skull. Could nearly hear bone crunching.

His stomach fluttered at the thought of being free of the innard-devouring woman who'd consistently and thoroughly beaten him down psychologically, emotionally, and physically.

Surreptitiously, he moved his gaze around the farm. The Ross's closest neighbor was a good mile away. Margo's demand for secrecy was so strong, she certainly hadn't told anyone where they were going. No one knew where they were.

People could just up and disappear. It happened.

During one of their earlier visits to the farm after Digger's death, Cleg had spotted an old, unused septic tank some distance from the house. Though it was partially caved in, there was still plenty of room for a body. Two shovels of quick lime, and *voilà*, within days flesh and bone would have completely dissolved. It would be as if that person had never existed.

Tantalizing images of freedom leapfrogged across the silver screen of his imagination, and he took a deep breath as seeds of mutiny landed on the fertile soil of his mind.

Margo had reached the house and stood peering back at him, her anger radiating like a force field. She jerked her hands up in exasperation, palms up, as if demanding to know what was taking him so long.

Cleg forced his face into a bland expression, gripped the shovel and hammer, and shuffled toward his wife.

Chapter Thirty-Nine

As David pulled into Mrs. Potter's driveway, he scanned the area for either of his aunts' cars. Unsure of whether to be relieved that neither was there or even more alarmed because they weren't, he parked behind a new pickup, walked to the front door, and knocked. When no one answered within several seconds, he knocked again.

Porch boards behind him creaked at the same instant someone spoke. "You need something?"

Taken off-guard, David whirled.

"Whoa, Slick." An impossibly wrinkled, elderly woman no more than four-and-a-half feet tall stood glaring at him like he'd just pissed in her flower bed. "You're trespassing, or are you yet another failed product of our exemplary public education system?" She jerked her head toward the gate. "There's a sign posted."

David started to reach for the credentials in his pocket.

But before he could complete the move, the old woman pulled a shotgun from the folds of her plaid flannel dressing gown. Although she kept the barrel pointed downward, there was no mistaking the move. "Maybe you'd best keep your mitts where I can see them."

David threw his hands up. "Okay, okay, slow

down. You must be Mrs. Potter."

The old woman pursed her lips but remained silent.

"Are you godmother to a little girl named Jillian Ross?"

Mrs. Potter hesitated but held the shotgun steady. "How do you know—"

"Her sister Beth told me." David pointed toward his coat pocket. "I'm Detective David Ruiz. May I get my ID?"

Mrs. Potter nodded, her eyes glittering with suspicion. "You might want to move slow. I'm old, and my trigger-finger might just up and take a notion to twitch."

David pulled out his wallet, opened it, and held it for the woman's inspection.

After several seconds of squinting at the credentials, Mrs. Potter nodded. "Personally, I don't hold anyone's career against them. Hookers, druggies, IRS agents, cops, they're all God's children."

In spite of himself, David smiled. He nodded toward the shotgun. "You mind pointing that somewhere else?"

The arm holding the shotgun relaxed, and the barrel lowered. But just barely. "We've had a slew of home invasions and auto thefts in this area. It pays to be careful."

"Understood."

"What can I do for you?"

"I'm looking into—"

"Stop right there," Mrs. Potter interrupted. "If you're re-opening the investigation into that hateful Digger's death, you can just turn around and go back to wherever you came from. That little girl was only protecting her sister from one of the most miserable excuses of a human being it's ever been my misfortune to run across."

"You're not the first person to say that. No, that's not why I'm here." As David filled Mrs. Potter in on what he'd learned about Jillie's situation and his missing aunts, the woman's facial expression ran from distrust to disbelief to anger.

"You mean Jillie's been on her own all this time?" Mrs. Potter shook her head. "I tried to get custody of her, but I'm not a relative, so that was a no-go. I couldn't just sit and do nothing, so I got certified as a foster parent in case Beth didn't make it. When Jillie turns twelve in a few weeks, she'll have something to say about where she lives. That child belongs with someone who cares about her, not in some stranger's house."

"Can you see the Ross place from here?"

"I can see their lights at night. And the road to their house runs along the west side of my hay field. I can usually tell when they have company, but that's about it."

"Have you seen either a red convertible sports car or a tan coupe this morning or last night?"

"Are those what your aunts drive?"

David nodded.

Mrs. Potter shook her head. "I'd remember a red rag-top, a tan coupe not so much. It's possible one or the other of them drove over there during the night. I sleep like the dead, so I'd never know. Are you thinking Jillie might try to find her way back here?"

"It's possible."

"So your aunts have been out all night looking for

her?"

"One of them has; the other is out looking for her sister."

"Okay." Mrs. Potter nodded her head thoughtfully. "I'll keep my eyes peeled."

"Based on what Beth said, Jillie will stay close by, somewhere between here and Albuquerque. I've checked with a couple of friends from school, but they haven't heard from her." David pulled a business card from his pocket and held it out. "If you hear from Jillie or see either aunt, I'd appreciate it if you'd call my cell."

Mrs. Potter frowned and squinted her eyes, her lower jaw jutting out. "You thinking of putting my Jillie back in that lockup for youthful offenders? A gentle, sweet kid like that, she couldn't handle it again."

"We're both on the same side here, Mrs. Potter. Besides, according to the folks at the hospital, Jillie's sister will be coming home soon."

The old lady accepted the card and stuffed it into a side pocket of her gown.

"If you remember something or think of someplace Jillie might have gone—"

"Got it. I'll call." Mrs. Potter's words said one thing, but her facial expression broadcast something to the effect of: *No way, Slick.*

David opened his mouth to say something, but the old woman interrupted.

"Something else?" She opened her eyes wide, blinked a couple of times, and smiled.

Exasperated, David shook his head and returned to his vehicle.

Surely Mrs. Potter had no reason to lie about

whether or not she'd seen Jillie; she'd been too surprised to hear the girl had run away. But she obviously had something up her sleeve. And now he was faced with the dilemma of either staking out the old woman in hopes she'd lead him to the little girl or getting on with his search for his aunt.

David ground his teeth hard enough to kick-start a headache. Hoping he was making the right decision, he pulled onto the road toward the Ross farm.

Chapter Forty

Jillie sat on the tool chest, her mind jumping from thought to thought. She had to make herself focus, had to figure out someplace to hide out. The feeling in her stomach was that she was running out of time.

She'd need to stay within walking distance of the Elliotts' to search the house every day or so. And she needed to be someplace safe and warm.

She'd never had a problem with cold weather, had always enjoyed it. But this frigid weather was beginning to get to her.

There had to be a place...

She rubbed the crust from her burning eyes as her stomach shoved a bad taste up her throat. Her nose ran, and her fingers and toes felt like cubes of ice. Grit and dust from the burlap bags had sifted into her mouth, coating her teeth and throat.

She took a long draw from her bottle and sloshed the water around her mouth. Then she remembered the sleeping bag she'd spotted while doing the Elliotts' laundry.

Carelessly tossed among the empty jars, piles of plastic shopping bags, smashed boxes, and old magazines that littered the floor, the thing had appeared almost new. If she had to sleep rough for a while, at least she'd sleep warm.

She slipped from the shed and sprinted to the

house. She'd just stooped to climb through the basement window when the hole-in-the-exhaust-pipe roar of a pickup sent panic sizzling up her spine.

Wildly, she flung herself through the window. Her frantic mind moving quicker than her feet, she bumped against the open window before dropping against the ladder then bouncing onto the concrete floor beneath, biting her tongue in the process. The resulting thump and clatter echoed into the still air.

Fighting to keep from crying out, Jillie rolled around on the floor, the taste of blood in her mouth. Then she sat up and rubbed her throbbing shins.

"What was that?" Mort's voice wafted through the open window.

Someone mumbled something unintelligible in response.

"No, it's not my imagination, Tobes, I heard something."

"Sometimes you act like a six-year-old girlie-girl," the person Jillie assumed to be Mort's cousin Toby said, "afraid of everything that moves."

"But what if it's the kid?" Mort said. "What if she came back for revenge?"

"Revenge? What are you talking about?"

"For the way Maggot treated her. You weren't there; you didn't see it. And that kid sure took care of Digger pretty good."

"She couldn't get away from here fast enough. She's not going to hurry back any time soon. Come on, I'm starved."

Frantically, Jillie searched for a place to hide in case the men decided to come to the basement. She hurried to a built-in cabinet against one wall, opened one of its accordion-like doors and stooped to climb into the tiny dark space beneath the counter.

Something small and furry darted out the opening, scampered across her feet, and disappeared into a pile of trash. She clamped a hand over her mouth, but not before she'd let out a small shriek.

Instantly, the door to the basement was flung open.

"Didn't you hear that?" Mort said, his voice coming from the top of the stairs. "I'm telling you, someone's in the house…maybe down in the basement."

Terror clawed up Jillie's throat, and her heart rate shot into the stratosphere, making her feel like she might pass out.

"Yeah?" Toby said. "Then why don't you go down into that dark hole and check it out? Be warned, I think a bobcat's made a nest down there."

Mort said something Jillie couldn't hear.

"I thought so," Toby said. "Come on, we've got things to do."

After one of the men slammed the basement door closed, Jillie's knees gave way. She sat on the floor and took a deep breath.

A couple of minutes later, pickup doors slammed, an engine fired, and tires spun in the gravel.

Jillie hurried to the corner where she'd spotted the sleeping bag. Tightly rolled up and wrapped in a protective cover, the thing looked inviting. She hefted the bag by its nylon handle, shoved it through the window and then climbed through after it.

Once back inside the shed, she gathered her belongings. She kissed Mickey, stuffed him into her backpack, slung the sleeping bag over one shoulder, and headed for the door.

But again, the crunch of tires on gravel made her freeze mid-step. Vehicle doors creaked open then slammed shut. The cousins' voices neared the shed.

"Why'd you turn around?" Mort's voice sounded high and tight. "I thought we were going to find some women and party."

"No choice," Toby said. "It has to be done sooner rather than later."

"But why the wild hair to move it now, after all this time?"

"Because that was your sweet mama on the phone. She said a policeman came out earlier asking questions about the kid and some old woman who's missing."

"So?" Mort said.

"Sometimes you remind me so much of your old man it's not funny. Think about it, if the police don't find the kid, they'll be back. And they'll leave no stone unturned. I don't know about you, but I have plans that don't involve doing hard time. And lest you forget, you'll be right there with me."

"Where are you going to put it?" Mort's voice sounded resigned.

"I'm going to rent a storage shed as soon as the place opens this morning." Toby laughed, an ugly sound. "Don't worry, cuz, if someone finds out, it'll be because you can't stop flapping your gums to impress the girls."

Mort mumbled something.

Toby laughed. "Come on. The sooner we deal with this, the sooner we can grab something to eat. Hurry up, before your gene pool gets back."

After several nano-seconds of heart-stopping

indecision, Jillie laid her backpack and the sleeping bag on the floor in a corner then slung a couple of burlap bags over them. She dropped to the floor in the opposite corner and pulled one of the bags over her head. A cloud of dust flew in her eyes and up her nose. She pinched her nostrils closed to keep from sneezing, breathed through her mouth, drew herself into a ball. With any luck, she'd look like another bag of mulch.

"This place is creeeeepy." Mort's voice coming from just outside the door sounded high-pitched.

Toby laughed. "Afraid of ghosts?" He made a *whooo* sound.

"Very funny. I'll wait for you out here."

"What's this?" Toby's voice drew closer as he poked his head through the gaping door and into the shed. "You been spending time here on your own?"

"You're kidding, right?" Mort's voice sounded like his throat was about to slam shut.

The door *shushed* across the dirt-covered floor as someone pushed against it.

"Well, well," Toby said under his breath. "What have we here?"

"What'd you say?" Mort said from outside the shed.

"Just talking to myself," Toby said. "Give me a minute."

"Sure, take all the time you want," Mort muttered.

"Ho, ho, I spy with my little eye…" Toby sang the child's rhyme softly, his voice hanging overlong on the *s* to sound like a snake hissing. "Peek-a-boo, I see you."

Jillie bit her tongue to keep from screaming as the sound of approaching footsteps moved across the shed and stopped in front of her.

Chapter Forty-One

Cussing himself for a fool, Cleg pulled up another floorboard. He'd had the perfect chance to rid himself of The Shrike but had been too weak to carry through, just another lost opportunity in a lifetime filled with lost opportunities.

Like a woman possessed, Margo ran through the house, pointing here and there, ordering him to dig under any floorboard that seemed remotely loose. When Cleg made the mistake of commenting that it seemed to him old man Ross would have hidden the map someplace easy to get to, she'd threatened him with the hammer. Lucky for Cleg the house was old enough to have wood floors, or she'd have had him hammering through a concrete slab. Margo had even insisted he pull all the electrical sockets from the walls after announcing she'd seen a false socket hidey-hole advertised on television. But effort after effort came up empty.

The worst part was working through lunch. Other than begrudgingly allowing him a few sips of water, The Shrike hadn't let him take a break. He'd nearly passed out from the exertion.

Then Margo spotted something shiny in one of the holes in the floor. She'd yelped that maybe it had been an actual treasure all along instead of a map, and dropped to her knees, her hands shooting like pistons in and out of the hole.

When the shiny thing turned out to be an old nail, she'd cursed the air a brilliant blue and called Cleg every name she could think of. But for an instant, the back of her bowed head had been right in front of him, within shovel's reach.

It was like the heavens opened, clouds parted, angels sang, and a shaft of sunlight lit up the room. Just one good chop, and all his worries would be over.

But he'd vapor-locked at the crucial instant.

The Shrike stood and looked at him as if she knew what he'd been thinking. Her upper lip curled in disgust, and she yanked the shovel from his hands. "Useless. Bring me the thermos of coffee. It's freezing in here."

Like early morning dew in the hot desert sun, every tiny droplet of hope evaporated. He'd blown his chance, now he'd slog through who-knew-how-many-more-years before dying a miserable, unhappy lump of failure.

Tears of frustration and self-pity clouded Cleg's vision as he walked to the pickup. He stopped every few steps to rest, his wheezing breaths grating in his ears. How he hated the sound of his physical weakness.

He'd been a strong young man—strong as an ox. Able to take any of the locals in arm wrestling. Able to work hard all day and never break a sweat.

But then he'd made the mistake of angering Margo-The-Shrike while she held a can of silver metallic spray paint. He didn't even remember what he'd said wrong, but she pointed the can at him like a gun and emptied it into his face. Before he had time to react, he'd breathed in enough of the paint and toxic fumes to result in permanent lung damage and the need for oxygen twenty-four seven.

Without a word of apology, she shrugged and said, "Look for a silver lining, isn't that what you always say?" She'd laughed. "Silver lining, get it? Now you'll qualify for total disability. It'll be nice to finally have a reliable income."

Cleg retrieved the coffee canister from the pickup. His shoulders drooping, eyes downcast, and feet shuffling, he started back to the house.

Chapter Forty-Two

Jillie could almost feel Toby staring down at her through the burlap bag, as if he had x-ray vision. She held her breath, every muscle taut as she fought to keep from throwing off the sack and running from the shed. Toby's sudden chuckle made the hairs on her arm move.

"Hey, Cuz," Toby's voice sounded as if he stood directly over Jillie. "Do me a favor and back your truck up as close as you can to the shed door."

Keys jingled then abruptly stopped as if thrown through the air then caught.

"My truck? Why not yours?"

"Low gas. Just do it."

Mort's response was cut short by the ringing of a cell phone. For a nanosecond, neither of the men moved. Then Mort whispered, "I gotta take this, it's Maggot."

"Of course you do." Toby's voice was filled with disdain.

"Yeah?" Mort's words were followed by several seconds of silence. "I'm pretty busy right now, can it wait?" This was followed by a longer silence. "Okay, okay. I'll be there in a few."

"So? What does she want?" Toby said.

"I gotta go. She's got a bee in her bonnet about something or other. You got a sledgehammer in your truck?"

"Yeah, on the floor behind the front seat. Why?"

"I need to borrow it."

"What for?"

"Who knows." Mort's mumbled response was followed by the sound of retreating footsteps.

Toby moved around the shed, jiggling implements and rustling bags while emitting an occasional chuckle. "Hmmm, seems Uncle Clot's 'toe sacks have heaped themselves into a pile. And my old sleeping bag has not only transported itself from the basement but has brought along a backpack for company." He yanked the bag off Jillie's head, pulling several hairs out by the roots in the process. "You must be the kid everyone's looking for. I figured you'd be in Timbuktu by now. What're you doing hanging around here?"

Jillie opened her eyes and stared down at the boots planted in front of her. "I'm not leaving without my sister's ashes."

"You think Maggot and Clot are going to have your sister cremated and then bring her ashes back here?" Toby chuckled. "I guess anything's possible, Maggot being Maggot." He snapped his fingers in front of her face, nearly touching her cheek. "Hey, I'm talking to you."

Jillie jerked her head back, painfully banging it against the shed's wall. As she rubbed her head, her gaze traveled up Toby's unusually small hands and long arms. Then her breath caught in her throat as she stared into the face of the man she'd seen entering the trailer behind her—the trailer where the radio said that horrible old man had been murdered.

"Have we met before?" Toby said. "Seems I've

seen you somewhere…."

Jillie lowered her gaze, a sudden buzzing in her head. "No, not that I know of."

Don't let on you know. If he killed one person, he'd kill another.

"I gotta hand it to you, kid, you've led everyone on a wild goose chase. And you had old lady Maggot chewing her nails out of fear you'd go to the police." He bent over so his mouth was only a few inches from Jillie's ear. "But I won't tell her about your hidey-hole if you take me to your dearly departed daddy's treasure." He straightened and smiled. "And don't try that *it doesn't exist* line with me. After Digger married your sister, I did some research, more out of curiosity than anything. Turns out there are several stories from the eighteen-hundreds about treasure hidden here in New Mexico. I figured those stories were pure fiction, but I'm re-thinking that. There's a couple of reputable sources claiming that over sixty-million dollars in gold bars is buried somewhere around the Manzano Mountains, just up the road from your place. I figure your old man found it." Toby picked at a fingernail absently. "Pretty smart of him to squeeze it out bit by bit rather than spend it all out at once. But I'm not greedy, just a couple of bars should do it."

As if her brain was stuck in an unending loop, Jillie repeated the only words it sent to her mouth, "I won't leave without—"

"Your sister's ashes, I know. Here's a proposition, you just tell me where he hid the goods then you can wait here as long as you like." A sly smile crept across Toby's face. "Although you might be here a while."

Jillie shook her head. "But I don't know—"

Toby held up his hand in a shushing motion. "Don't tick me off. You have no idea who you're dealing with." He sucked air in through his teeth and jerked his head up at the sound of approaching footsteps. His eyes riveted on Jillie's, he whispered, "Don't move." He pulled the bag back over her head.

"Who're you talking to, Tobes?" Mort's voice grew louder as he stood in the door. "You're freaking me out. You haven't been chatting with her again—"

Toby interrupted, "You're hearing things."

"Heads up," Mort said. "Looks like I'll be busy for most of the day, so I'll take my truck."

"Text me when you're done. We have to get this done by tonight."

As Mort's footfalls grew faint, Toby pulled the bag off Jillie's head. He pointed his index finger at her like a gun. "Stay right there. I'll be back soon as I take care of some business." He pulled the lock from its place on the door jamb and hooked it through the u-bolt. "We can't have you running off before we finish our chat, now can we?"

The sounds of squealing hinges and the metallic sounds of a lock being forced into position echoed through the shed.

As the engine noise of both pickups faded into the distance, Jillie ran to the door and pulled at the knob with all her strength. But even though the wood looked rotten, it was still strong enough to hold firm.

Panic roiling in her stomach, her eyes fell on the metal tools. The shovel would have been her first choice if the handle hadn't been broken off. But maybe she could use the hoe to dig a hole under the door frame, then use the shovel handle as a lever. Her science teacher once said with a fulcrum and a long enough lever, she could move the earth. And all Jillie needed to do was force the door open enough to get through. She grabbed the hoe and hurried to the door.

Her internal clock anxiously ticking the minutes away, she brought the hoe down onto the floor just in front of the door's frame. But the sound of metal striking metal, accompanied by an arm-numbing jolt, meant the floor wasn't made of dirt as she'd assumed. She threw the hoe onto the floor and bit her lip to keep from crying out in frustration.

The toolbox again caught her attention. Its hinges appeared to be rusted into globs, so it most likely would squeal like a dying animal when she tried to open it. But she was running out of options.

She dragged the surprisingly light box a few inches from the wall and bent to study the lock dangling from the lid. Fully expecting to have to spend precious minutes banging away at the thing with the shovel blade, she nearly exclaimed out loud to find it unlocked.

Please, God, let there be a tire tool or jack in there.

Mentally crossing her fingers, she opened the lid. The surprisingly well-oiled hinges opened without a sound.

But hope evaporated at the sight of what appeared to be the most realistic-looking Halloween skeleton she'd ever seen. Gaping eye sockets stared out from an amber-colored skull, the left side of which had been crushed. Tufts of straggly, dark hair rested on a small stained pillow; arm and leg bones nestled on top of faded fabric that had been neatly folded alongside the torso.

You haven't been chatting with her again…

Jillie dropped the lid as if it were red hot. The resulting clang still echoing in the small space, she ran to the farthest corner, squatted on her haunches, and began rocking back and forth.

She'd been eating on top of a dead person…had read Beth's book, drawn pictures of wild flowers, and sipped water while sitting on a dead person.

Jillie's stomach heaved, and something sour shot up her throat. Panic took control, and she ran to the door where she feverishly pounded against the splintery wood until the muscles in her arms cramped. Then she dropped to her knees and clawed at the floor, ignoring the pain radiating up her arms from torn fingernails. Finally, exhausted, she slumped against the door and sobbed until she could sob no more.

She was still there some time later when tires again crunched on gravel. The tiny hairs at the back of her neck moved, and her breath caught in her throat. A vehicle's door creaked open and then slammed. After an interval of several minutes, footfalls approached the shed.

Without thinking, Jillie snatched up the shovel handle. She took a position in front of the door, her legs slightly bent at the knees and weight balanced on the balls of both feet as she'd seen a martial arts professional do on television. Gripping the pole in both hands as if it were a sword, she aimed its broken, pointed end at the door and waited.

Chapter Forty-Three

With Margo's command to *get his ass to the Ross farm* ringing in his ears, Mort drove well under the speed limit. He'd probably pay for that bit of rebellion, but at that point he just didn't give a rip. Once he got his hands on the treasure, he'd take off and never look back.

He pulled into the Ross drive and parked behind Cleg's pickup. Leisurely, he turned off his engine, exited his truck, and sauntered toward his parents.

Cleg stood leaning against the side of the house, a shovel and hammer on the ground at his feet. With one arm against the wall at shoulder level, his head bowed and his face a rich magenta color, he gasped and wheezed. "I got to sit down."

Maggot stood facing her husband, her arms slashing through the air like the blades of a high-powered fan. Her voice loud enough to travel through steel plating, she jutted her face into Cleg's and shouted, "Worthless. It's not even ten yet, and you've already conked out."

"Yo." Mort stepped onto the porch. "I'm here. What's so important?"

Maggot whipped her head toward him. "You bring a sledgehammer?"

"Yeah."

"Bring it into the house." She sneered and jerked

her head toward Cleg. "Worthless there can't swing a hammer worth a flip, let alone a sledgehammer."

Mort sucked air in through his teeth then said, "What're we—"

"Just do as you're told." Maggot strode toward the back door. "Move it," she hollered over her shoulder.

Cleg turned toward his son. "You'd best do as she says." He plopped onto the steps, taking in deep, sucking breaths of oxygen through his nasal cannula. "You know how she can get."

Mort shook his head. "You should have left her years ago, when you had the chance. What are you still doing here?"

"I don't—"

Mort held up his hand. "You don't have to explain. I decided a long time ago you must enjoy getting beaten up."

Cleg flinched as if he'd been struck. "Is that what you think? You think I like getting hit, kicked, and bitten? Nobody likes that, at least, no sane person." Cleg coughed then got a thoughtful look on his face. "Fear, I guess. I've just been afraid to leave."

"So, you're a wuss." Mort shook his head. "Wow, what a role model."

"Mort." Maggot's voice could have pulverized boulders. "Get in here."

"Coming," Mort shouted. He looked at Cleg, his upper lip curling.

People said he was like his old man, but he wasn't. He'd never let anyone treat him the way Maggot treated his dad. He couldn't wait to put as much distance as possible between himself and the witch who'd birthed him. And nothing or nobody was going to get in his way.

He returned to his truck and hefted the sledgehammer from the passenger side floor, then headed back toward the house.

Maggot stood just inside the doorway tapping her foot. "You took your time."

"I'm here now."

Moving her arm in a sweeping arc, Maggot said, "We've got a whole house to work our way through, and I don't care if we tear the place to the ground, we're going to find that map."

"You figured out where it's hidden?"

"I just put my mind to it, that's all." Maggot looked into Mort's eyes. "Same as anyone else could do, if he had half a brain."

As if time suddenly leapt backward, Mort was a kid of twelve again. In crystal clear detail, he felt the churning in his gut as Chlorine yelled at Toby and him, calling them names, threatening to hurt them, threatening to make them wear diapers because they were such babies. He relived the fear he'd felt as the rage-filled, red-faced, screaming monster bore down on them, a wooden slat gripped threateningly in her hands.

He remembered the hammer laying on the ground, and Toby, with a blank look on his face, casually picking it up. And he remembered the sudden silence that followed.

Maybe he was more like his old man than he wanted to admit. Maybe Maggot was right when she said he was a gutless, spineless wonder. Why else would he have just bowed his head and accepted all the hateful words the screeching woman threw at him over the years?

Like a light at the end of a long dark tunnel, the promise of escape drew his thoughts. He took a deep breath.

Escape and payback—two for one. What better way to get revenge than to let the Hated Ones do the work of finding the map, then taking it for himself.

Mort gripped the sledgehammer and followed his mother into the house.

Chapter Forty-Four

By the time Dix pulled into the Elliotts' driveway, the sun was just coming up. Her earlier caffeine jolt had long since worn off. Her eyes burned, and acid reflux ate at the lining of her esophagus.

She turned off the engine and studied the house. Although lights shone through the windows on the bottom floor, the early hour meant she'd most likely not receive a warm welcome and offer of coffee and scones. At the thought of what might become a heated exchange, she sucked a deep breath in through her nose then blew it out through puckered lips.

What excuse could she offer for being there? Since the Elliotts had elected to keep quiet about Jillie's running away, they most likely wouldn't look kindly on her interference. And the fact that the child had shown true terror when speaking of the dark, soulless woman named Margo meant Dix would have to tread softly.

With few exceptions, she'd never been much use in a confrontation. Had, in fact, always tried to steer clear of it. But like a hologram, images of Jillie's blistered heels and torn fingernails shimmered onto Dix's memory-screen.

She interrupted the loop of internal monologue that mocked her pseudo-bravado, exited the car and approached the house. Shoving aside unwelcome images of her body plummeting through the porch's screeching, groaning planks, she stepped to the front door.

Remnants of the shattered, brown plastic doorbell switch too small for Dix's finger to press, she knocked. As she did so, hinges squealed, and the door swung open a couple of inches.

She opened the door farther and poked her head through. "Helloooo, anyone home?"

Silence.

"Hello?"

Lights on, door ajar, no one home. The tiny hairs on Dix's forearms moved as if she'd fallen into a bed of fire ants. Regretting for the umpteenth time her decision not to use the all-night gas station's phone to call either Lil or Davie, she started back to her car.

She scanned the decrepit place Jillie had so aptly described. Her eyes slid past a small gardening shed then were pulled back. Without making the conscious decision to do so, she walked to the outbuilding and tugged at the lock.

Something shuffled just inside the door.

Dix heard herself croak, "Is someone there?"

She jiggled the doorknob and nearly jumped out of her skin when a tiny voice said, "Is that you, Miss Dixie?"

"Jillie?"

"Please, can you get me out?" The plea was followed by a deluge of words tumbling over each other in a chaotic stream, consistent only in their terror and something about a dead man in a trailer and bones in a toolbox.

Rage flamed from the soles of Dix's feet and blazed its way like an erupting volcano up her body.

"Did those horrible people lock you in here?"

"Please hurry, I don't know when they'll be back."

Dix cast her eyes on the ground around the shed in search of something to use as a tool. "I don't see anything—"

"Here," Jillie said. "Try this."

A long, wooden bar reminiscent of a broom handle shot through a crack in the boarded-up window and landed at Dix's feet. She picked it up, stepped to the door, and searched for an opening large enough to gain purchase.

"Get ready to squeeze through," Dix said. "I'm not sure how long I can hold it."

She jammed the end of the pole into a warped spot between the door and its frame. After several tries, she managed to work it deep enough to bring pressure to bear. With her full weight behind it, she pushed. Her confidence rising with the squeal of tortured wood, she redoubled her efforts. Suddenly, the termite-ridden door jamb pulled away from the surrounding wall, the door still held firmly in place by the U-lock.

Jillie ran out the opening and into Dix's waiting arms. "We have to call the police."

"You bet your boots we do," Dix said. "But first, you and I are going to the hospital to see your sister."

Jillie's head jerked up, and she studied Dix's face. "What?"

"Those people lied to you. Beth's awake and getting stronger every day."

"Beth's alive? She didn't get burned up?" As if an unimaginable weight had dropped from her shoulders, Jillie swayed; she leaned against the shed for support. "I knew Margo was lying." She wiped tears from her cheeks as a smile lit up her face. "Can we go see Beth?"

Dix nodded. "Absolutely."

Jillie took a step toward Dix then stopped, as if something had occurred to her. "Just a minute." She hurried back into the shed. When she returned, she was wearing her backpack. "You have your phone? We have to call the police, we have to tell them—"

"Tell them what?" Spoken from only a few inches behind Dix, the sudden sound of a young male voice sent her heart rate into the stratosphere.

Dix whipped her head around toward the speaker as the child whimpered and pressed against her.

Between her excitement at finding Jillie and the noise she'd made while forcing the shed door open, she'd obviously not noticed the sound of a returning vehicle. Not her brightest moment.

"Who are you?" The young man cocked his head toward Dix.

"I'm a friend of Jillie's, and I'm taking her to see her sister."

"So, you're the old lady the police are looking for."

"The police?" Had Lil been so angry she'd called Davie, and then had Davie reported her?

"It was your nephew," Jillie said. "He came here looking for you."

The tension in Dix's neck relaxed a bit. "We'll call him from the hospital." She put an arm around Jillie's shoulders and started toward her car.

"Oh, I think not." The young man stepped in front of Dix.

"Get out of my way. This child has been through enough."

"Well, *this child* and I have some unfinished

business to attend to."

Dix gave Jillie's shoulder a nudge. "Run," she whispered as she moved to stand between the two.

A pistol suddenly appeared in the young man's hand, and he pointed it at Dix's midsection. "Go ahead, Kid, run. But then whatever happens to your granny friend will be on you."

Jillie cried, "Stop it, Toby, leave her be."

"I have an idea." Toby waved the pistol at Dix, motioning for her to walk in front of him. "Let's take a little road trip. Granny will drive. The more the merrier; many hands make light work, as they say."

"We're not going anywhere with you." Dix lifted her chin. If she could just get a bit closer… It'd been three decades since she'd taken a self-defense course, but surely, she could still…

"Oooo-ho, she's getting ready to make a move. I'm quaking in my boots." Toby smiled, a rictus that sent chills up Dix's spine. "Who do you think you are, Granny Bonecrusher?"

Jillie cleared her throat. "There's a problem with your plan."

Toby cocked his head. "Really? And what do you know about my plan?"

Jillie took a step toward Toby. "It's just some things you don't know, things I heard the Elliotts talking about."

"Oh?" Toby's eyes were riveted on Jillie, but the gun never wavered from Dix's midsection. "Then why don't you clue me in."

As the two talked, Dix began inching toward Toby. With her eyes riveted on him, she failed to sidestep a small twig. The subsequent *crack*, though tiny, was loud enough to attract the young man's attention.

Growling, he whipped his head around toward her. "Stop, I'm dead serious." Toby shifted the pistol until it was aimed at Jillie's head. "How much are you willing to risk?"

Dix held both hands up. "Okay, okay. Just don't hurt her."

Toby smirked. "I don't want to, I really don't. But I will if you make me." He jerked the pistol, motioning Dix and Jillie toward the pickup. "Let's go. Old Yeller's gassed up and ready to go."

Sleep-deprivation, hours of adrenaline-suffused hyper-vigilance, and just plain rage flowed through Dix. With a battle cry that pulsed upward from the soles of her feet, she lunged at Toby and chopped down with the side of her hand, aiming at his wrist.

But the same conditions that had made her fearless, had made her slow. Toby pivoted then brought the pistol down in an arc that ended against Dix's temple.

Her vision went gray. She took a stumbling step forward and fell to her knees.

Jillie screamed her name, then everything went black.

Chapter Forty-Five

When Dix regained consciousness, it was to a raging headache. Disoriented at first, she struggled to sit up while her eyes slowly focused.

"Miss Dixie?" Jillie's voice sounded muffled, as if she'd been crying.

"I'm here." Dix tried to smile as she reached for the child's hand.

"Well now," Toby drawled. "A mere flesh wound, as they say. Let that be a lesson."

"You know this isn't going to end well for you, right?" Dix looked up at the young man holding a pistol in her face.

"I know nothing of the kind," Toby said. "I do know, however, that by the time you have a chance to go whining to the police, I'll be long gone."

Dix bit back a retort. She grimaced and raised her hand to the side of her head, her sweat-salty fingertips lighting fire as they came into contact with broken skin atop a growing lump. She studied her fingers, grateful that there was very little blood.

Okay, then, just a minor concussion. Ringing in her ears, but no severe nausea and no serious mental confusion. Hopefully, no lasting damage.

"Did-ums granny fall down go boom, get a booboo?" Toby taunted.

"Stop being mean," Jillie said. "She's hurt."

He whirled toward Jillie. "Oh, she'll be a lot more than just hurt if you don't cough up your old man's stash."

Jillie started to say something, but clamped her mouth shut at the warning look Dix shot her.

Toby bent at the waist to bring his eyes close to Dix's. "I'm doing you a favor, you know."

Taken aback, Dix squinted up at him.

"You're on a fixed income, right? Think about it, while I'm poolside in someplace known only to God and Marco Polo, you'll be negotiating with a major publisher for your story. *My Twenty-Four Hours in Hell* has a nice ring to it, don't you think?" He held up his hand, palm out. "No need to thank me, just a mention in your acknowledgements will do. That's Dinkins, with an *i*. Of course, within a week that'll no longer be my name, so knock yourself out."

"What now?" Dix said.

"As I said, we're going on an outing." Toby jerked the barrel of the pistol upward, motioning for Dix to stand. "I hate to add insult to injury, but you'll have to drive." He pointed the gun at Jillie.

"I won't do anything unless you move that gun away from her. Point it at me, if that makes you feel better."

"You're telling me what to do, you interfering old witch?"

"That'd not be real smart, since you're the one with the pistol. No, I'm just passing along some information, that's all. If you keep holding that gun on her with your finger on the trigger, you risk a sympathetic jerk, and that would put an end to your plans."

"A what?"

"A sympathetic jerk as a result of muscle memory. I'm assuming you've actually spent time practicing with that thing?" Dix struggled to keep her voice calm.

"What if I have?"

"Then your muscles will eventually do what they've done every time you've practiced, but they'll do it on their own. Muscle memory."

Toby frowned but shifted the pistol barrel toward Dix. "Better?"

Right then, Dix would have been thrilled to see Lil. But her sister had been so angry when she left to find Jillie, she'd probably packed all Dix's stuff and thrown it into the street.

Dix took a deep breath and, with Jillie's help, got to her feet. For several seconds, she remained motionless to regain her balance. With what she hoped to be a calming smile at the child, she shuffled toward the pickup.

Whistling a happy tune from a children's animated movie, Toby fell into line behind them.

Chapter Forty-Six

As Lil turned into the dirt, circular drive that lead to the Elliott house, the beams from her headlights moved across the yard, highlighting dead trees, weeds, and peeling paint. She followed the light's path as it reflected off the house's front windows then came to rest on the windshield of Dix's red sportster.

Fighting to keep from hyperventilating, she pulled up behind her sister's car, jammed the gearshift into park and jumped from the still-shuddering vehicle. She strode to Dix's car and laid the palm of her right hand on the hood.

How long would it take an engine to cool completely? An hour? Two?

The image of her twin's body either slumped against the steering wheel or crumpled onto the seat peeled away a layer of Lil's anger as she hurried around to the driver's side. She tightened her lips and opened the door.

The bright overhead light came on as the car's key-in-the-ignition warning bell chimed. Dix's purse and empty cell phone lanyard lay on the passenger seat. A huge, empty Styrofoam coffee cup sat in the built-in drink holder.

Feeling as if a maniac had begun knitting her insides, Lil sucked in a deep breath through her nose then blew it out through her mouth. Dix's car had been broken into a couple of years earlier, and she'd never again left her purse, or anything else, inside a car—especially an unlocked car.

She squinted at the house. An unpleasant tingle crept up her spine at the sight of the slightly ajar front door and the lighted entryway.

Gripping the handle of her Taser in one hand, she lightly caressed the pepper spray's trigger mechanism with her other and headed toward the house.

The rickety porch squealed like a pinched nerve, making the hair on her neck dance. Fighting down her gag reflex at the miasma of odor oozing through the door, she stepped over the threshold and into the house.

A phrase she'd once read sprang to mind: *Abandon hope all who enter here.*

"Hello?" she said into the stillness.

Fearful of what she might find, Lil cautiously moved from room to room. The smell. The urn. The lock on the pantry door. She hated to admit it, but everything was turning out just as the kid had said.

Once satisfied that no one was around, she hurried back outside and strode to her car. Along the way, she shot one last look around the yard at the shadowy shapes now highlighted by early dawn sunlight.

The tin, corrugated roof of a dilapidated shed, unnoticed in early morning darkness, caught her attention. She strode to the out building, noting the shattered door jamb.

Small footprints near the front of the door mingled with two sets of larger prints. The small prints looked like they could have been made by a child's tennis shoes. Of the larger prints, some were in the pattern of Dix's favorite cork-soled footwear, and some appeared to have been made by a man's boots.

Lil murmured, "Not good, sis."

She stuck her head through the shed door and waited for her eyes to grow accustomed to the dark interior. Tools and gardening supplies—no surprise there. But there must have been dozens of the same small footprints on the dirt-covered floor inside the shed she'd seen outside. Though there were none of Dix's footprints inside the shed, there were several boot prints—some of which were on top of the kid's.

"Kid?" Lil stepped around a pile of bags and into the shed beyond.

Her glance fell on a rusted-out tool box, the lid of which sat canted at an angle atop a burlap bag hanging half inside and half out. At four or five feet long, the thing was more than big enough to hide a kid's body. Or Dix's.

Barely able to control her shaking hands, Lil opened the lid. She gasped, and her knees nearly gave way at the same time her brain refused to believe what she was seeing.

Two gaping eye sockets stared up at her from a crushed skull. Large bones nestled in folds of faded and stained fabric carefully placed along each side of the rib cage. No flesh, and no odor of putrefaction meant old, desiccated bones.

*Oh, the head bone's connected to the (pause) neck bone; The neck bone's connected to the (pause) shoulder bone…*The words and melody of the old song tumbled unbidden through Lil's head as she fought back an unexpected giggle.

Get a grip, Lil. You lose it, and you're no use to anyone.

She dropped the lid, hustled back to her car, and pulled Dix's cell phone from her scabbard. Once in the driver's seat, she punched in her nephew's number. Accompanied by periodic bursts of static that sounded like someone trying to straighten a wad of cellophane, the call went straight to voice mail.

"Davie, I'm at the Elliott place. I'll apologize later, but I've got a feeling something bad is going down. Dix's car is here, but she's not." Lil's voice broke, and she cleared her throat. "The place is deserted, but there's a shed and a toolbox with a skeleton in it. I think it's real, doesn't look plastic. Anyway, I think someone was held captive in the shed, maybe the kid, judging by the small footprints." Fearing that the phone was nearly out of juice, she hurriedly added, "I'm headed to the Ross farm. GPS says it's in the sticks, so I may not have a signal. Just wanted you to know."

Lil ended the call and glanced at the tiny battery icon. Just as she'd suspected, the thing was completely dead. She could only hope at least some of her message had gotten through.

Riving the air with every four-letter word in her repertoire, Lil tossed the useless phone onto the passenger-side floorboard. With what Davie had long ago dubbed her "twin-ESP-thing" shooting canon ball-sized lumps into the pit of her stomach, she cranked up her engine, floored the pedal, and shot down the drive.

I warned you that kid was trouble.

Chapter Forty-Seven

Dix gripped the pickup's steering wheel so tightly the muscles of her arms spasmed. Jillie sat next to her, unmoving and silent, while Toby sat in the back seat holding the pistol against Dix's neck.

"You know the penalty for kidnapping, right?" Dix grimaced. Her voice sounded like it could barely squeeze past the invisible clamp tightening around her throat.

Toby didn't respond.

Emboldened by the silence, Dix added, "You can still back out; it's not too late."

Toby shot forward in his seat and brought his mouth close to Dix's ear. "Shut up. You hear me?"

Dix swallowed hard and nodded.

Toby said, "I hate club cabs. But when my old lady bought this, they'd just come out, so she had to have one. Knees up around my ears, scrunched up in a wad. I'm not happy right now, so you might want to keep your yap shut and just drive."

"Leave her alone, Toby."

"I want to, I really do. But life dumps on all of us, it's just plain reality. And your reality is that your granny friend is going to get hurt if you don't do what I tell you. Now shut your mouth, or I'll shut it for you." Toby turned to Dix. "Exit at the sign and bear right."

By the time Dix pulled the pickup onto the Ross

property, she'd considered then discarded several ideas for escape. If she'd been alone, she might have made an attempt, but any risk to the child was unacceptable.

"Pull around the back," Toby said. "A little privacy is in order."

Dix did as commanded.

"What the hell…?" Toby shot forward in his seat.

Two pickups, one rusty brown and the other sun-faded red, sat parked near the back porch. A woman and two men stood between the vehicles, deep in conversation. All three heads jerked toward the newcomers; then, the woman broke away from the group and strode toward them.

"Say anything, and the kid gets it. Clear?" Toby hissed in Dix's ear. The hand holding the pistol was withdrawn and the back window powered down.

"Hey, Aunt Margo, what's up? Didn't know there was a party going on."

Unspeaking, the woman stomped around the pickup to the passenger side and yanked open the door. Her hand shot out, grabbed Jillie's wrist, and gave it a painful twist. "So glad to see you've finally decided to come home." Her voice sounded more like a hissing snake than a human. As if she suddenly realized there were others present, she dropped Jillie's arm, stooped, and smiled through the open window. "Toby, dearest," she said. "What are you doing here?"

"I found the kid and grandma snooping around your place. The kid set up a whine to come home, and grandma suggested it would be therapeutic. What about you?"

"The place needs some cleaning up. We figured today's as good a day as any." Margo glared at Jillie and her lips twitched. "You've made the police take an interest in us, and that's something I just won't tolerate."

"And you told me Beth was dead, that makes us even."

"The way that policeman looked at us." Margo shook her head as if she couldn't believe her own words. "The police would treat us like criminals, you know that? But *you're* the guilty one. We're the victims." She took a deep breath. "And yet here you are, just going about your business as if you'd done nothing wrong, as if you hadn't killed my Digger."

"Digger was hurting Beth."

Margo cocked her head and studied Jillie's face. "Well now, we can't ask him for his side of the story, can we?" She looked at Dix and sneered. "And you must be that policeman's old aunt."

Before Dix could respond, the man she figured to be Cleg, judging by the oxygen tank slung over his shoulder, started toward Toby's pickup.

"What's up, Lotus Blossom?" he said. "Is that our little Jillie?"

Margo ignored her husband. "Mort," she hollered over her shoulder, "bring the shovel."

Cleg's face wore a worried expression. "What're you going to do, Babykins? Shouldn't we go home now? We could come back later. Maybe we should just go home—"

Margo emitted something like a growl and whirled on her husband. "I've come too far to stop now we're so close." She hauled Jillie out of the pickup.

Dix reached out as if to pull the child back inside the vehicle. "Stop that, you're hurting her. Haven't you horrible people done enough to her?"

Margo glared at Dix then snorted. The skin tag Jillie had described flapped like a bed sheet in gale force winds. Veins standing out on her neck, she shrieked, "Mort, get over here." She whipped her head around toward Jillie. "Now you're going to pay for what you did. It's time for a little home-grown justice."

The young man Margo had called Mort approached the pickup. "What's up?"

"A meeting of the minds, that's what." Margo laid a hand on Toby's forearm.

Toby instinctively jerked away, as if his aunt had just wiped a snot-coated finger on his arm. His nostrils flared; then he instantly replaced the look with one of mild boredom.

Margo pretended not to notice the rebuff. "There's more than enough to share. If we stick together, we can get this done and be out of the country before anyone's the wiser. You in, or out?"

Toby chuckled, all pretense of being a disinterested bystander dropped. "Well now, it's like I told the kid, I'm not greedy."

"You packing?" Margo said.

Toby lifted his pistol, its barrel pointed upward. "Always."

"Good. You cover grandma. If the girl gives us any grief, shoot the old lady."

Toby's eyebrows lifted in an unspoken question.

"You don't have to kill her," Margo said. "Just pop her a couple of times." She shot a look at Jillie and Dix to make sure her words had the desired effect.

Jillie cried out, "No. If you hurt Miss Dixie, I'll never tell you about the treasure." She glanced sideways at Dix, the imploring look on her face begging for understanding.

Cleg chose that moment to clear his throat. "It's almost dinner time, Sweetums. This might take some time, and we'll need our energy."

Margo whirled on her spouse. "I've heard about enough from you. If you're not careful, I'll leave you behind with the old lady and the girl."

Cleg flinched as if his face had been slapped. He muttered something apologetic, ambled back toward the house and stood on the porch, shifting his weight from one leg to the other, a troubled look on his face.

Dix swallowed hard. She'd have to step up her game. The look on that hideous woman's face left no doubt as to what she had in mind.

"Mort, take Grandma into the house." Margo turned toward Toby. "You got any rope in your truck?"

"Some nylon cord," Toby said.

"Thick enough she can't chew through?"

Toby smiled and shot a smirk toward Dix. "Not unless granny has a chainsaw hidden in her britches."

"Good," Margo said. "Tie her to the kitchen stove or a chair, anything heavy."

Toby ran the pistol's barrel up and down Dix's neck then turned and looked at Jillie. "Time to learn a life lesson." He looked toward his cousin. "Let's go. I'm right behind you."

"I didn't sign on for violence," Mort said. "I just want that to be understood."

"All that's required for evil to prosper is for good men to do nothing." Dix looked pointedly at Mort.

Refusing to look directly at her, Mort grabbed Dix's forearm and pulled her toward the house. Toby followed, his pistol held at waist-level.

"No more lies," Margo said to Jillie. "Time to pay the piper."

Dix moved slowly, willing Toby to get close enough for her to make a grab for his pistol. As if he sensed what she intended, he kept his distance.

Nearing the house, Dix looked at Cleg. "You need to make this stop."

Cleg opened his mouth to respond, but Toby interrupted, "Oh no." He held his left hand up to his mouth in mock terror. "Not the dreaded *divide and conquer* tactic." He snorted. "You've been reading too much Sun Tzu."

In a last-ditch effort, Dix pretended to stumble in front of Cleg, forcing him to look at her. "Please—"

"Shut it." Toby jabbed the small of Dix's back with the pistol.

Cleg moved his lips like he was chewing gristle. Then he frowned, dropped his gaze, and studied the tops of his shoes.

Dix's stomach sank. If she and Jillie were going to get out of this mess, it would be up to her.

Chapter Forty-Eight

David stopped at every all-night gas station and convenience store on the road between Albuquerque and Belen, but no one had seen either his aunts or a runaway. As he drove, his eyes moved back and forth, alert to signs of a road mishap. With one ear tuned to his police scanner and the other to his phone, he tried to keep from thinking of all the things that could have happened to his aunts and the little girl.

He walked into the last all-night gas station before Belen just as a young male employee was clocking out. The tired-looking young man pulled a backpack from under the counter, slung it over his shoulders, and headed for the door.

"Excuse me," David said. "Are you the night clerk?"

The young man nodded. "I'm on my way home. If you need something, you'll have to talk to the manager. She's in the back."

David pulled out his identification and held it up for the clerk's benefit. "Actually, it's you I need to talk to. Have you seen two elderly women, one in a red sports car and the other in a tan coupe? That would have been either last night or this morning."

"Yeah, the one in the red convertible. Nice ride. Is she your grandma?"

David's heartbeat sped up. "Did you talk to her?"

"Not really. She fell asleep in her car over by the air pump. Scared the hell out of me." The young man eyeballed David. "Did she do something bad, like rob a bank?"

"She's missing. When did you see her, at about what time?"

The kid grew thoughtful. "Oh, I'd say it was about five or six this morning. I thought she was in trouble or something, so I went out to her car and tapped on her window. I think I woke her up."

"Was she alone, no little girl in the car with her?"

"No, she was by herself. I thought, you know, she might be senile or something and just forgot where she was, but she seemed okay."

"Did she happen to say where she was going?"

The kid shook his head. "Like I said, we didn't really have a conversation."

"Did you see her leave, notice which direction she went?"

"She drove south, towards Mountainair."

"Thanks for your help."

"No problemo." The young man headed for a motorcycle chained to an upright metal pipe cemented next to the door. "Good luck."

David hurried back to his car. A southerly route meant his aunt had either been headed to the Elliott place or the Ross farm.

I'm right behind you, Auntie Dix.

He pulled his cell phone from the holder attached to his dashboard. He needed to update his aunt Lil as well as find out where she was.

He prepared to punch in his aunt's number, but his phone's flashing green light announced he'd missed a call. Berating himself for forgetting to take his phone out of silent mode earlier, he tapped the screen to retrieve a message from his Aunt Dix's phone.

But static and an occasional dead interval made his aunt's message nearly impossible to decipher.

...at   the   Elliott   place...Dix's   car's here...deserted...held captive in the shed...

His stomach doing a pirouette and heart pounding, David replayed the message several times in hopes of making sense of it. Then he tried to call Dix's number again, but it went immediately to voice mail.

...held captive in the shed...

The snippet of message sent a chill up his back. Had that garbled message been Aunt Lil's call for help? Had his aunts been locked in that shed during his visit? No, that didn't make sense given neither of his aunts' cars had been there at the time of his visit.

David sucked air through his teeth. Had he been so caught up inside his own head that he'd driven past one or both of his aunts' vehicles on the highway?

He'd noticed that shed earlier, had even considered looking into it. But because of the Elliott woman's offhand attitude about it, he'd dismissed it as being inconsequential.

David pounded his palm against the steering wheel. One step forward, two steps back—like fighting his way up the side of a steep sand dune. If anything happened to his aunts or that little girl because of his short-sightedness, he'd never forgive himself.

David called dispatch and gave Betts an update.

"What're you going to do?"

"I'm going to find my aunts and the runaway."

"Do you need backup?"

"If I do, I'll be in touch." David ended the call

He pulled onto the road that would take him back to the Elliott house.

Chapter Forty-Nine

During the drive to the Ross farm, Jillie sat ramrod straight, her mind a chaos of thought. Everything seemed unreal.

One day she and Beth were happily planning to go away; the next, Beth was in the hospital, and Jillie was eating lunch on top of a skeleton while everyone in the world was looking for her.

All she wanted was for her life to go back to the way it was before Pops died, before someone started that stupid rumor about a treasure. But like in *Pandora's Box,* all the evil had been let out, and nothing could put it back.

Once the treasure rumor had caught on, everything changed. Kids at school suddenly wanted to become Jillie's friend. People they hardly knew invited the family to dinner and talked about the weather for a second or two before asking pointed questions about Pop's trips, while pretending only passing interest. Then as time went on and Pops didn't magically produce a treasure trove to share with everyone, the rumor mill turned nasty.

And now, with what she'd discovered in the shed, it was obvious the Elliotts were playing by a different set of rules than the ones by which Jillie'd been raised.

One thing was obvious: she couldn't keep denying there was a treasure. Even if that were true, it wouldn't work with those people. And neither she nor Miss Dix would be able to talk their way out of the fix they were in. Just like in the true crime stories she and Beth used to watch on television after Pops had gone to bed, she and Dix could be made to disappear. And they'd never be found in the miles and miles of open desert—at least not by anything human.

Unwelcome scenes from those television episodes flashed into her mind—images of sun-bleached bones scattered and carried off by predators, of dried, leathery skin and crushed skulls, made not so horrifying by the calm, matter-of-fact voice of the narrator. And, of course, on television there'd been no smells.

The worst part of those episodes was that a lot of the murdered people had willingly gotten into cars with their murderers. And many of them had been killed by people they'd once loved.

Searing pain and the taste of blood made her aware she'd started chewing her nails again. Gingerly, she wiped the pads of her fingers on her jeans and thought about the skeleton in the toolbox.

Jillie decided that the bones belonged to a woman, since she couldn't picture anyone putting a man on a folded flower-print dress. And the hair had been long.

The mental picture of those teeth and the skimpy hair attached to a dried, crusty-looking scalp made her shiver. The image would no doubt make an unwelcome addition to her nightmares.

You been chatting to her again?

Those words meant either Mort or Toby murdered the tool chest person, or maybe they both did it.

Regardless, although Jillie hadn't actually seen Toby kill the man in the trailer, she knew he had. And as soon as she got the chance, she'd turn her drawing over to the police.

But just then, she needed to revise her plan of escape. As she mulled over tidbits of information, some of it learned from her favorite forensic television shows, slivers of thought bubbled up from her survival-brain.

The most important thing was to say nothing about what she found in the toolbox to anyone other than Miss Dixie; there was no way to know how many of the Elliotts were involved in the murder.

Next, she had to pretend the treasure was real; hopefully, that would buy some time.

Finally, she had to figure out a way to get Miss Dix to Moms Potter's so they could call the police; not only was her godmother a tough old lady, but she had a shotgun and could keep the Elliotts from hurting anyone until the police could get there.

Jillie had heard that the best ideas were usually the simplest. She'd also heard that people see what they expect and want to see.

So, if the Elliotts wanted and expected to see a treasure, that's what she'd promise them.

By the time Miss Dix turned the truck up the farm's drive, bits and pieces of an idea had begun to grow. If her plan worked, they might at least have a chance.

And it had better work; Beth was depending on her.

Chapter Fifty

Cleg stood on the Ross's back porch and watched the goings-on. Things were spiraling out of control—that's what The Shrike had said, and that's exactly what was happening. She, Mort, and Toby had become obsessed with finding old man Ross's treasure, and nothing seemed likely to stop them from getting it.

The more Cleg thought about it, the more he figured that might not be such a bad thing. As sure as God made little green apples, if Margo found a pile of money, she'd light a shuck out of his vicinity. That's what she'd said, and once that woman set her mind on something, it was as good as done.

Like a flower-scented breeze, the thought of freedom from The Shrike sent sweet images of happiness whistling through his head.

Freedom. Cleg rolled the word around in his mouth, savoring it like a plateful of mashed potatoes and cream gravy. Dreamlike images leapfrogged through his mind. Images of him enjoying unrestricted access to television while eating anything he wanted, as much as he wanted, any time he wanted. Him sitting in his big, easy chair for days, if he chose, while *no one* badgered him about his weight, and *no one* shrieked orders. Him saying whatever he wanted to say and thinking anything he wanted to think without fear of being berated. And best of all, he saw himself free from worrying about the next unexpected outbursts that would end in him getting a beating.

He watched the people who made up his family as they discussed what to do with the old woman and argued about the best way to make the girl tell them where to look for the treasure. It was as if scales fell from his eyes, and he saw them for who they really were—a gaggle of selfish, hateful strangers.

What had happened to that gentle, sweet kid named Mort who'd only ever wanted to be good at something? Or to the brave young Toby who'd lost his mother? When had they turned into such sharp-faced, hungry-eyed, worthless lumps of humanity?

But worse than that, whatever happened to that young Cleg who'd been so filled with the joy of life? What had he ever done bad enough to condemn him to the years of hell he'd spent with The Shrike?

All he ever wanted was a loving wife, a nice family, a good and peaceful life. He didn't want the treasure, didn't give a rat's patoot about it. But his life would be so much better if Margo got her hands on it.

Cleg didn't want to hurt anyone. He'd never even been able to bring himself to discipline Mort or Toby. But things were changing, and he had some tough choices to make.

He'd actually kind of liked the little girl, never even considered hurting her. The Shrike had done enough of that for both of them. Nevertheless, she had to be made to tell where her daddy had hidden the map.

The girl clearly cared about that old woman who'd just shown up out of the blue. That made the woman leverage—Cleg's ticket to freedom.

Maybe his luck was about to change. After

shooting one last glance at the people he no longer knew, he shuffled toward the kitchen door.

Chapter Fifty-One

By the time David arrived back at the Elliott house, he'd worked himself into an iridescent fireball of fear and frustration. Barely slowing, he took the curve into the driveway, shoved the gearshift into park, leaped from the Jeep, and ran to his aunt Dix's car.

No blood or any other sign of struggle meant whatever had happened to his aunt had taken place elsewhere. But the keys dangling from the ignition and the purse shouted that she'd not gone of her own accord.

David made a quick auditory and visual scan of the area. Complete silence—no birdsong, no rustle of undergrowth. Although light shone through the lower floor windows, no movement was visible either from inside or outside the house. It was as if all life had fled the area.

The front door of the house stood ajar. Light poured through the opening and into the yard, where it highlighted dirt, weeds, and rocks.

He adjusted his shoulder holster and approached the house. With the squealing porch planks tracking his progress, he stepped to the door.

Taking care to follow departmental protocol, he shouted his identification through the opening. When no one responded after two more shouts, he went in.

Like a checklist, he verified each bit of his aunt

Lil's message.

…deserted…

Beginning with the upstairs, he did a quick search of the house. After scoping out the basement, he hurried outside.

…held captive in the shed…

Engaging the photo app on his phone as he moved, David strode to the outbuilding. He took several photos of the four sets of footprints outside, careful to leave them undisturbed, then squeezed through the shattered door. Stepping as close to the walls as possible, he surveyed the interior, noting the small footprints mingled with, and in some places covered by, large boot prints about the same as David's size elevens. Only a few prints from a second adult, a woman's, judging by their size and shape, led from the door to the tool chest and back outside.

It looked like someone, most likely one of David's aunts, had broken into the shed. But who did the boot prints belong to? Had a man waited inside the shed while one or both of David's aunts pried the door open?

Who'd lock himself inside that tiny shed and hope for someone to come along and rescue him? Get your brain in gear.

It seemed more likely that someone had locked the child in the shed then left. He'd then likely returned in time to witness the door being jimmied.

The sight of a large-enough-to-hold-a-body toolbox kicked up sand in the pit of David's stomach. With a knot in his throat, he stepped to the box, opened the lid, and peered down at its pitiful contents.

In his tenure with the police department, he'd seen some fairly hard-core murder scenes. But aspects of what he was looking at shook him worse than some of the most vicious calls he'd worked.

The careful positioning of the leg bones upon neatly folded, blood-stained fabric. The caved-in skull almost lovingly nestled on a discolored pillow. The telltale saw and knife kerfs and gouges at the joints—especially deep and numerous up and down the neck, as if the frenzied killer had symbolically removed the head over and over again.

Whoever the poor creature had been—a woman judging by the floral fabric—she'd obviously been dead for years. Someone, most likely the murderer, had expended a huge amount of time and energy cutting her up, and arranging her pieces into an almost perfectly symmetrical mosaic.

That much anger would be hard to keep hidden. The sick feeling in David's gut told him the little girl Jillie and one or both of his aunts might be the catalyst to set the murderer off.

He gently lowered the lid and returned to his vehicle.

The absence of his aunt Lil's car might mean she was still out searching for her sister. But it could just as easily have meant the boot-print-man had forced Aunt Lil to use her car to transport the twins and child to another location—someplace more isolated and far removed from the Elliott house.

In his experience, fear and paranoia were constant companions to those who took another person's life. After years of looking over his shoulder, whoever killed the woman in the shed would most likely assume the little girl and David's aunts had discovered the skeleton. Not only would the killer need to move the body to another hiding place, he'd feel compelled to make sure there were no witnesses left behind.

David could wait for the killer to return for the body, then he could pounce for a quick arrest. But, of course, that would most likely not take place until *after* the killer had dealt with the child and his aunts.

Taking precious minutes to call dispatch, he reported the skeleton, the evidence he'd found of a child's being held captive, and his aunt's abandoned car. He described his other aunt's car, then suggested an Amber alert for Jillie Ross. After offering physical descriptions of the three, he requested both aunts be listed as *missing and suspected of being in danger*.

On the off chance his aunt Lil might answer, he tried to call one last time. He wasn't really surprised when the call went immediately to voicemail.

"Aunt Lil, if you get this, please stop the car as soon as you can safely do so and call me." After a pause, David added, "I'm worried, Auntie. I don't know if you're still searching for Aunt Dix, but if you find her and the little girl, call me. Don't approach whoever has them. This is not a person who'll listen to reason. He has nothing to lose." He punched the disconnect button and sat staring at his dashboard.

Based on what he knew at that point, it seemed his aunt Dix had driven from the gas station to the Elliott house. Once there, she'd been caught and taken somewhere else—either in someone else's vehicle or in Aunt Lil's. The surrounding desert was huge, home to places so isolated they didn't even appear on the map. So, if Lil was taken captive with her sister and Jillie, David's window of opportunity for finding them was rapidly closing.

But if his aunt Lil *hadn't* been caught at the Elliott house, where would she have gone next? A logical and systematic thinker, she would have considered all the data, made a deduction, and then acted on it.

David was certain that wherever one of his aunts turned up, the other would be close behind. All he had to do was to put himself into one of their heads.

As if conjured by his need, Beth's words floated into his mind. *The Elliotts are vile, truly evil. They'll stop at nothing to get what they want.*

Then, as if struck by lightning, David sat bolt upright and half-shouted, "And what do they want? They want the treasure, and where do they believe the treasure is?"

He cranked the ignition, shot down the drive and out onto the road that would take him to the Ross farm.

Chapter Fifty-Two

Dix pushed her feet against the floor to lift herself off the chair to which she'd been tied. Even a few inches leeway should allow her to frog-hop the chair to the kitchen counter. Maybe she could get a drawer open and find something sharp to cut the nylon bindings.

But her calves cramped into granny knots. Pain shot through her legs, then held, so intense her eyes teared up. Tugging against her restraints, she worked her toes and moved her feet in a circular motion to loosen the muscles. Finally, after several minutes, the pain subsided.

The hinges on the screen door squealed, and Cleg entered the kitchen. His portable oxygen tank hanging under one arm, the cannula slightly askew in his nostrils, he looked like he'd just run a marathon.

Cleg stood in front of her, breathing hard, his lips a mottled purple. "You got to...*wheeze*...make that girl...*cough*...tell them where the treasure map is."

Dix shook her head. "There is no treasure, and there is no map."

Cleg took a step toward her, his facial expression unreadable. "That story's not going to wash, not with those people. If the girl sticks to it, there's no telling what they'll do."

As if it had been only yesterday rather than four decades since Dix studied crisis intervention strategies, her training kicked in.

"Your name's Cleg, isn't it?" *Call him by his name.*

The man nodded.

"My name's Dixie." *Make him see you as a person with a name.* "I don't believe Jillie knows anything about a treasure. But I do know you're unhappy about what's happening here." *Make it personal.*

His mouth tightening, Cleg looked unsure.

"Cleg, look at me." Dix waited for him to make eye contact. "My nephew is a detective with the Los Lunas Police Department. He won't stop searching until he finds Jillie and me. And he won't rest until anyone who hurts either of us is in jail."

Cleg's gaze dropped to the floor. "I don't see what I could do."

"Help us, and I'll paint a clear image of you to the police." *Reflect to the client whichever of the five senses he uses to express himself.* "They'll get the picture."

Surprised and gratified to see a tear drop from Cleg's downcast eyes, Dix pounced. "Your life has been tough, anyone can see that."

A small nod.

"Cleg, you have a chance to do something good here. Will you help us?"

The man looked over his shoulder toward the door. "How?"

"Either untie me or give me something sharp to cut this rope; then, distract them. Give me the keys to your pickup, so I can get Jillie away from here."

Cleg licked his lips. "If that woman gets wind of what I'm up to—"

"She won't. We'll make it look good, like I got the

best of you. It won't be your fault."

Cleg drew in a deep breath through his cannula and pushed the air out through pursed lips. He stepped to the kitchen counter, where he opened and closed several drawers before finding one that contained what he was searching for. A thoughtful look on his face, he reached into the drawer and retrieved a butcher knife. Gripping the handle of the lethal-looking blade in one hand, he approached Dix.

"Thank you, Cleg." Dix smiled her most winning smile as gratitude sent her spirits soaring.

Sweat beading along his upper lip, the man played the pad of his thumb lightly along the sharp edge of the knife. He turned it this way and that, staring at the light flashing along its steel blade.

"Cleg?" The beginnings of fear dug into Dix's solar plexus. She had to interrupt his string of thought, or she was going to lose him. "Cleg, you're doing the right thing. You're going to be a hero."

But Cleg remained unmoved, as if he hadn't heard. Almost to himself, he said, "If that girl thought someone was going to hurt her friend, she'd tell them what they want to know." Thoughtfully, the man looked back and forth between Dix and the knife. "It wouldn't have to be really bad, just enough for the girl to know those people mean business. I mean, I don't want to hurt anyone; I'm not a violent person."

"Cleg—"

"Once they got hold of the treasure, they'd leave me alone."

Dix's breath caught in her throat and she hiccupped. *Steady.* "They're all going to prison for a long time, Cleg. You'll have years and years to do whatever you want. Years, Cleg, just think of it."

The man stood motionless in front of Dix. Then, as if a clog suddenly slipped into place, he smiled and raised the knife.

Dix's eyes widened in horror as Cleg's arm muscles bunched, ready to the bring the knife down.

Chapter Fifty-Three

Margo couldn't believe it when the old woman and the girl showed up at the farm. She'd wanted to drag the kid from the pickup and pound her until she told them where the treasure map was hidden. Her impulse had been so strong, her fake nails punctured holes in the palms of her tightly fisted hands.

But the sight of Toby sitting in the back of the pickup he'd inherited from his mother calmed her. Even as a kid, he'd been the spitting image of his father Johnnie Dinkins—the man Margo almost married. And as a grown man, the resemblance extended beyond physical appearance to include mannerisms: The way he cocked his head when deep in thought. The way he smiled at her when she'd done something special for him.

Margo glanced at her son and ground her teeth. Except for the mouth he got from Cleg, Mort didn't even remotely resemble either of his parents. Instead, by some perverse nastiness of the universe, he could have been Chlorine's twin. From the moment of his birth, Margo had been unable to hold or hug him without the urge to throw him into the fireplace. So, she'd left his care to Cleg.

Of the two sisters, Chlorine had been their mother's favorite. Whenever the sisters fought, which was often, their mother took Chlorine's side. Whether or not Margo was guilty didn't seem to matter. Margo was never given the opportunity to tell her side of the story before the girls' mother yanked the horse quirt— her favorite instrument of punishment—from its nail on the wall and whipped Margo until she confessed. Chlorine, on the other hand, was rewarded for betraying her sister. Margo could still see Chlorine sitting on the porch swing licking an ice cream cone and smiling.

Margo stared at her shambling husband and remembered the days she'd spent as Johnnie's girl all those years ago. She'd fallen so hard and fast, the rest of the world had faded into unreality. It was as if she lived and walked inside a cloud of sparkling woofle dust.

All the girls had wanted to be Johnnie's girlfriend. Tall, dark, and handsome, he could have snapped his fingers, and a dozen would have flocked around him. Instead of detracting from his looks, his small hands and over-long arms added a kind of magnetic, primal element.

And he'd chosen Margo to be his girl, at least, for a while.

The look on Chlorine's face had been priceless when Margo showed her Johnnie's ring hanging from a chain around her neck. For days, she basked in her sister's radio-active jealousy, enjoyed the bitter verbal jibes, and smiled at the constant put-downs. She even managed to convince herself that she'd finally outdone her sister, finally gotten possession of something of her own—something Chlorine couldn't take away from her.

The dream ended when Margo made the mistake of introducing Johnnie to her sister.

Within the next two weeks, Margo's precious times

with Johnnie grew more and more sporadic before stopping altogether.

She'd burned up the phone lines calling him, pleading with him to come see her, to tell her what was going on. She'd even shown up at his house at all hours of the day and night, until his mom put a stop to that.

One night, unable to sleep, Margo called Johnnie and left a message that she was on her way over, and for him to please meet her. But when she rang the doorbell, his mom instantly flung the door open, threw a huge pan of ice water over Margo, yelled something obscene, and slammed the door in her face.

The next day, Margo was served a restraining order. She'd raged then cried her heart out while reading some judge's command that she have no further contact with Johnnie, or she'd suffer legal consequences.

No further contact. She'd been devastated and angry enough to choke someone.

The humiliation had been hard to take, but not as hard as when Chlorine announced her engagement to Johnnie. Whoever coined that phrase *Hell hath no fury like a woman scorned* knew his beans. Margo could have incinerated the town and all its inhabitants with her barely controlled blast furnace of anger.

And all the time, there stood Cleg with his tongue hanging out, hoping for a bit of her attention. In a last-ditch effort to make Johnnie jealous and show her sister up, Margo turned her attentions to Cleg.

But Johnnie hadn't batted an eye. On the contrary, he'd pounded Cleg on the back and congratulated him.

Then Margo discovered she was pregnant. That had been the toughest pill of all to swallow.

With nothing left to do, she'd asked Cleg to marry her. He'd been so excited, she thought he was going to wet himself. He'd agreed to all her requests for the wedding and honeymoon.

The wedding was top shelf. It bested Chlorine's by a mile, and people talked about it for months. Except for Cleg's clumsy fawning, the honeymoon in Paris had been okay.

Surprisingly, marriage to Cleg hadn't been so bad at first. He'd been attentive, obliging, willing to do whatever he could to please her. He even went so far as to set up revolving charge accounts at a local dress boutique and beauty shop.

After a couple of years, he changed. Where he'd once been strong-willed, he became like a wilted celery stalk—flavorless and weak. Where he'd been attentive, he began questioning her purchases. When he canceled her charge accounts, he placed himself firmly and irrevocably on her list of enemies.

Then, joy of joys, after only a few of years of marriage, Johnnie left Chlorine for a local barmaid. Rumor had it the thirty-something barkeep knew things other women didn't know about sex, stuff she'd read in some book called the Something-or-other *Sutra*.

Chlorine had flown into a rage the likes of which the town had never before witnessed. She snarled at everyone, even the hapless folks who made the mistake of showing a bit of sympathy. It didn't take long for the townsfolk to begin to steer clear of her.

Margo smiled to herself at the memory. *Good times.*

She'd call her sister on the phone and yell things like: *How does it feel to be kicked to the curb? How do*

you like being thrown out with the rest of the garbage?
What do you think Johnnie's doing with his barmaid
right now?

After Chlorine got an unlisted phone number,
Margo resorted to showing up at her trailer house. The
face-to-face taunting had been delicious but short-lived
when Chlorine stopped answering the door.

Margo had been pleased beyond measure when her
sister disappeared. She enjoyed the locals whispering
and speculating that she herself had been responsible.
She reveled in the mixture of fear and intrigue on
people's faces.

She'd never wondered where her sister went, never
questioned whether it was foul play, and never
wondered who might have been involved. As far as she
was concerned, if Chlorine had been a victim of foul
play, the person or persons unknown should be given a
reward.

Of course, even though her own marriage was a
mess, she'd never considered leaving Cleg—not for an
instant. Cleg, the house, and the land was all hers, and
she never gave *anything* away.

Now, after all the years of struggling to pay the
bills, of shopping at discount clothing stores, and of
doing her own nails, now she had a once-in-a-lifetime
chance at Wealth, with a capital *W*.

That was something worth killing for.

Chapter Fifty-Four

Dix whimpered as Cleg lifted the butcher knife, apparently aiming the blade at her chest. With an intensity she'd rarely seen, even in her most disturbed clients, he stared into her eyes. But at the last instant, instead of following through with a thrust into her abdomen, he arched the knife blade down toward her hands and severed the orange-colored nylon rope with which they were bound.

Her hands shaking so badly she could hardly control them, Dix threw the segments of cord onto the floor. "Thank you, Cleg."

The man reached into his pocket, pulled out his pickup keys, and dropped them into Dix's open palm. "It's the old brown banger." Then, before Dix could stop him, he pushed the knife blade into the meaty part of his forearm.

As if mesmerized, he cocked his head and stared at the trickle of blood oozing from the wound. Moving in slow motion, he withdrew the blade and pointed it toward his chest, a far-away look in his eyes.

Dix instinctively grabbed Cleg's hands. Gripping them as tightly as she could, she pulled them down until the knife blade pointed away from the man's body. "This isn't the only way to freedom, Cleg." Gently, she removed the knife from his hands. "Untie me from this chair; you've been hurt enough."

Tears pouring down his cheeks, Cleg fumbled with the cord. "I've lost my chance. Now I'll never get shut of her."

Dix shifted the knife to her left hand and put her right on Cleg's unhurt forearm. "You've already taken the first step." Dix stood. Hurriedly, she scooted the chair to which she'd been tied across the floor and positioned it next to the still-open drawer. "This will make it look like I managed to drag myself to the cabinet for the knife."

Cleg nodded once.

Dix studied the man's wound. "You managed to miss everything major, by the looks of it." She found a dishtowel in one of the drawers and held it toward Cleg. "There's not a great deal of blood, but enough to back up your story."

Cleg surprised her with a shy smile. "You mean I did something right?"

"Oh, you didn't just do something right, you did something truly wonderful. I meant what I said. As soon as Jillie and I get away, I'll call the police and tell them how you helped us."

Once Cleg had dabbed a convincing amount of blood onto the towel, Dix laid the knife on the counter. She was taking a chance by leaving it where Cleg could get to it, but it would offer credence to his story. And the hopeful light in the man's eyes told her he'd moved beyond his self-destructive impulse.

"After I've gone, knock over the chair and yell for help. When they come running, tell them I said I was taking Jillie to stay with an elderly family member." Dix smiled. "Thank you, Cleg. You're saving our lives, you know."

Cleg's face lit up, and he squared his shoulders. "Yeah, I know."

Dix hurried through the house and out the front door. Sticking close to the stuccoed walls, she sneaked around toward the back where the three pickups were parked and peered around the corner of the house.

Beyond the driveway, the group of adults surrounded Jillie. Voices floated on the light autumn breeze.

"What are we going to do with her?" Mort said.

Margo's lips pulled themselves into a smile. "We're going to make a deal, that's what." She jerked her head toward Jillie. "You either give us the treasure, or we'll throw you and the old lady into the septic tank." She waved her hand in an arc. "All the way out here, no one'll hear you scream. And no one will ever find you. For a day or two, the news will be filled with the story of a poor little lost orphan and an old woman who disappeared. But pretty soon, you'll be forgotten." She looked at Toby. "How long you reckon it'll take them to die in there?"

Toby looked thoughtful. "I'm thinking they'd die of thirst before starving to death, so maybe two or three days." He looked at Jillie. "Three days of standing in all that wet, smelly stuff up to your armpits...not a pretty way to go."

"How do I know you'll let her go if I tell you about the treasure?" Inside the circle of angry adults, Jillie stood like the Biblical David facing down Goliath.

"You really don't have a choice." Margo said.

"I'll only show you where it is after you've let Miss Dixie go." Jillie folded her arms across her chest, lifted her head, and jutted out her lower jaw.

Mort moved closer to Jillie. "Come on, kid. All you have to do is—"

Suddenly Cleg let loose a war whoop from inside the house. "Help, someone help. She's stabbed me."

All heads swiveled toward the sound. Then, after an instant of indecision, the three adults rushed toward the house, leaving Jillie behind.

From the corner of the house, Dix waved her arms above her head to get the child's attention then sprinted toward Cleg's vehicle. No sooner had she climbed into the driver's seat than Jillie vaulted into the passenger's side. Jubilant, Dix jammed the keys into the ignition, fired the thing up, pointed its nose toward the open road, and stomped on the gas pedal.

The vehicle had only gone a few yards before it coughed and died. Frantically, Dix turned the key over and over, but the engine only sputtered in response.

"Out of gas," Dix said.

"Miss Dixie, Toby's—"

Jillie's warning was interrupted by the sudden tap of metal against the driver's window. Dix whipped her head toward the sound just as Toby yanked her door open.

"So predictable." Toby made a *tsk, tsk* sound. "But then, how could you know Uncle Clot's gas gauge is busted?" He moved the pistol's barrel until it pointed at Dix's right eye. "Out of the pickup, ladies."

"Wait," Jillie twisted in her seat and leaned forward to peer at Toby. "I'll show you where the treasure is if you let us go." She nodded toward the house. "More for you if we leave before the rest of them get back."

Toby cocked his head. "You take me to the

treasure first, *then* I let you go." He glanced toward the house and licked his lips. "Make it fast."

Jillie rapidly nodded her head. "I can show you a sample of the stuff Pop found. He gave me a few things, just in case I ever needed some fast money. He said the best place to hide things is in plain sight."

Sample of the stuff? Dix's stomach did a pirouette.

"I'm listening," Toby said.

"It's in my backpack."

"Ah, and here was me thinking you only insisted on bringing the thing because you couldn't be separated from your teddy bear."

And you've bought her story, hook, line, and sinker. Dix shook her head as Lil's words blasted through her mind. Could she have so completely misread the child?

"Let's get moving," Toby said.

With Dix leading the way, the three hurried to Toby's pickup.

"You drive again, Granny. I want to be long gone before Team Elliott discovers they've been had."

Dix climbed behind the steering wheel as Jillie jumped into the passenger's seat. Toby again took up his position in the back, his pistol aimed at Dix's head.

Barely able to control her shaking hands, Dix fired the engine, backed up, then whipped the steering wheel toward the open road.

They'd traveled only about a quarter of a mile when Toby jabbed the pistol barrel into Dix's neck. "Turn right here." He motioned to a dirt, farm-to-market road. "Pull around behind that group of juniper trees. We wouldn't want anyone to interrupt our discussion, now would we?"

Dix did as she was told.

"Stop the engine." Toby retrieved Jillie's backpack from the seat beside him and shoved it over the seat toward her. "We're not going any further until I see what you have."

Refusing to look at Dix, Jillie opened the backpack and pulled out a small wooden box engraved with tiny roses. She opened the lid, took out a couple of stones, and held them toward Toby in her open palm.

"What're those supposed to be?" Toby said. "They look like clear white rocks to me."

"They're what my pop called rough diamonds. That's what they look like before they've been cut and polished."

Toby's gaze riveted on the stones. He nodded and smiled. "I knew it. I knew your old man found treasure. I read about the lost diamond mine at Encino. That must be where these came from." He blew air through his open mouth, then whipped his head back around to Jillie. "Where's the rest?"

"I don't know."

Toby's face contorted into a mask. He raised his hand with the obvious intention of backhanding Jillie, but Dix threw her hand up and blocked the blow.

"Oh, now, you oughtn't have done that." Toby snarled and lifted the pistol toward Dixie.

"Stop," Jillie cried. "I said I don't know where the *rest* of the treasure is. Pops only brought home a few stones at a time; he said some of them are big as walnuts."

Toby licked his lips, his eyes bright. "So, if the treasure's not at your place, where is it?"

"Pop left a map."

"A map." Toby chuckled. "Okay then. You got that in there, too?"

Jillie shook her head. "Pop left it with my godmother for safe keeping. She's our neighbor just up the road."

Toby nodded, a crooked smile creasing his face. "Now it's all making sense. You ever see the map? You know where the mine is?"

"I've never actually seen it, and I haven't been to the mine. But Pops said there were enough of these just lying on the ground to take care of us in style for the rest of our lives." Again, she lifted the stones toward Toby.

Toby smirked, grabbed the stones and dropped them into his shirt pocket. "Let's go. The quicker I get the map, the quicker you and Granny can get on with your useless lives."

At Dix's hesitation, Toby prodded her neck with the pistol barrel. "Quit stalling. I said, let's go."

Her insides screaming for her to do something, anything, Dix started the engine. If she were going to make a play, it had to be soon. Contrary to Toby's words, she had no doubt his plans didn't include allowing the two of them to go free.

Chapter Fifty-Five

After recalculating for the fourth time in as many minutes, the female, robotic voice of Lil's ancient GPS commanded her to "Bear left at the next curve. Your destination will be on the right."

"Finally," Lil said to the one-time expensive piece of electronic junk sitting in its cradle on her dashboard. "Tell me again why I need you when a paper map works just as well, is cheaper, and allows me to opt out of taking the longest, most circuitous route possible?"

With a blossoming suspicion that her desired destination and the place to which she'd been directed might not be one and the same, she pulled up the driveway and parked behind a shiny white, late-model Ford 350 pickup.

A quick scan of the house and grounds reinforced her fears. The yard was carefully groomed. Artistically arranged plantings, trimmed bushes and professionally pruned trees dotted the area. No holes pockmarked the yard, and no weeds were in evidence.

"You lying bimbo," she mouthed toward the now-silent device.

An elderly woman wearing a heavy plaid jacket, blue jeans, and boots stepped out onto the porch. Unsmiling, she stood and stared at Lil.

Lil powered down her window. "I'm pretty sure I'm lost."

"I'm pretty sure you're right," the old woman said. "Where do you want to be?"

"I'm trying to get to the Ross farm."

The old woman pursed her lips and squinted. "You and just about everyone else in Belen. Who might you be?" She stepped off the porch and walked slowly toward Lil. "And what business do you have at the Ross farm?"

Her hackles rising at the woman's tone of voice, Lil commanded herself to be civil. "I'm looking for my sister. She looks like me, maybe with a kid in tow?"

"How old?"

"Same age as me."

"Not your sister, the kid."

"Eleven or twelve. You know her?"

The woman nodded. "And I'm guessing you're the twin to the woman who's spent the night searching for this *kid.*" The woman bent at the waist and peered through Lil's open window.

"Maybe," Lil said.

"Nice young man came 'round looking for Jillie and your sister. You just missed him." She stuck out her hand. "Beverly Potter."

Lil ignored the hand. "Reverend who?"

At first, the old woman looked taken aback. Then her face broke out into a wry smile and she chuckled. "No, certainly *not* Reverend, just Beverly Potter."

"Just a sec." Lil reached into the pocket of her shirt and extracted a small square black box, from which she pulled two tiny, flesh-colored bulbs. After inserting one in each ear, she scowled at the Potter woman. "Am I anywhere near the Ross place?"

Mrs. Potter motioned toward the road. "Yep."

"So, have you, or have you not seen a little old lady and kid." Lil pursed her lips. The other old lady's attitude was not only beginning to irritate her, but it was wasting her time.

"Like I said before you put in your plugs, I didn't see them, but your police-kin came 'round asking questions."

"I see." If Davie had talked to Mrs. Potter earlier, he could already be at the Ross place. Although Lil had utmost respect for Davie's detective-instincts, he could find himself in a whole mess of trouble if the contents of that toolbox was any indication of the kind of people the Elliotts were. "Would you be kind enough to point me in the right direction?"

A speculative look on her face, Mrs. Potter remained silent.

"Okay, fine, thanks." Lil nodded toward the woman and started to power up her window.

But Mrs. Potter put her hands on top of the rising glass and narrowed her eyes. "I think we should talk."

"I don't have time to chat, or did you not understand what I said about their being in danger? You can either take your hands off my window before I close it or learn if you can run fast enough to keep from losing your fingers."

"And what if you find Jillie at the same time you find your sister; what'll you do, call that young cop?"

"What's that to you?" Lil squinted her eyes.

"Maybe you'd leave Jillie for someone else to take care of, someone like her godmother?"

Lil studied the woman's face. "Seems to me a godmother would be a good person for that kid to stay with, at least until her sister Beth could claim her."

Mrs. Potter nodded. "Good answer. What's your plan?"

"My sister's car is at the Elliott place, but no one's there. The kid had been there, I'm pretty sure, locked in an outbuilding. The only thing I can figure is, based on what the girl told us, the Elliott clan is going to try to make her take them to some kind of treasure."

Mrs. Potter's face assumed an expression that didn't bode well for those responsible for hurting the kid. "The Elliotts," she said through clenched teeth. "I never met any of the others, other than Digger, that is. Digger, now, he was a real piece of work. The most foul-mouthed, meanest, laziest snake I've ever known. He cut Beth and Jillie completely off from the rest of the world." She shook her head. "True to his name, that waste-of-space was. He dug up nearly every inch of that yard. There never was any treasure; that was just a rumor."

Lil nodded her head. The fact that this crusty old woman cared so much about Jillie said something about her *and* about the kid.

Mrs. Potter frowned. "I drove to the hospital several times to see Beth. Tell the truth, I was surprised that I never saw Jillie there. Those two are more than just sisters; they have a special bond. I called the Elliott house several times to talk to Jillie, but there was always some reason she couldn't come to the phone. Beth, now she's one of the sweetest people I've ever known. That whole Ross family was. You know their dad used to help build barns and out buildings for local folks? The economy out here's pretty stagnant, but Mister Ross never charged a penny for his services. He brought his own tools, too."

Lil held her hand up to stop the flow of words. "Much as I'm enjoying this, I need to get going."

"Well, then, we'd best get a move on. Come in, I was just about to get my gear when you pulled up."

"I don't have time—"

Mrs. Potter moved her hand in a shushing motion. "Now don't go off half-cocked. Your nephew might or might not be at the farm yet, but if that's where those folks have taken Jillie, I guarantee you, she's in trouble. I'm going to get my nun chucks."

"My sis got into that martial arts stuff some years back. Are you any good?"

Mrs. Potter smiled. "Oh, I have my moments. Come in, I have all kinds of stuff you can choose from, if you want." Muttering under her breath something that sounded like *I should have known something was up...all that traffic*, Mrs. Potter hurried toward her house.

Lil shut off her engine, exited the car, and followed. "You have two minutes, then I'm leaving, with or without you."

Chapter Fifty-Six

Cleg waited as long as he dared before hollering for help. Getting into his role as a stabbing victim, he flopped around on the floor, dabbing spots of blood here and there. By the time Margo and Toby rushed into the house, he'd worked himself into a lather of pseudo-outrage.

"She stabbed me then took off. Threatened to finish me off if I so much as peeped before she got away."

Margo stooped, studied Cleg's wound. "I've cut myself worse with my toenail clippers." She snorted and sneered into her husband's face. "Could you possibly be more of a wimp?"

"I could've been killed—" Cleg whined.

Margo lifted her foot and stepped down on her husband's wounded arm. "But you weren't, were you?" She smiled at Cleg's pain-filled yelp, then spoke over her shoulder. "Toby, you go get the kid. Mort and I'll catch Granny; she can't have gone far." She turned back to her husband. "Get up. We've got work to do."

Puffing, grunting, and groaning, Cleg made several attempts to get up, but flopped back onto the floor after each effort. "I can't get up, Cream Puff. I gotta have some help."

"Oh my Lord. Mort, help your father."

Mort stooped and grabbed Cleg under his arms. "You gotta put some weight on your own feet. I can't lift you by myself."

After a spate of cursing and flailing, Cleg stood upright.

"Let's go." Margo grabbed her husband's arm. Ignoring his groans, she pulled him toward the door. "Where's Toby?" she asked Mort.

"He took off after the old lady, I think," Mort said.

"And where's the girl?" Margo raised her fist toward Mort. "You just run in here and leave her alone?"

"Same as you," Mort snarled.

"You search every inch of this place. Start with the barn." Margo pulled on Cleg's arm. "We're going to drive up and down every road between here and Wyoming, if we have to."

"The old lady took my keys, Honeydew. We'll have to take Mort's truck."

"How am I supposed to get home?" Mort said.

"Call Toby to pick you up." Margo-The-Shrike shoved Cleg out the door and onto the back porch. With her hand clamped on his upper arm, she pulled him across the yard toward Mort's pickup. "If we lose out because of you, I'll make you wish you'd never been born."

Suddenly, like a slide show run amok, memories of his mistreatment tumbled through Cleg's head. Margo hitting and berating him, pulling his hair and slapping his face. Taunting him, questioning his manhood. He ran his fingers over a scar on his forearm—a bite mark, barely dimmed, even after all these years.

Thirty years of his life gone, vanished into a black hole.

He couldn't do it any longer. Not for one more day.

Even if he had to get another mortgage on the house to pay for a divorce, he'd do it.

As Margo dragged him near a thick sumac bush, he jerked free from her grip, pretending to lose his balance. When she automatically made a grab for him, he shoved her, hard as he could, toward the bush. He giggled as Margo's subsequent fighting-to-stay-upright jig failed, and she fell headlong into the sumac. A few pokes and scratches from the sharp twigs would serve her right. As rebellion went, it wasn't much, but it made him feel ten feet tall.

"You pig, I'll rip your—" But Margo never finished her threat.

To Cleg's surprise, the bush came alive. Leaves rustled, and branches moved at the same instant a dozen or so rattlesnakes of all sizes covered Margo's upper body. She screamed and thrashed as what appeared to be a startled mama snake and her writhing new-born babies repeatedly plunged their poison-filled fangs into the woman's face, neck, and shoulders.

Margo's screams brought Mort rushing back from the barn. Standing side by side, he and Cleg stared in shocked silence at the macabre dance playing out in front of them.

"We have to get her out of there," Mort said. He made a move to grab Margo's ankles and pull her out of the den.

But Cleg knocked Mort's arms aside. "If you get too close, they'll come after you, too. You'll be no use to anyone then. It's best to wait a bit."

Mort nodded. "Right, you're right."

Father and son stood spellbound until Margo stopped screaming and lay limp on the ground. As if on cue, the snakes pulled their fangs free and slithered away in different directions.

Cleg squelched a chuckle and wondered if the snakes had any idea how lucky they were to escape before Margo could bite them back. At Mort's shocked expression, he regained his composure.

He'd heard about that thing called Karma, but never really believed in it, at least, not until then.

"We ought to call an ambulance," Mort said. "We should do it now, before she comes to and starts moving around. If she starts moving, it'll make the venom move through her body faster." He pulled his cellphone out of his hip pocket and punched the screen.

Cleg nodded. "That's the thing to do, Boy, you go ahead and call for help." He breathed in the clean desert air and looked around the farm.

It was a nice place. People had been happy there. At least, they had before Digger managed to mess it up. That was just one of many unhappy outcomes to be laid at The Shrike's feet.

By the time the ambulance arrived, Margo's face had begun to swell, and her breathing was rapid and labored. She'd vomited a couple of times.

Unable to look away from her swollen, nearly unrecognizable face and soundlessly moving lips, Cleg whistled a golden oldie and mentally sang the only lyrics he could remember: *Now I'm free...*

Cleg's dad once told him about a man who was bitten by a Western Diamondback Rattlesnake. The guy hadn't realized how bad it was for several hours, so he didn't get to the hospital for the antivenin that would have cleared it up. When the skin around the bite swelled and started turning black, he realized he was in trouble. By the time he got help, irreversible damage had already been done. At some point, his kidneys shut down. Of course, that was before the time of dialysis machines. Though it had become rare for anyone to die of snakebite, without immediate help, damage to vital organs could send a person into his endgame.

Endgame.

Unable to hide the joy erupting from every pore, Cleg's face creased in a huge grin. Even if Margo survived, she'd never be the same. She'd be weak, vulnerable, unable to care for herself. She might even need round the clock attention, the kind of attention found in a convalescent home. And by the time she got out, he'd be long gone.

Reflecting that he should have been feeling guilty, angry, worried, or some other heavy emotion, Cleg tried to gin up a smidgen of sadness. Instead, like an unstoppable tidal wave brought on by an undersea earthquake, he felt only relief.

Life was suddenly worth living.

Chapter Fifty-Seven

Dix was backing the pickup in preparation for pulling from behind the juniper trees, when screaming sirens flew down the road toward the Ross farm.

"An ambulance? The old man didn't look like he was hurt that bad," Toby said under his breath. "Soon as they get past, get a move on. There's way too much activity around here for my liking."

Once they were back on the road, Toby chuckled. "Maybe all the commotion isn't such a bad thing. It'll keep the rest of them occupied and out of my way for a while. Always look for the silver lining, that's the one thing I learned from Uncle Clot."

As Dix turned up the Potter's drive, Toby exclaimed, "I thought you said the old lady lived alone."

"She does," Jillie said.

"Then she must be worth a few shekels." He motioned toward two vehicles parked one behind the other. "A pickup *and* a car."

Dix sat bolt upright at the sight of the tan car parked behind a white truck. It was so like Lil—just in time to become part of the problem.

"Here's the plan," Toby was saying to Jillie, "you and Granny walk ahead of me. Once we're in the house, you bring me the map. If I see any signs you're misbehaving, I'm going to have to hurt someone." He jabbed the pistol barrel against Dix's neck. "Oh, and, act natural, got it Granny?"

The three stepped out of the truck and Jillie led the way up the drive. They'd just stepped onto the porch when a tiny, prune-faced woman flung the door open.

A huge smile creasing the woman's face, she grabbed Jillie in a bear hug. "Oh my, what a wonderful surprise." She turned to Dix and Toby. "And you've brought friends. Welcome, welcome." She stood to one side and held the door open then closed it behind them. "Come in. I've just pulled a loaf of cinnamon bread out of the oven. Two coffees and one milk coming up." Mrs. Potter held her hand out toward Dix. "I don't believe we've met."

Dix took the extended hand and, following the unspoken cue, said, "I'm Dixie. Jillie's told me all about you."

Mrs. Potter smiled and extended her hand toward Toby, who automatically began to offer his left hand. Before he could complete the move, the old lady grabbed his arm and twisted it behind his back in one of the smoothest Tang Soo Do Arm Bar moves Dix had ever seen. "Welcome to my house, Slick." Forcing Toby's elbow to bend backward, she twisted the arm upward until he howled. "Drop your weapon, or I swear I'll break if off at the shoulder."

Dix's head swiveled toward a movement behind Mrs. Potter, and Lil stepped into the room. Holding a Taser in her right hand, Lil gave her sister a short side-of-the-body hug.

Meanwhile, Toby had managed to move his hand so his pistol pointed at Mrs. Potter's kneecap. His face contorting in a grimace and sweat popping out on his upper lip, he snarled, "Is that all you got? My old lady could have taken you in her sleep."

Before Toby could fire, Lil raised the Taser toward his torso and pulled the trigger. Two prong-tipped wires attached themselves to his shirt and pulsed fifty-thousand volts into the young man's chest. He jerked, stiffened, then crumpled onto the floor. He flopped around like a fish out of water, dropping the pistol in the process. After a few seconds of convulsing, he lay still. As if unable to decide what to do next, the four women encircled Toby and stared down at him.

Dix stooped and picked up the pistol before glancing at Mrs. Potter. "Where'd you learn that move?"

"I'm retired, not dead. I started taking martial arts a few years ago. An old woman living alone is a magnet for every bad actor in the area."

Toby chose that moment to stir.

Dix grabbed the Taser from her sister. "That wretched human being was going to kill Jillie." She pulled the trigger, igniting the prongs that were still attached to Toby's shirt.

Again, Toby flopped and jerked, his teeth clenched. In full battle mode, Dix continued to jerk the trigger, her intention to fire until the battery ran down.

"Dix, you keep that up, and you could kill him." Lil yanked the weapon out of her sister's hands and motioned toward Toby. "You may have already, if he has a heart problem."

As if awakening from a dream, Dix looked at her twin. "I wanted to kill him. God help me, I wanted to." She held her hands out and stared down at them as if they belonged to someone else.

Lil patted her sister's shoulder. "But you didn't. Welcome to the real world, Sis."

Mrs. Potter stepped into another room, then immediately returned with two extra-long zip-ties. "Handy things. Never know when you'll need some of these babies." She pulled Toby's arms behind his back, tightly ratcheted one tie closed around his wrists, then tied his feet together at the ankles with the other.

"How'd you know we'd be coming here?" Dix asked Lil.

"We didn't," Lil said. "In fact, we were about to head for the Ross place when you drove up. Beverly, Mrs. Potter, told me about Davie's visit and said there seemed to be an awful lot of traffic headed toward the farm." Lil glanced toward Jillie then back at Dix. "I found your car and the toolbox in the shed. I called and left a message for Davie."

Speaking to no one in particular, Mrs. Potter gestured toward Toby. "We going to stand here jawing, or are we going to call the police?"

"How about none of the above." All heads spun toward the open door where Mort stood holding a shotgun.

Chapter Fifty-Eight

At the sound of Mort's voice, Dix stepped in front of Jillie and pushed the child behind her in one smooth move. "Hide," she said out of the corner of her mouth.

But instead of running, Jillie scooted over to stand behind Lil.

"What took you so long, Cuz?" Toby held his bound wrists toward Mort. "Get me out of these things; I'm feeling distinctly anti-social. You're going to want to get my pistol from Granny."

"Which one?" Mort said.

"The one standing next to the short old lady."

Mort motioned with the shotgun toward Dix. "Drop it on the floor."

Dix did as she was told.

"Came as quick as I could, Tobes. While you were hurrying off to find the treasure, I had to call an ambulance."

"Your old man's a wuss. From what I saw, he wasn't hurt that bad."

"The ambulance wasn't for him." Mort shifted the barrel of the shotgun a fraction of an inch toward his cousin. "Maggot got snake-bit." He shook his head. "Never seen anything like it. You would've paid money to see that." He sniffed. "After I called for help, I noticed you'd hauled ass. Then I spotted your truck on my way back into town."

"You got your pocketknife?" Toby asked Mort.

"Yep." With his left hand, Mort pulled a bone-handled knife from a small scabbard attached to his belt. He tossed the knife onto the floor next to Toby. "Cut him loose, Kid." He moved the shotgun barrel to point at Dix's mid-section. "Sorry, but you know how it is, family being family and all."

Her fingernails chewed to the quick, Jillie struggled with the tiny, fingernail-shaped indentations in the exposed portion of the blades. By the time several seconds had elapsed, the atmosphere in the room had become so charged, Dix almost expected to see everyone's hair stand on end.

"Let me do it." Dix took the knife from Jillie's hands.

Toby shrugged. "I don't give a jolly care who does it. Just do it."

Dix opened the larger of the two blades and moved toward Toby. Although she commanded herself to keep a benign expression on her face, she must have failed, because Toby chuckled.

"Now, now," he said. "Just think of all the commotion you'll make if you try to do me damage."

"Please don't test me," Mort said. "I'd do almost anything to get out of this hell-hole, and a cut of the treasure is my way out."

Dix stooped and ineffectually hacked at the bindings.

"She could have gummed these things to pieces quicker than using that thing," Toby said. "Don't you ever sharpen it?"

Once Dix finally managed to sever the plastic ties, Toby shook the remnants off his wrists and ankles and then removed the Taser's prongs from his shirt front. After a couple of false starts, he managed to stand.

"Where's the treasure map?" He turned his full attention to the women.

Mrs. Potter piped up, "There is no treasure map."

"I've had just about enough of your stalling," Toby said. "Like the big green guy used to say on television, don't make me angry, you wouldn't like me when I'm angry."

Mrs. Potter just shook her head.

His face turning red, Toby sucked on his teeth. "I'll bet you decided to keep it all for yourself after the old man died. Is that how you managed to pay for that new truck out front?"

Jillie took a step out from behind Lil. "Pop made her swear never to tell. But I know where it is. If you let them all go, I'll show you."

"Oh, you'll show me where it is, all right." Toby lifted the pistol. "Or I'll shoot your granny friend; then I'll pop your godmother; then I'll take my time with the biddy who tazed me. No more negotiations."

"You'd better do what he says." Mort looked at Jillie. "You really don't want to tick him off." He turned to Toby. "Maggot's out of the running, and Clot doesn't care. That means it's just a two-way split."

Toby smiled. "Oh, is that what it means?" In one smooth movement, he turned the pistol on Mort and pulled the trigger.

A surprised look on his face, Mort sighed and looked down at his thigh. As if the shotgun suddenly weighed a ton, its barrel dipped toward the floor, and his finger spasmodically pulled its trigger.

The unexpected second explosion resounded

through the house, and the three women gasped. Jillie screamed.

Mort dropped the gun and pressed his hands against the sudden blossom of blood on his thigh. "Why'd you…" His knees buckled, and he fell to the floor.

"Sorry, about that Cuz," Toby said. "That'll hurt like hell for a few days, but at least you'll live, family being family, and all."

Mrs. Potter hurried to the fallen man, knelt, and put pressure on the wound.

"Tourniquet the leg, if it'll make you feel better," Toby said. "Then get over there with the rest of the Golden Girls." He pointed the gun at Mort's head. "Or I'll finish him off. You want the kid to have to see that in her dreams for the rest of her life?" Toby motioned toward Mort. "Use his belt."

Mrs. Potter tugged Mort's belt free, then carefully tightened it around his thigh. "What kind of man shoots his own kin?"

"The determined kind." Toby motioned toward his cousin. "He'll be okay. I just need him out of commission long enough for me to evaporate into thin air." He turned toward Jillie. "You go get the map. You've got two minutes before I start shooting your friends." He made a big deal out of looking at his watch and pointing the pistol at Dix.

"It's in a vase in the front room," Jillie said. "That's the room behind you." She stepped around Toby.

The pistol never wavering, Toby watched Jillie's movements.

Lil shot a look at Dix, then suddenly jabbed her

index finger into her sister's chest. "We wouldn't be in this mess if you hadn't broken my phone."

Dix smacked her sister's hand away. "I wouldn't have broken your phone if you'd done what I asked. But I gave you mine, so why didn't you call for help?"

"Shut up," Toby said, his eyes pin-balling back and forth between the women and Jillie's retreating form as a look of recognition dawned in his eyes. "I knew it; I knew I'd seen that kid somewhere before."

Jillie jerked to a stop and turned back toward Toby, a look of pure fear on her face.

"Go on," Toby said to Jillie. "You got nothing to be afraid of if you bring me that map. I'll be long gone before you can tell anyone about anything you might think you know."

"You never charge your phone, that's why," Lil was saying. "It's dead as a mackerel." She grabbed a handful of Dix's hair. "You're so busy saving the world, you can't be bothered with—"

"I said shut up!" Toby shifted his pistol slightly.

Dix slapped Lil's face then grabbed her ear and twisted. "And you're a heartless old crotch who hates the world."

"I'm going to shoot the next—" Toby then made the mistake of shifting his attention away from the child and toward the twins.

Before Toby could react, Jillie pointed a small black canister at his head and pulled the trigger. Instantly, his eyes started pouring tears, his nose began to run, and he had to struggle to breathe. He stumbled a couple of steps then fell to his knees.

"Pepper spray," Lil said. "You won't die, but you'll sure wish you could for about an hour or so."

Unable to see, Toby fired the pistol in random directions until the clip was empty. One bullet found its mark, and Lil yelped.

From a sitting position on the floor, Toby scrubbed at his burning, swollen eyes with the palms of his hands. He coughed and gagged as his nose ran uncontrollably, dripping goo down his shirt front.

Jillie ran to Dix, who pulled her close. "It's okay," Dix said. "You're going to be okay."

"Or not," Toby managed to say between coughs. "I'm going to kill all of you."

Chapter Fifty-Nine

As David pulled out of Mrs. Potter's drive, he considered waiting for backup. But the Ross farm was miles from town, and no one knew better than he how thin local law enforcement manpower was stretched. It could take half an hour for someone to answer his call, and a lot could happen in that amount of time.

He'd only gone a few hundred yards when his scanner crackled to life.

We have an emergency on a farm near mile marker sixty-five off highway three-fourteen. The caller says an elderly woman is unconscious as a result of multiple rattlesnake bites. Valencia County Sheriff has requested help. Any first responders in the area should also be advised a man has reportedly sustained a knife wound.

His insides turning to ice water, David floored the gas pedal. Scenery flew by in a kaleidoscope of color. A flash of something yellow in the midst of a stand of juniper caught at the periphery of his vision, but the instant his law enforcement brain registered it and sent up a red flag, he pushed the thought aside. Whatever it was could wait until he found out which of his aunts had managed to get herself bitten by a rattlesnake.

As he pulled up the Ross's drive, he saw Cleg Elliott and a younger man staring down at a bundle of something on the ground. David jumped from his vehicle and approached the scene.

Holding a towel dabbed with blood around one of his forearms, Cleg stood as if in a trance, his lips puckering and un-puckering like a blowfish.

The younger man glanced at David, then muttered something about having to go into the house. By the time David realized what the guy really had in mind, the young man was driving away.

Murmuring a quick prayer for whichever aunt had been so desperately hurt, David hurried toward the body on the ground. A nanosecond later, he allowed himself to breathe again. Although the face was swollen, Margo's telltale skin flap moved in and out with her every breath and moan.

David took a deep, relieved breath. He straightened and turned toward Cleg. "Are you okay?"

Cleg nodded, never taking his eyes off Margo's body. "I've never seen anything like that before. Snakes crawling all over her head, biting and hissing something fierce, even the little bitty ones." He cut off the beginnings of a chuckle and looked into David's face. "I don't know what's come over me." He cleared his throat. "It's a terrible thing; it sure is." He looked back at the now-mewling woman on the ground. "Looks like she's still alive." The tone of his voice wistful, he added, "So, that's that."

"An ambulance is on the way," David said. He motioned toward Cleg's arm. "What happened?"

Cleg looked down at his arm, a puzzled expression on his face. "Oh, this is nothing. I did it myself." He peered into David's eyes. "Your Aunt Dixie, now there's a woman, got an iron streak a mile wide. She's the one hatched the plan."

Electricity sizzled through David's body. "My aunt

was here?"

Cleg nodded. "Yeah, she was, but they've all gone now, gone and left me to deal with that." He motioned toward Margo.

"Where, Cleg, where have they gone?"

"I don't know, they just up and left. The kid, your aunt, Toby, they all scattered to the four winds." He looked around. "Mort was here just a minute ago, but I guess he's gone, too." He took a deep breath around the nasal cannula that ran from a portable oxygen-making machine hanging from a strap around his shoulder. "How long do you reckon she'll be in the hospital?"

"Cleg, I need you to think. Were they afoot or did they take a vehicle?"

"They must've taken Toby's truck."

"Describe it."

"Nineteen ninety-five Dodge Ram. Club cab, rusty yellow."

Yellow.

"Did my aunt tell you where they were headed?"

"She said if anyone asked, I was to say she was taking the girl to stay with an elderly family member."

David frowned. Beth said they didn't have any other family, at least none she knew of.

"Are you sure that's what she said?"

An offended look on his face, Cleg said, "I know what Dixie told me." He tapped an index finger on his temple. "She even made me repeat it so's I'd not forget."

His aunt had either hoped to throw the Elliott crew a red herring, or she'd left the clue for David's benefit. But it seemed she'd given him more credit than was due because he hadn't the foggiest idea what to make of her words.

Then as if a gong had been struck right next to him, he jerked his head up. Mrs. Potter—Jillie's godmother—next best thing to a blood relative.

"How long have they been gone?"

"I don't know, maybe thirty minutes."

David reached for Cleg's towel-wrapped arm. "How bad is it?"

Cleg moved the other arm in a dismissive move. "Dix said it wasn't bad enough to worry about."

"Maybe you should sit in your pickup until help gets here."

Cleg nodded and ambled toward his vehicle, chuckling every other step.

David hurried toward his Jeep. If he hadn't been out of his mind at the report of an elderly woman being snake-bit, he'd have checked out the flash of yellow he glimpsed just off the road. He'd lost all objectivity and was acting like a rookie.

The approaching wail of a siren disrupted David's self-flagellation.

Muffled sounds of a distant pistol shot followed by the blast of a shotgun floated on the gentle breeze. In one smooth move, David jumped into his Jeep, slammed the door, and fired up his engine. As if the hounds of hell were hot on his heels, he floored the pedal, peeled out of the Ross drive, and pointed his vehicle toward the Potter place.

Chapter Sixty

When Mort came into the house, Jillie's friend Dix had shoved her behind her back and told her to run and hide. But instead, she looked around the room in search of something she could use as a distraction.

When she spotted the top of a black cylinder sticking up out of Miss Lil's back pocket, she moved closer to get a better look. Spray paint? Bug spray? Hair spray? It didn't really matter, because any kind of spray might be just what she needed.

All Jillie had to do was get the canister from Miss Lil's pocket and then get close enough to the cousins to let them have it in the face. The challenge would be getting them both with the same shot because hitting only one would be a disaster.

But then Toby shot Mort, and during all the commotion that followed, Jillie managed to pick-pocket the cylinder out of Miss Lil's pocket. She'd palmed the thing and shoved it behind the elastic of her underwear in one smooth move.

When Toby told Jillie to go get the map, Miss Lil winked at her then picked a fight with her sister.

After Jillie gassed Toby, Moms Potter grabbed up both weapons and disappeared into the kitchen. When she came back, she was carrying more zip ties.

Since Mort wasn't in any shape to escape, she'd only bound his wrists. But like she'd done before, she bound both Toby's wrists and legs.

"You okay, Lil?" Miss Dix pulled a wadded-up tissue from somewhere in her bra, spit on it, and dabbed at the small spot of blood on her sister's shoulder.

Moms Potter inspected the wound. "Just a graze, she'll live to fight another day."

"I *know* you didn't just spit on a used tissue and wipe it on me." Miss Lil swatted her sister's hand away. "Don't you know the human mouth is one of the filthiest things on the planet?"

"Oh yeah?" Miss Dix said. "Well my mouth's a lot cleaner than yours."

"Would someone please call the police?" Lil said. "I've had just about all this fun I can stand."

"Will someone please drive me to the hospital to see Beth?" Jillie said.

"I believe that can be arranged," the police-nephew said from just inside the front door.

"Grand Central Station," Moms Potter said. "Come in and make yourself useful."

Within the next few minutes, Mrs. Potter's house was abuzz with people. A deputy sheriff showed up, followed by an ambulance and two EMTs.

After Mort's wound was bandaged, Miss Lil's shoulder was disinfected. Toby's swollen face was doused with bottled water until he was breathing better. Then the two cousins were handcuffed and taken away. The sheriff and his deputy took statements from everyone present, then left.

"It's going to take them a while to get those boys to the hospital," Moms Potter said. "The nearest one's in Albuquerque. We've got critical care places all around, but no hospital."

Miss Dix looked at her nephew. "Please don't yell at me. I've been awake over twenty-four hours; I can't be held responsible for anything I might say."

The policeman-nephew hugged Miss Dix and Miss Lil. "I'm not going to yell at either of you, not just yet, anyway." With a thoughtful look on his face, he added, "Life doesn't offer any guarantees, does it? I guess it's up to us to make the most of the time we have here, however long or short that might be."

Jillie tugged at David's shirt. "Can we go see Beth now?"

"You bet we can." David smiled at her. "You ever ridden in a Jeep complete with a siren and flashing lights?"

Jillie squealed and started for the car.

Chapter Sixty-One

Still wearing her hospital gown, Beth sat in the vinyl-covered chair next to her hospital bed and tried to keep her mind busy by watching television. As she'd done a thousand times within the past few hours, she glanced at the clock attached to the wall at the foot of her bed. Only three o'clock, yet it seemed days had passed since she learned Jillie was on her way.

She'd just turned toward the window when Jillie burst through the door, ran to her, and threw her arms around her neck. The sisters hugged each other, broke into tears, and simultaneously tried to speak.

Beth laughed then said, "You go first."

"I thought you were dead," Jillie said.

"And I thought you'd been kidnapped, or worse." Beth pushed her little sister back and looked into her eyes. "I'm so proud of you, Chili Bean."

"We all are." David walked into the room followed by Mrs. Potter and two other elderly women who looked identical, yet didn't. "Beth, I want to introduce my aunts Dix and Lil."

"I'm Dix, the nice one." Dix tapped an index finger against her chest then pointed to her sister. "She's Lil."

"The smart one," Lil said.

Beth smiled at the group. "I can't thank you enough, all of you." Tears poured down her cheeks. "If you hadn't—"

The afternoon charge nurse chose that moment to bustle into the room carrying a huge plastic bag bearing the hospital's insignia. She placed the bag on the bed and smiled at Beth. "The Physician's Assistant will review your aftercare instructions then sign you out after your doctor's final visit. He'll also answer any questions you may have, what to watch for, that kind of thing."

"Thank you for all you've done," Beth said to the nurse. "Everyone has been so good to me."

"It's been my pleasure. But you're the one who refused to give up." The nurse sent a smile around the group. "Everyone on the floor calls her *The Feisty One in Four-Ten.*" She stepped to Jillie and bent at the waist. "You must be Beth's sister. You know she hasn't stopped talking about you from the moment she woke up?"

Jillie beamed.

The nurse smiled back. "Have you decided what you want to be when you grow up?"

"I'd like to be a veterinarian."

"You'll be a good one." The nurse looked at Beth. "I don't know if you're aware of it, but some of the state universities offer full scholarships to kids who've been in foster care for at least one month. It's something worth looking into."

Doctor De Bruin came into the room as the nurse left. "One last check up." She looked around the group, smiled, and said, "It's great to see such a support base."

After the doctor left, the Physician's Assistant returned carrying a clipboard and pushing a wheelchair. Documents were signed, and conditions of aftercare were discussed. "Who'll be driving you home today?"

Beth looked confused. "I hadn't really thought about—"

"I'll be driving her," David said.

Mrs. Potter chimed in, "Beth and Jillie will be staying with me until they can decide what to do about the farm."

"And we'll make regular visits. She won't lack for caregivers." Dix patted Jillie's shoulder. "Neither of them will."

Mrs. Potter held a small overnight bag toward Beth. "We brought a change of clothes Jillie picked out. The police still have the outfit you were wearing when you were brought in."

Beth accepted the bag and stepped into the bathroom. Within a couple of minutes, she stepped back into the room. "It feels so good to be out of that bed. Let's go."

With Jillie walking beside the wheelchair and holding her sister's hand, the troop made its way toward the exit.

In the elevator, Lil cleared her throat. "Dinner tonight's at our place, and you're all invited." She smiled at Beth and Jillie. "Two sets of sisters have been reunited, and I propose a celebration."

Dix's mouth flew open, and she tapped an index finger on her sister's cheek. "Who are you and what have you done with my twin?"

Lil held her hands out, palms up. "Just because I'm right ninety-eight percent of the time doesn't mean I can't admit when I'm wrong the other two percent." She grinned at David and Beth, then patted Jillie's shoulder. "And from now on, you can call me Aunt Lil."

****

Per Jillie's request, dinner that night was spaghetti and meatballs followed by Banana Split Bread a la Dixie. The house rang with laughter as the new-found friends chatted and joked. After-dinner coffee was served on the patio.

"So, the skeleton Jillie found was Toby's mother?" Beth asked David.

"According to dental records it is," David said.

"What happened to her, how'd she die?" Lil said.

"Toby says he killed her accidentally, but Mort says otherwise. Mort said the two of them were building a fort out of scrap lumber lying around the back yard when Chlorine came flying out of the house, screaming and cussing, calling the boys everything but human. She claimed to have plans for the lumber that didn't include building a fort for two useless boys. After a few minutes of the tirade, Toby picked up a hammer and, cool as you please, bashed her head in. Then he bullied Mort into helping him bury Chlorine's body and all her stuff in the desert at the back edge of the Elliott property. They hauled rocks of all sizes to cover the grave, to hide the over-turned dirt."

"The thought of those two little boys digging a hole to bury a body..." Dix said. "How did they know to bury it deep enough so coyotes wouldn't get to it?"

"Television," David said. "But that's not the half of it. Sometime later, Toby dug up the body, dismembered it, then arranged it inside the toolbox. He made Mort help him move the chest to the shed."

"Why move the body when she was already so well-hidden?" Lil said.

"Mort says Toby wanted her to be close so he

could talk to her from time to time." David said.

"It's sad that no one reported her missing for several weeks," Mrs. Potter said.

David nodded. "It was long enough for the weather to settle the soil on the grave and make it invisible."

"Creepy," Jillie said.

"Didn't the police question that boy about his mother at the time she went missing?" Mrs. Potter said.

"Yes," David said. "But Toby told them she left without telling him where she was going. That rang true, given her background. And since all her stuff was gone as well…"

"I don't understand how it took so long for people to figure out she was missing in the first place," Lil said.

"Seems everyone in town steered clear of her," David said. "And she pretty well confined herself to her trailer after her husband left, so no one noticed. In fact, it seems the local populace heaved a sigh of relief when they realized she was gone."

"Why did Mort never come forward?" Dix asked. "They may have been kids, but they were old enough to know right from wrong."

"Whenever Mort's conscience acted up and he started making confession-noises," David said, "Toby threatened to tell everyone that *he* was the one who'd killed dear old mom. He claimed to have hidden the hammer with Mort's prints on it and wouldn't hesitate to take it to the police."

"So, Mort's been afraid he'd be the one going to jail for the murder," Lil said.

David nodded. "Remember, these guys were only kids at the time of the murder. And Mort *had* been using the hammer while Toby sawed up the lumber. By the time Mort matured enough to realized he'd been scammed, he thought he was already in too deep."

"Mort was always nice to me. He kind of acted sorry about the way Digger treated us," Beth said. "What will happen to him?"

"He's made a deal with the District Attorney," David said. "In return for his testimony, he won't spend much time in jail."

"What about Cleg?" Dix said.

"Probably not much to worry about there, either," David said. "He did risk his life to help Aunt Dix and Jillie escape, but on the other hand, he kept quiet after Jillie ran away in the first place, so that might come back to pinch him a bit."

"The words *Stockholm Syndrome* come to mind." Dix said. "That man was one of the most beaten-down people I've ever run across."

David looked at Beth. "You'll be interested to know that Margo Elliott was admitted to ICU at the same hospital you were in."

"Margo's in the hospital?" Jillie said.

"She's suffering from multiple organ failure as a result of snake bite," David said. "Her name will go on the lists for various organ transplants. But unless she gets an almost miraculous break, she'll be lucky to survive two or three years."

"…two or three years during which she'll have to spend three days a week undergoing hours of dialysis." Mrs. Potter said. "Sounds like Margo's life is going to be a nightmare."

After a couple of minutes during which the group digested Mrs. Potter's words, Dix murmured, "And

Cleg's finally free."

Jillie looked at Beth. "Margo told me they had to hire people to clean the house up. Should we pay Cleg back for that?"

"Not necessary," David said. "The cleanup didn't cost the Elliotts a cent. The county has a fund that kicks in when the victim's family can't cover those expenses."

Jillie shivered. "The day Digger hurt Beth so bad, I saw that big mama snake under the Sumac."

Mrs. Potter spoke up, "I read a bit about the Western Diamondback rattler. They give live birth to as many as eighteen little ones, all armed with venom and dangerous as all get-out until they learn how to tell the difference between a real threat and just some innocent intruder. Did you know the Diamondback is responsible for most deaths due to snake bite in the United States?"

"And to think, this whole mess got started because of a rumor," Dix said.

"I don't understand why Pops would care if people knew where he got the extra money," Beth said. "He taught us not to pay attention to what other people thought."

"We all have a glitch or two," Mrs. Potter said. "Your pa was a proud man. He couldn't stand the thought that his girls might think less of him because he couldn't make a decent living off the family farm. Working the oil rigs in Oklahoma and Texas paid good money, enough to provide the extras. Then when the rumor mill ginned up and everyone thought he'd found some missing treasure or other, he never denied it. I think it tickled him that everyone looked at him as an adventurous treasure-hunter."

"What about Toby?" Dix said. "Is there a statute of limitations? He was just a kid."

"There's no statute of limitations on murder. Toby's going to spend the rest of his life locked up for killing his mother. And thanks to DNA found at the trailer, along with Jillie's life-like drawings and written testimony, he'll be charged with murdering the man in the trailer. We'll see what happens after his psych evaluation. This whole episode seems to have finally pushed him over the edge."

Dix shook her head. "…so sad."

"Sad?" Lil *harrumphed.* "The guy was seconds away from killing all of us."

"Yes, sad. I'm not excusing him. I just can't help but wonder why no one recognized the warning signs when he was still a child, why no one stepped up to help."

"All I know is you're the reason I still have Jillie," Beth said to Dix. "If you hadn't been willing to risk your own life—"

"I didn't do much," Dix interrupted. "This amazing young lady saved our bacon with her quick thinking."

"I hate to admit it," David said to Dix, "but you did a good job of figuring out where to find Jillie."

"She's a real sleuth." Mrs. Potter clapped Dix on the back. "And nervy as all get-out. My kind of people."

A disgusted look on her face, Lil pushed her chair back, stood, and looked toward the garden. "Hey Gumshoe Granny," she pointed toward the herb patch, "is that a tiny space-boot print I see next to your chives?"

Chapter Sixty-Two

Jillie and Beth stood arm-in-arm near the cottonwood tree under which their parents' ashes were scattered while David, Lil, Dix, and Mrs. Potter watched from a respectful distance. A cool mid-October breeze rustled through the tree's bare branches.

"We miss you," Jillie said toward the tree. "But we're okay now."

"Yes, we are." Beth glanced over her shoulder at the group of friends who were busy putting food and utensils on a wooden picnic table. Her gaze lingered on David, and she blushed.

Jillie caught the movement and smiled. "In fact, we're more than okay." She held out her right hand, palm up. Sunlight glinted off a nickel left by one of the crows. "Aunt Lil says it's a rare 1943 war nickel, worth a lot of money. Enough so we can tear down the old house and build a new one at the other end of the property. There may even be enough to repair your car, Pops."

Dix turned to David, her words ringing clearly in the morning air. "I don't know if you believe in such things, but I like to think Jillie's parents showed one of the crows where to find that coin."

Lil rolled her eyes, but otherwise remained silent.

"That's a nice thought, Aunt Dix," David said absently. His eyes locked on Beth as he returned her shy look with a smoldering one of his own.

Jillie smiled at the tree and dropped her voice to a whisper. "David likes Beth, and Beth likes him back. You'd like him, too. He has lots of ideas about how to make this place pay for itself."

Lil took a deep breath. "Are we done here? That burrito I had at the Balloon Fiesta has long since worn off, and I'm hungry enough to eat a buffalo without horseradish."

"You mean the *three* burritos you ate," Dix said.

"I'm with Lil," Moms Potter said. "I vote we get down to the business of eating that delicious-looking birthday cake and ice cream."

Beth hugged Jillie so tightly all the air whooshed out of her lungs. "Happy belated twelfth birthday, Chili Bean."

Jillie returned her sister's hug. "It was the best birthday ever."

A series of caws coming from the cottonwood drew Jillie's attention upward. "Thank you," she mouthed to the glossy black crow watching from one of the lower branches.

With a final caw, the crow flew upward, circled the group, then flew away.

Amid laughter and smiles, the troop headed toward the table.

A word about the author...

Olive Balla makes her home near Albuquerque, New Mexico with her husband Victor. When not writing, she enjoys woodworking.

Visit her at:

http://omballa.com